DUST AND OBEY

Squeaky Clean Mysteries,
Book 10

By Christy Barritt

Other Books by Christy Barritt

Squeaky Clean Mysteries
#1 *Hazardous Duty*
#2 *Suspicious* Minds
#2.5 *It Came Upon a Midnight Crime*
#3 *Organized Grime*
#4 *Dirty Deeds*
#5 *The Scum of All Fears*
#6 *To Love, Honor, and Perish*
#7 *Mucky Streak*
#8 *Foul Play*
#9 *Broom and Gloom*
#10 *Dust and Obey*
#11 *Thrill Squeaker*
#11.5 *Swept Away* (a novella)
#12 *Cunning Attractions* (coming soon)

The Sierra Files
#1 *Pounced*
#2 *Hunted*
#2.5 *Pranced* (a Christmas novella)
#3 *Rattled*

The Gabby St. Claire Diaries (a tween mystery series)
#1 *The Curtain Call Caper*
#2 *The Disappearing Dog Dilemma*
#3 *The Bungled Bike Burglaries*

Holly Anna Paladin Mysteries
#1 *Random Acts of Murder*
#2 *Random Acts of Deceit*
#3 *Random Acts of Malice*
#3.5 *Random Acts of Scrooge*
#4 *Random Acts of Greed*

Carolina Moon series
#1 *Home Before Dark*
#2 *Gone By Dark*
#3 *Wait Until Dark*

Suburban Sleuth Mysteries
#1 *Death of the Couch Potato's Wife*

Standalone Romantic Suspense
Keeping Guard
The Last Target
Race Against Time
Ricochet
Key Witness
Lifeline
High-Stakes Holiday Reunion
Desperate Measures
Hidden Agenda
Mountain Hideout
Dark Harbor

Standalone Romantic Mystery
The Good Girl

Suspense
Dubiosity
Disillusioned
The Trouble with Perfect

Nonfiction
Changed: True Stories of Finding God through Christian Music
The Novel in Me: The Beginner's Guide to Writing and Publishing a Novel

DUST AND OBEY

CHAPTER 1

Finally my life was getting back on track. I was looking forward and not behind. I was pressing on. Running the race. Considering my trials pure joy.

Then my phone rang.

I climbed into my van, in a hurry to grab some lunch before I had to be back for the next training session for my new job, and glanced at the screen. When I saw Riley Thomas's phone number, my nerves ratcheted from a-day-at-the-beach calm to New York City crazy. He was my ex-fiancé, the man who'd crushed my heart, turned my life upside down, and left me wandering aimlessly for the past few months.

Why is he calling me?

I cranked the engine and let some air blow on me. Unfortunately, the air was still hot. Springtime was unreasonably muggy here in Raleigh, North Carolina, and I needed all the Freon possible to help me chill.

I stared at the phone another moment in contemplation. What possible reason could Riley have to call me? I already knew he was moving back home to Norfolk, taking up his former residence in the apartment across the hall from me. Just like old times. Not that *he'd* told me that little update.

My best friend, Sierra, had been the one to mention it. Not that I was bitter about it or anything.

Just when I thought I'd gotten over Riley and the way he'd broken my heart like a Greek engaging in some celebratory plate smashing, the man decided to reenter my life. Lucky me.

I sighed and, after a moment of hesitation, decided to get this conversation over with.

"Hey, Riley." I leaned back in my ripped seat, trying to deny the fact that my heart raced.

"Gabby." His voice sounded smooth and warm. "How are you?"

"I'm . . ." I almost said "hanging in," but that sounded weak.

Instead, I glanced out the bug-splattered windshield at the new facility where I'd spent the majority of my time the past two weeks. I was now working as a representative and instructor for Grayson Technologies, a leading provider of forensic equipment and supplies. I'd begun a new chapter in my life, and that should equate with hope.

"I'm doing great," I finally said.

"I'm glad to hear that. Listen, I know it's been a while, but I have a proposal for you."

"A proposal?" As soon as the words croaked out of my mouth, I wished they hadn't. I knew how Riley could interpret them, but my quip wasn't about a lingering desire to marry him or our broken engagement or me longing after him. I rubbed my forehead and wanted a redo.

"Yeah, you know, an idea." His voice didn't hold any judgment or even sarcasm, but instead he sounded earnest.

I released the breath I held. Thank goodness he'd been gracious enough to let that one slide because it could have easily made it onto my top ten most embarrassing list—and I had some doozies up there. "Okay, shoot."

"I was going to wait until you were back in town, but I'm

afraid it will be too late by then. This . . . *proposal*," he seemed to hesitate before using the word, "actually involves this upcoming weekend. Sierra said you'd be back home tomorrow, so I'm hoping if you say yes the timing will work out."

"I'm sorry. Our connection is lousy. Did you say you want to elope this weekend?" My words contained a slightly devious edge. This time I purposefully wanted to make him uncomfortable because I was immature like that sometimes in matters of the heart.

"Uh . . ." he started.

I heard him waffling around in agony, and I thought I'd get more pleasure from his discomfort. My negative feelings had really just risen to the surface over the past couple of weeks, and I wasn't sure why. I suppose it tied in with the stages of grief. I had been in denial for a long time, and now I was wafting back and forth between anger and acceptance.

I prayed that I was edging closer to acceptance, but some days I questioned whether that was true.

"I'm just kidding, Riley." I needed for him to know that I was over him and that his return to Norfolk wasn't going to affect my mental well-being in the slightest.

In theory, at least.

Riley let out a short, clipped laugh. Had I made him nervous?

I was more curious now than ever as to where this conversation was going. "Anyway, all joking aside, what's going on?"

"You know how I started working for the law firm up in DC? One of the law partners has a brother named Brad. Long story short, Brad and his wife were having some problems, and they went to therapy. In the middle of the process, Brad's wife died. The police have ruled it a suicide. Brad doesn't believe that's true."

"That sounds terrible and tragic, but what's this have to do with me?"

"Well, I just happened to be telling my friend about you."

Riley had been talking to his friend about me? Now *that* was interesting. But he'd probably just been telling a crazy ex-fiancée story. I'd given him a lot of material.

". . . and your investigations," Riley continued. "You've got a great track record for getting to the bottom of things and finding answers."

"Yes, I do." That was mostly because I was stubborn and sometimes foolhardy, so I really wasn't bragging on my brilliance or anything. I also had a talent for putting my foot in my mouth and looking foolish—in the end it was a wash.

"Brad wants to hire someone to investigate his wife's death. It will require going undercover at this retreat center. However, there's a catch."

"What's that?" I fanned my hand toward my face. What was wrong with my AC? Did I even have money to fix it? And was smooth sailing ever in my future?

"It's at a couples retreat center."

I let that sink in quickly. "So I need to be a part of a couple? Who in their right mind is going to sign up to do that with me?"

"Obviously, you can't go alone to investigate. You'd need someone to go with you since the program is for husbands and wives."

"So you volunteered yourself?" I said the words jokingly, fully expecting him to deny it.

"Maybe I did," he said, his voice surprisingly relaxed and at ease.

That only piqued my interest. It really didn't sound like Riley. At least not like the Riley I used to know. "Go on."

"When Brad and his wife had to . . . drop out of therapy, for lack of a better term, a spot opened up. Brad pulled some strings, and we can get in—under assumed identities, of course. The retreat takes place on the weekends at a place about an hour-and-a-half from Norfolk."

"You're really up for doing this?" I had to make sure I understood correctly because it was so out of the realm of what I'd expected.

"I am. Are you game?"

I thought about it a moment. I was free this weekend. Sure, I'd started a new job, but it was part-time and I didn't have any work to do until Monday. And I was moonlighting as a crime-scene cleaner still, but since I'd given up ownership in the company I was now free to accept or reject jobs as I pleased.

"You don't think that would be awkward? You and I working together? Pretending to *be* together?" I finally asked, curious as to how he'd respond. There were a lot of unspoken issues between us. Knowing Riley, he had to feel awkward to a certain extent about this. He was conscientious like that.

"I think we're both mature enough to handle it, Gabby."

Mature. That's right. Doing this could prove to Riley that I was over our breakup and that I was emotionally healthy enough to be around him. In other words, I was She-Ra.

"So, what do you say?" Riley asked. "Are you game?"

I was never one to turn down a challenge, even if it did require having my heart torn out and trampled. "I say . . . let's do it."

He let out a little breath. A sigh of relief, maybe? "It will be like old times."

I could hear the pleasure in his voice, and the sound

sent a shiver up my spine.

Drats!

And it *wouldn't* be just like old times. In old times, we were a couple. Now we would be two people working together, *pretending* to be a couple. I had to keep that at the forefront of my mind as I went into "Operation Protect My Heart" mode. Failure was not an option here.

"So what do I need to know?" I forced myself to focus. My lunch break was quickly ending, and I'd had no food. I rolled down the window and let some fresh air waft inside, wishing it would offer nourishment and not just comfort.

"I'll fill you in on the way there tomorrow. We'll have an hour-and-a-half to talk on the drive. What time will you be home?"

"Around eleven tomorrow. Does that work?"

"It's perfect. I'll meet you at the apartment at one. You'll need to pack for two days overnight. And dress to impress. Most people at this retreat center make an income in the high six figures."

Oh, I was going to fit in *so* easily there. Struggling to make ends meet came as naturally to me as walking did for most people.

I resisted a sigh. "It sounds like a plan."

But as I hung up, I wondered what exactly I'd gotten myself into.

I could hardly wait to find out.

CHAPTER 2

I was more nervous than I should be the next day as I stuffed some clothes into my suitcase. I'd finished my training, checked out of my hotel, and driven home in record time. I'd had way too much time to think during those hours.

Mostly, I'd been thinking about Riley and what his reemergence into my life might mean. The bottom line: only bad things. I didn't see any other way around it.

Finally, I pulled up to the little apartment building where I'd lived for the majority of my adult life. It was an old Victorian that had been cut up into five units. The building was located in an eclectic area of Norfolk, Virginia, where things were always interesting. It seemed to match my life well. A little too well at times.

My first problem at the moment went back to my task at hand: I was *stuffing* clothes that I *already* owned into a *ratty* suitcase.

Dress to impress? High six figures? I was going to have the most trouble pulling that that off. I wasn't an upper-crust kind of girl. I never had been. And I didn't care if I ever was. I was content with who I was, even if that meant my luggage frayed on the ends and might even be missing a wheel.

I stared at my clothes and sighed. The people at this retreat center would be looking for name brands, for neatly pressed blouses and pampered garments. I mostly owned well-worn threads that I didn't mind getting dirty. I *had* been a crime-scene cleaner for most of my adult life. That didn't afford many opportunities to dress up.

I glanced at the outfit I had on now. I was wearing designer jeans I'd found at a thrift store and a silky pale-blue blouse. I'd actually taken the time to straighten my unruly red locks. I always thought the effect was more elegant than my hair in its natural state—my natural state being Medusa-like red curls that sprang from my head.

Just then I had a light-bulb moment. I walked to my dresser and found my mother's old set of pearls in my jewelry box. I owned very few pieces that were the real thing. Most were imitation. There were even a couple pieces I'd gotten out of a bubble-gum machine, if that told you anything.

With a little bit of finagling, I clasped the strand around my neck. I glanced in the mirror, surprised with the final result. I looked halfway elegant. I hoped this was good enough for Riley, not because I wanted to impress him but because I wanted to pull off this investigation.

With one more nervous glance at the clock on my table, I realized it was time to go face my ex and have my "Circle of Life" moment. I grabbed my suitcase and walked toward the door. *Here goes nothing.*

As soon as I stepped out, I spotted Riley striding onto the landing between our apartments. My heart skipped a beat. I hadn't seen him in a solid two months, but he looked just as handsome as ever with his dark hair and baby-blue eyes. His hair had grown back nice and full, and I couldn't even tell he'd nearly died from a gunshot wound in the head almost nine months ago.

Something else seemed different about him also, but I couldn't pinpoint what exactly. The look in his eyes maybe? The way his muscles filled out his azure golf shirt?

"Gabby, you look great." He offered an approving nod before reaching forward to give me a hug.

I forced my arms to move and offered an awkward embrace. I refused to get too close. But still, as my chin went over his shoulder, I got a whiff of his leathery aftershave. I loved that scent. And I'd missed it.

As soon as that realization hit me, I recognized I'd lingered in the hug way too long. Quickly, I pulled back and rubbed my hands against my jeans, trying to look composed and unaffected.

"You ready to go?" My voice trembled slightly. *Stupid voice.*

"Yes. But first . . ." He reached behind him into his apartment. "I brought this for you."

He held out a glossy, hard-sided suitcase with all wheels intact and no frayed edges. Something about it screamed, "Expensive. Upper crust. High six figures."

"For me?" I questioned. He might as well have offered me a diamond necklace. This suitcase probably cost as much, and it was way more practical.

He nodded. "We are supposed to be married so having different kinds of luggage might set off some alarms. Besides, Brad Thorn paid us an advance in case we needed stuff like this. I hope you don't mind that I picked it out for you. I knew you were kind of busy."

"No, I like it. But, speaking of this retreat: Don't most couples share suitcases? And rooms, for that matter?" That question had dawned on me as I'd been driving back from North Carolina this morning. It had made me feel panicky with dread. If I was going to make this ruse of a relationship work then I'd need some time away from Riley to decompress.

"Not here. We're staying separately as a part of the plan of therapy."

Relief filled me.

But then it hit me what he said, and I gave him one of those "something doesn't smell right" looks. "Isn't that weird at a marriage retreat for couples not to stay together?"

"Some might say so, but that's the rule."

"Works for me." I was so grateful that I didn't have the time or energy to ponder what he said. I only knew I wouldn't be trapped in a room with him for most of the weekend. "Let me go get my bags switched. I'll be out in a minute."

"By the way, I put your half of the check in the suitcase."

As I slipped back inside my apartment, I noticed my hands were trembling. Maybe I wasn't prepared to do this. It had seemed like a good challenge when Riley presented the idea, but being with Riley in just those five minutes had already left me reeling off balance. All those feelings of having my life back on track disappeared.

Consider it pure joy, I reminded myself. That would be my theme verse.

When I opened the luggage and spotted the check, my eyes widened. I didn't know P.I. work could pay this well. I mean, the amount scribbled on that check was *really* nice. As in, "I could potentially get that new car I'd been eyeing" nice.

I switched my last shirt into the new suitcase and closed the lid. This aerodynamic masterpiece of travel leisure definitely put my ratty one to shame. Riley was right—no one would buy it that we were married if my luggage screamed Kmart Bluelight Special and his elegantly stated I-make-more-money-than-I-know-what-to-do-with-so-I-bought-a-Louis-Vuitton.

I set the suitcase on the floor and noted that my hands

still trembled. I was even more nervous now than before. Seeing Riley had definitely shaken me up more than I'd anticipated. I mean, I was over him. There was nothing to feel awkward about.

But even I couldn't convince myself that my mental pep talk was true.

I swiped my hair behind my ear, plastered on a smile, and stepped back into the hallway. As soon as I spotted Riley again, my nerves intensified.

Gabby St. Claire, you've confronted killers and haven't been this nervous. You're a professional—a professional investigator, not a professional escort.

Why in the world did I feel the need to clarify these things when I was the only one hearing the conversation play out in my head? *Obviously*, I knew what I meant.

Welcome to my world.

"Let's go."

Riley smiled, took my suitcase, and carried it down the stairs. "So, how was your training? I can't wait to hear about this new job."

"It went . . . great. I really learned a lot. There's some new amazing technology out there to help police forensically. It's changing all the time, and the advancements are groundbreaking." I'd recited, nearly word for word, a bulleted talking point from my training. But what I'd said was true. Even I had been impressed as I'd learned about the improvements in forensic science.

He cast a grin over his shoulder. "That's great."

He wedged the door to the apartment building open with his hip and held it for me. I slipped outside into the searing April day. By the time I reached Riley's sensible sedan, he'd already stowed the suitcases and closed the trunk. He hurried around to the passenger side and opened my door. Only after I was snug inside did he jog around to his side and climb in.

Had other women sat in this seat since we broke up? Had he opened their door? Made them feel like a million bucks?

I shook the thoughts from my head. I couldn't go there. I'd been cheated on so many times that I felt programmed to expect it. Not that Riley would have been cheating because we'd broken up. But still.

He put the car in reverse, slipped his arm across the seats as he looked behind him, but paused before moving. "You sure you're ready for this?"

As a quiver raked through me at his nearness, I realized that was an excellent question.

CHAPTER 3

After swallowing hard, I finally nodded and slid on my sunglasses. "I'm always up for an investigation."

Riley nodded. "Good."

With that, we started down the street, a certain awkwardness setting in between us. There was so much I wanted to ask him, so much I wanted to know. But I didn't want to jump into my questions. I needed to seem chill. Unaffected. Like anything *but* what I actually felt inside.

So I did the next best thing: I asked about the case. I figured I couldn't go wrong talking about an investigation, and it seemed much safer than any other conversation.

"So where exactly are we going?" I forced my thoughts to remain focused. I had to refuse to think about the memories this spic-and-span car brought to mind. Not the good-night kisses. Not the wild goose chases. Not the near-death experiences.

And that pretty much summed up our past relationship.

"We are headed to a little retreat center in the Chesapeake Bay."

"In the bay?"

He nodded. "It's on an island."

"Even better." Islands were good, right? I mean, there was *Fantasy Island*. *Gilligan's Island*. That island from the TV show *Lost*. Or the island where Tom Hanks was stranded in

Castaway.

Just because you were surrounded on all sides by water with no means of escape didn't mean anything . . . right?

Besides, Riley seemed so relaxed about it. In fact, he seemed laid-back in general. That realization made me happy because, deep down inside, I wanted the best for him. But it also bothered me because it meant he'd moved on without me. I wished I could honestly say the same.

"It's called Love Birds Marriage Retreats. A therapist named Dr. Richard Turner started the program. He takes four couples at a time, and they meet every weekend for six weeks. He says going for a week straight would disrupt life too much and that missing work could also add to marital stress, especially if there's already tension because of finances."

"Are we starting at the beginning?"

"No, three weeks of the program have already been completed, so we're coming in right at the middle. Dr. Turner let us in as a favor to the man who owns the island. Brad Thorn has a connection to him and convinced him to pull a few strings."

"You said this is a pretty expensive place?" Virginia Beach blurred by on the interstate, a mix of contemporary, vinyl-sided houses and strip malls mixed in with some golf courses and churches.

"It costs twenty thousand dollars for the entire six weeks."

My mouth nearly dropped open. "Wow. That's major cash. I don't suppose insurance covers anything."

"Not a program like this. That's why most of the people who attend have quite a bit of money. Dr. Turner also believes that if you pay out the cash to be there, you're more likely to take the program seriously."

I settled back in my seat. "Okay, so you told me all that, and it sounds credible enough. Why is it at the center of a murder investigation?"

"Brad Thorn and his wife, Anna, were attending. Brad is convinced there's a connection between her death and those therapy sessions."

"Is there any compelling evidence to support that?"

"We're meeting with Brad before we go, so hopefully he can tell us. Either way, I think her death is worth looking into."

I chewed on what he'd told me so far. "Why the retreat center? Couldn't Anna have been murdered because of some other aspect of her life? Did she work? Could her death be random? I'm just trying to get a feel for all this."

"The police are in agreement with you. They questioned everyone, but also cleared everyone."

"Well, I'm intrigued. What's our cover?" I fully didn't expect Riley, a good boy through and through, to have thought of that. Deceit didn't come easily to him. That was why I'd given him the nickname Church Boy when we'd first met.

Since then, I'd become a bit of a church girl. If not a church girl, then definitely a Jesus follower.

Despite the harm Riley had done to my heart, he was also the reason my heart had mended in other ways not related to him. He'd shown me Jesus, answered my endless questions about the Bible, and even endured my badgering at times.

So there was that.

"I figured we should still go by our first names. Otherwise, it just gets confusing, you know? Last name St. Thomas? Both of our names together, St. Claire and Thomas?"

"We're practically a celebrity couple when you put it like that. Watch out Brangelina. It's Ribby. Or does Giley have a better ring to it?"

He chuckled. "You still have that sense of humor."

Did he think I'd abandoned it when I lost him? I didn't ask but instead shrugged. "What can I say? Anyway, so when did we get married?"

"I figured it could be the day we met. September 9 two years ago."

He remembered that. Interesting.

"We can say we met while trying to save a lost parrot, just like we really did. The closer we can stay to the truth, the better. Don't you agree?"

"Absolutely." I crossed my arms. "So, are you going to stick with being a lawyer as part of your cover story?"

"I think that would be best."

"And I should be a . . ."

His lips turned downward. "I think it would be better if you don't mention a career in forensics. It might put some people on edge, and we want to get them to trust us."

It was the reason I often made more progress than the cops. People were more likely to open up to a crime-scene cleaner than someone with a badge. I wasn't sure about the psychology behind it, but I'd seen it happen time and time again.

"I can see that viewpoint. So what should I say?"

He shifted in his seat as we started across the Bay Bridge Tunnel, a twenty-mile span over the Chesapeake Bay. "It would probably be most believable if you said you stayed at home."

My eyebrows shot up. "What?"

He inhaled deeply. "Well, like I said, most of the couples are wealthy. Most of them have husbands who work a lot and make a lot of money. The wives generally stay home and see to the affairs of the house, not to mention shopping, spa dates, and staying current on the social scene. That's the life most of these people are living. It's a subculture within itself."

Something about how he said it didn't settle well in my gut. The image that formed in my mind wasn't pleasant: women who lived lives of luxury, who cared more about the kind of purse they carried than the kinds of kids they raised, and who viewed life as one materialistic pursuit after another. These weren't my kind of people.

Maybe I was off base. But I'd worked with my share of wealthy people. I'd seen how many of them operated. Maybe my assumption wasn't fair, but it was honest.

"I see."

"What kind of 'I see' was that?" he asked.

The sun hit Riley's side of the car, illuminating his face. I'd practically memorized his features at one time, and now I wanted desperately to unremember all of them. Like how silky his hair felt beneath my fingers. Or what his cheeks felt like when he hadn't shaved for a day. Or how his hands felt amazingly strong and calloused for someone who sat behind a desk for the majority of his days.

I shrugged, remembering his question. He could still read me a little too well. I needed to keep that in mind this weekend. "I'm just soaking everything in. Absorbing it. Taking on this new persona that's so unlike me."

"Can't see yourself as a housewife?"

"Only as a desperate one." I flashed a smile, not wanting to go there. "So anyway . . . when someone asks why we're there, what should we say? What issue has brought us to this point in our marriage?"

It could have been my imagination, but Riley looked uncomfortable for a moment. He shifted, and his grip tightened around the steering wheel. Was it the long drive on a narrow bridge surrounded by water? Or was it this conversation?

"I thought we could say that we rushed into our marriage without truly knowing each other and that's led to problems."

I wondered if he was still trying to keep his answers as close to reality as possible. Did he think we'd hurried things before? Did he think we didn't really know each other when we'd been engaged?

I didn't ask the questions. Maybe I didn't want to know the answers.

Instead, I looked out over the water. I'd always loved the bay. It was peaceful and significantly calmer than the raging waves in the Atlantic. I stared across the glimmering expanse now, trying to collect my thoughts.

Several boats cruised the area, some with fishermen clutching long poles and wearing floppy hats. Other boaters were simply enjoying the exceptionally warm spring day. Seagulls soared. Cirrus clouds streaked high overhead.

For a moment, I felt serenity.

Then Riley spoke again.

"So tell me more about this new job you have."

I drew in a breath, wondering what exactly I'd gotten myself into by agreeing to his proposal. This was all a bad idea. That simply became clearer and clearer as the car ride continued. But I was such a sucker for both mysteries and for Riley. You might as well slap a wrapper on me and label me a "Cherry Firecracker" lollipop.

"I'll be teaching police departments in the region how to use various crime-scene investigation equipment and technology."

He stole a glance at me. "Really? Now that sounds

perfect for you. How'd you get the job?"

Garrett Mercer had helped me to get it. I didn't want to tell Riley that, though. Garrett was the guy I'd kinda sorta started seeing after Riley ditched me. At the moment, Garrett was in Africa helping to dig wells to provide people there with clean water.

Garrett was a great guy. So why did I feel guilty right now? Garrett and I weren't really together, and working with Riley for this investigation wasn't cheating on Garrett.

Emotions were so confusing at times. Especially when it came to men. Argh.

"I got the job through various connections," I finally said, skirting around the exact details. "I can set my own hours based on the workload for the week."

"I'm really happy for you, Gabby."

Silence fell for a moment. There was a time when it would feel like the most natural thing in the world to reach over and grab Riley's hand. To stay quiet while we rode because we were comfortable enough with each other that we didn't always have to fill the silence.

But right now I was keenly aware of every second that ticked by without conversation. I was unsure what to do with my arms. Crossing them seemed so closed. Keeping them open I felt exposed. When I left my hands in my lap, I fiddled with my fingers.

This was going to be a long weekend. And maybe one of the biggest tests of my faith yet.

CHAPTER 4

Only a few minutes after we exited the Bay Bridge Tunnel, Riley took a left and we pulled into the small town of Cape Charles. Golf carts cruised the old-timey streets, people walked their dogs along the warmly decorated sidewalk, and the bay glimmered in the background.

"This is where Brad said he would meet us," Riley said. "Just for a frame of reference: Anna was buried yesterday. This is all fresh still."

"Noted."

He parked on the street, and we scrambled across the road, dodging golf carts—okay, not really, but the image amused me—until we reached a bistro. A man was seated outside at a wrought-iron table. A colorful, green umbrella perched above him, and cheerful plants lined the sidewalk around the area. Too bad the man looked anything but cheerful. A sweaty glass of iced tea on the table looked like it hadn't been touched.

He nodded ever so slightly at Riley as we approached.

I knew without any introduction that this was Brad. I could see the heartache in his gaze, in the heaviness on his shoulders, in his lackluster expression.

My heart panged for a moment. I knew what grief was like, and seeing him brought those emotions rushing back. There was nothing I could say to ease his sorrow. Only time would do that.

Riley extended his arm and, without any fluffy greeting, the two men shook hands. Some kind of silent understanding passed between them.

"This is Gabby," Riley said.

I simply offered a smile and started to sit across from him. Riley nudged my chair out for me before I was fully seated. It was such a simple action, but it always made me feel special. If Riley acted like a big jerk, it would be much easier to dislike him.

This was Riley's gig, so I wanted him to take the lead. He knew more of the details and people involved than I did. But I was so used to being the pushy one when it came to investigations that I had trouble remaining quiet.

"Thanks again for meeting us," Riley said.

I leaned back, observing Brad. The man was good-looking. He had thick blond hair with gentle gray strands washed through it. His tan seemed to indicate he liked to be on the water. The crow's feet around his eyes were white streaks the sun never touched. I imagined him squinting on a boat as it sped across the water after a long day of fishing.

But he also had an air of distinction about him. It was the way he carried himself, I decided. The expensive texture of his coral-colored golf shirt. The fancy watch on his wrist.

"Thanks for taking this on." Brad shifted in his chair. A smile hadn't touched his lips or eyes since we'd arrived. "I hope you both realize what you're getting into here. You're dealing with someone dangerous, someone who's willing to kill to keep his secrets quiet."

A shiver niggled up my spine at his proclamation. Danger. Secrets. Almost dying. It all seemed right up my alley.

"His?" I asked. I brushed my hair away from my face and

27

pushed my *Top Gun*-style sunglasses higher on my nose. It was better this way: He couldn't see my eyes and know I was eyeballing his tea. I'd neglected my lunch in my haste to get ready.

"Most killers are men, so I feel like that's a safe bet. However, it's anyone's guess at this point." He raised his palms in the air.

His observation made it apparent he was well educated and researched. I'd intended to ask Riley what the man did for a living, but I'd forgotten.

Riley shifted, angling his body away from the sun. "I was hoping you could tell Gabby your side of the story here. It will mean more coming from you."

The man's gaze fell on me. He was scrutinizing me, I realized, and trying to determine whether or not I could be trusted. Trying to ascertain if I was as good as Riley claimed. He finally looked away, no conclusion in his gaze. I supposed I'd have to prove myself. You'd think I'd be an expert on that at this point in my life.

I mentally cued "Never Surrender" by Skillet. That song had been on my playlist a lot lately. I was confident I could win Brad over. Well, at least 95-percent confident. I'd seen too many people get cocky and fail. It was a delicate balance.

"My wife, Anna, and I were going to counseling through Love Birds Marriage Retreats," Brad started, his shoulders rigid and his jaw tight. "This was actually our second time around with Dr. Turner. We thought we were making progress after we went through the sessions the first time. We really wanted to make our marriage work—if for nothing else, for the children's sakes."

We stayed silent, waiting for him to formulate his thoughts. Brad absently rubbed the side of his glass, his gaze pensive. His wife's death had obviously affected him. He had cared for her, I realized. He was carrying too much pain for him not to have loved her. That probably seemed like a callous thought, but I'd seen a lot in my nearly thirty years. Nothing surprised me any more.

"I really thought we'd crested the wave, that we'd gotten over the humps and the biggest hurdles we faced. I thought things were looking up. After our first weekend session, I woke up that Saturday and went to meet Anna in the dining hall for breakfast. She didn't show up. I continued to wait, but when she still didn't appear, I asked her roommate to go check on her. She said she hadn't seen Anna all morning and assumed my wife was downstairs. That's when a full-out search began." His voice cracked. "They finally found her body. She was in the boathouse. She'd overdosed on some prescription pills."

I let a few seconds pass before gently asking my next question. "Were they her pills?"

He nodded, a muscle flexing in his jaw. "She struggled with depression and anxiety. But she would have never taken those pills herself and overdosed. Never."

"How do you know?" I tried to remain sensitive, but I needed this information. It was essential to this investigation.

Brad's gaze finally met mine, and I saw the determination there. "I know because of our kids. She wouldn't put them through this. I know her better than that. Our kids were her whole world. What they're going through right now . . ." He swung his head back-and-forth, his shoulders hunched.

I could accept his answer, yet I knew that when people weren't in their right frame of mind, they could act in out-of-the-ordinary ways. Who really knew how desperate Anna was feeling? Or what kind of emotions she'd bottled deep inside?

I wouldn't bring that up right now, though. He had

enough on his mind. "Did you tell the police that? I'm assuming there was an investigation."

"I did tell the police, but the note Anna left meant they didn't put as much time into considering the idea that this was something other than a suicide."

"Anna left a note?" That changed things. Could a person be forced to compose a note? Of course. But there would be signs and clues within their handwriting that they were writing it under duress. I'd taken one class on handwriting analysis, but I wanted to take more. The concept and science behind it was fascinating.

"That's correct." Brad swallowed hard and pulled out his phone. "I wrote down what I could remember, but I wasn't able to keep the note myself. The police haven't released it back to me."

He held out his phone, and I read the words he'd typed. Riley leaned in beside me. As his arm brushed mine, my body went into survival mode. I jerked away a little too fast. Realizing that my actions had slipped out of my control, I cleared my throat and focused on the words on the screen.

I'm tired of the struggle. I'm tired of the guilt. I can't live under this pressure any more. I'm sorry for what I've done and that my selfish actions have torn my family apart. I don't deserve forgiveness.

I frowned at the desperation in the words. "Selfish actions?"

Brad winced and sat up straighter in his chair, almost as if he had to gather his courage. "Anna was a good woman. But she cheated on me."

I blinked. That was unexpected.

"Tell me more," I prodded. I hated to ask, but I had no choice. Not if he wanted answers. Investigations required some discomfort. It was like paring down a block of wood as you sculpted a masterpiece—the process was painful, but the end resulted in a clear, discernable image.

He let out a sigh. "I'm a developer. Office buildings, skyscrapers. Things that are a big deal. My job kept me from home too often. I take responsibility for that. Anna was lonely, and she met a man—more like a boy, truth be told—down at the marina where she'd started taking kayaking lessons. The affair lasted for three months, and she left me for part of that time. That's when we went to counseling for the first time."

"She ended her affair?" I asked.

"She did."

"We'll need this man's name," I said.

He reached into his shirt pocket then pushed a piece of paper toward me. "Here it is. The guy's name is Jason Sparrow. He lives up in Onancock. It's about an hour north of here."

"Was the note she left handwritten or typed?" I asked.

"Handwritten," Brad said. "And, yes, it was her scrawl. She had a distinctive way of writing, with lots of loops and fancy cursive. She liked to do calligraphy as a hobby so she took a lot of pride in how her letters looked."

I stored away that information. Interesting. I could be pursuing a case that really wasn't a case at all. This could really be a suicide.

***

A waitress had appeared, and Riley and I ordered some iced coffee. That gave me some time to collect my thoughts, and to adjust my poker expression. Thank goodness for these sunglasses—otherwise Brad may have seen my doubt.

These glasses also gave me the chance to observe Riley

a moment. My heart rate sped at the sight of him. He seemed at ease here with the gentle breeze, the bright sunlight, and the bay in the background.

I had to admit that being here also made me feel like I was in my element. Cowboys had rodeos. Football players had games. I had my mysteries. This was my passion, the thing I loved to pursue, and the hobby that kept me up at night.

"Do you have any suspects?" Riley rested his arms on the tabletop, his full attention on Brad. "You obviously think this is related to the retreat center somehow. Why?"

"The island is secluded, so there are only a few options as to who could have done this. All of the other couples should be present this weekend for week three of this program." Brad pointed to the paper he'd shoved toward us. "I've listed their names on the paper. One is Atticus Griffith. Atticus owns a major technology firm—Griffith Innovations. Perhaps you've heard of them."

I nodded and took a sip of my chilled caramel latte. Everyone had heard of Griffith. The company made a new smart phone that people raved about.

"His wife is Farrah, and the couple is very pretentious. They didn't get along with anyone at the retreat center. They definitely didn't get along with each other. I've seen ice cubes warmer toward each other than the two of them."

"And how about Bo and Angelina Daniels?" I pointed to the next name on his list.

Brad frowned. "No one could understand why the Daniels were there. He works for a construction company. He doesn't own it. She works part time at a gas station. There's no way they should have been able to afford the retreat. They were on a different . . . level."

He said the words with disdain. What would he think of

me if he knew the details of my past? Definitely that we were on different "levels." But would he also feel that I was beneath him?

"So maybe they got a scholarship or someone supported them in going?" I questioned.

"Dr. Turner doesn't give scholarships," Brad explained. "He feels people appreciate the therapy more if they pay for it. But there were rumblings that this couple wasn't as innocent as they seemed. At least, that was my wife's theory. She thought they were hiding something."

"You think Anna discovered something and either Angelina or Bo confronted her, maybe?"

He shrugged. "Maybe. I haven't ruled anything or anyone out. Besides them, there were Jim and Ginger Wagnor. They seemed the most normal of all the couples there. But I saw Anna arguing with Jim the day she died. I asked her about it, but she brushed me off. But I could tell something was bothering her."

In my mind, Jim was already my first suspect. They had a history of conflict. Conflict could lead to violence, even death.

"Those are the only people who were there?" Riley asked.

"Well, of course, there was Dr. Turner, his assistant Blaine, Captain Leroy, and a couple of housekeeping staff, as well as the cook. I can't say I ever had any negative interactions with any of them, though."

"The secluded location at least narrows down the potential suspects," I said. "Provided her death is connected to the retreat."

"It is." Brad's voice left no room for doubt.

He took a long sip of his drink. I could practically see his thoughts churning. Finally, he set his glass down with a clunk, flexed his jaw again, and glanced at Riley then me.

"I should also let you know that there was a reporter from up in Baltimore who started looking into this," Brad continued. "Her name is Rae Gray."

"So you have more than one person investigating?" I clarified.

He shook his head. "No, she disappeared. I haven't heard from her in several days. Granted, I didn't officially hire her. I contacted her about a potential story. These retreats are based out of Baltimore, plus we live in that area."

"Do you suspect foul play in Rae's disappearance as well?" I asked, curious as to how this all fit together in his mind.

"I have no idea. She has no obligation to contact me, but she seemed very interested. She said she was going to dig deeper. It makes me cautious that she's not returning my calls."

"I can see why," I said.

Brad picked up his phone, tapped on the screen a few times, and then held it up for us to see the photo. "This is Anna. She deserves justice. Please say you'll help."

That seemed to be his stamp of approval. I'd passed his test, and he trusted me to investigate for him. Now I just had to hope I didn't let him down.

I stared at the picture of his wife. Anna looked vivacious, with intelligent brown eyes, glossy chestnut-colored hair, and an overall cultured look, all the way down to the leopard-print scarf tied like a headband around her head. She was on a boat in the photo, and the sun hit her hair in a way that made the picture look like a magazine cover.

Yes, Anna's life had ended too early.

"I'd look into this myself," Brad continued. "But I'm afraid if I found the person who did this, I'd kill him myself."

As his words lingered in the air, there was no

34

uncertainty that he'd spoken the truth.

CHAPTER 5

"So, what did you think?" Riley asked when we were back in his car.

I pulled out the paper Brad had given me and stared at the information there as Riley put his car in drive. Just being in such close proximity to him again with no barriers between us—no other people, no table, not even a cup of coffee—had me feeling unnerved again. I needed to get used to this because I was going to be with him a lot this weekend.

I pulled myself together, though. I always did. And I always would.

I knew I was loved by my Creator. I would never find my wholeness in anyone but Him. So I pressed on. Beneath the humor and sarcasm and self-deprecating comments, I knew where my purpose came from, and it wasn't Riley Thomas. All of these struggles in my life were building my character one painstaking step at a time.

"It looks like we have four suspects to start with," I told him, glancing at my notes. "The snooty Griffiths, the redneck Daniels pair, the happy Wagnors, and boy-toy Jason Sparrow. But there's one other thing we have to consider."

"What's that?"

"That Anna possibly did commit suicide. She left a note that was clearly her handwriting, and the police don't seem to suspect any foul play. When people commit suicide, family members never want to accept it. It's too difficult to come to terms with the idea."

Riley frowned. "At least maybe we can prove that, right? Some answers are better than no answers."

"I agree." I was an answer person. I liked knowing what really happened. And I was under the strict belief that the truth could set us free. However, dealing with that truth could initially be quite a struggle.

Riley took his eyes off the road long enough to glance at me. "You handled yourself like a pro back there."

I shrugged, like it wasn't a big deal, but I secretly glowed under his compliment. I'd come a long way since my initial days as a nosy crime-scene cleaner. Education and experience and a lot of errors—I couldn't forget to mention them—had gotten me to this point.

"You weren't too shabby yourself," I finally said. And it was true. He'd been a good balance of listener and interrogator. He'd been curious but not overly anxious. His laid-back vibe made him seem comfortable and confident.

For a moment, we'd felt like partners. Like Mulder and Scully. Monk and Sharona. Castle and Beckett.

I had to nip those thoughts in the bud, though. This was strictly professional, and I'd be wise not to forget it.

***

Forty minutes after leaving Cape Charles, we pulled into a gravel lot adjacent to a sturdy pier on the bay. There were five other cars in the parking area, and one boat at the dock. As we stood there, a strong wind whipped around us. I'd like to think it was just the breeze coming off the water, but the dark clouds in the distance told a different story. A storm was approaching.

Hopefully that wasn't an ominous sign of things to come.

"You must be Mr. and Mrs. St. Thomas." A man who looked like Captain Stubing of *The Love Boat* fame approached Riley and me as we lifted our suitcases from the trunk. The shiny, aerodynamic suitcases. Those accessories needed a security detail all their own.

Okay, I was exaggerating, but I did have a strange love for that new luggage.

Riley smiled affably. "We are. And you're . . . ?"

"I'm Leroy." He raised his chin and reached for our luggage. "I run the boat back and forth from the island. We were waiting for you before we started the journey over. Let's get you boarded. Your car should be fine here until Sunday."

I couldn't resist humming the theme song from *The Love Boat* as Leroy took our luggage and put it on a large pontoon boat waiting by the pier.

Riley leaned closer, so close that his breath feathered across my cheek. "I've missed that."

Something about the exchange caused a shiver to wiggle down my spine. Not a good sign.

Remember, Gabby. Failure's not an option. Protect your heart. Be in control.

"It's show time," I muttered under my breath.

"You've got this, Gabby," Riley said.

I didn't feel like I "had" anything, but I decided to keep that quiet.

Riley helped me onboard before climbing in behind me. Another couple was already sitting on a padded bench near the bow with their backs toward us. They didn't bother to look our way as we boarded.

Riley and I exchanged a look before finding a cushioned seat on the perimeter. As the captain geared up to go and ran through some general safety precautions like the location of life preservers, I braced myself for the ride.

I glanced at the front of the boat where the other passengers sat. How strange was it that they hadn't even mumbled a greeting or acknowledged us. Was this how all the couples at this retreat center would act? Would they all sense that they were somehow above everyone else because of their padded paychecks and fancy cars? Did rich people think they were better than other rich people?

I stared at the couple's backs for a moment. They weren't sitting lovey-dovey. In fact, there was a good six inches between them. They looked stiff as they stared straight ahead, neither of them speaking.

The woman had ashy blonde hair, and, when she turned her head ever-so slightly, I could see the fine wrinkles along her eyes and mouth. She wore a long-sleeved white sweater that she had pulled over her hands. The man had salt-and-pepper hair slicked back, and he wore a Northface parka. They had to be Atticus and Farrah Griffith. The Daniels were too redneck and the Wagnors too happy.

Riley struck up a conversation about fishing with Captain Leroy. I tuned out what they were saying and, instead, studied Riley a moment. Why did he have to be so handsome? Would he be easier to dislike if he was repulsive looking? Honestly, probably not because it wasn't his looks that had drawn me toward him. I felt like our spirits connected.

I was just getting my life on track when he'd returned.

God, are you trying to teach me something? Show me some kind of fault in myself that I need to correct?

If I were smart, I'd concentrate on my new job and ignore the emotions trying to capture my heart and mind. That would be the smart thing. However, I'd never been very wise in matters of the heart.

And I had a feeling that would be my ultimate downfall.

Before I could dwell on that thought too long, I saw the man pull something from his pocket. His cell phone.

The boat suddenly jostled. I glanced at the sky. That storm was not only on its way—it was upon us. As if to confirm my thought, the wind gusted over us and sent a spray of water with it.

Even the birds seemed to recognize that things would get treacherous. They squawked overhead as they made a mad dash for the mainland.

When the boat jostled again, the man's phone clattered from his hand and skidded toward me. Quickly, I darted up and grabbed it for him. Right before I handed it back, I glanced at the screen. A text message was still there.

This isn't over. Don't think for a second I'm letting you get away with this.

CHAPTER 6

The man I assumed as Atticus Griffith snatched the phone from me.

Oops. I guess I hadn't been all that subtle about reading his message.

"Here you go," I mumbled. "By the way, I'm Gabby St. Thomas."

He simply grunted, mumbled something that sounded vaguely like "Atticus," and stomped back to his seat.

What had that message been about? It was definitely suspicious, especially in light of everything I knew so far.

At that moment, Riley and Captain Leroy's conversation floated to my ears.

"It's about a twenty-minute boat ride," Captain Leroy said, looking over the water as we puttered across the bay, the waves and wind urging us to go back. "Unless it's a big storm, we can usually go back and forth between the island and the mainland without any problem. This boat is big enough to handle it."

I still couldn't believe that I was headed over to an island in the middle of the bay with no means of escape other than this boat. It seemed like the perfect setup for a really horrific experience. Add the stormy weather to that, and it was just the wrong mix.

"Tell us about Bird's Nest Island. We're excited to see

it," Riley continued, not missing a beat, even as the wind caused more water to splatter into the boat.

Riley would fit in easily here. His parents were fairly wealthy. He'd grown up in a different world than I had. That was probably one of the reasons he'd broken up with me. He'd never said so, but I'd always suspected it deep down inside.

"Oh, it's a great place. Not very large. It used to be a playground for the wealthy. There's an old lodge where hunters and fishermen stayed."

"What happened?" As I asked the question, my hair nearly suctioned itself to my face. Just as I removed several strands, several more grabbed at my features. So much for straightening it earlier. By the time this weather finished with it, I'd look like I stuck my finger in a light socket.

"The lodge closed down in the late thirties after the stock market crash. It was never revitalized until about five years ago. Now the owner, Mr. Robinson, rents it out to groups like Dr. Turner. But, of course, you know all this, correct? Because you're friends with Mr. Robinson?"

Riley nodded. "That's right."

In truth, Brad Thorn knew the man personally and had pulled some strings.

"We are, but he never told us the history of the place," I said. Thunder rumbled above us and caused me to tremble.

Captain Leroy nodded, unaffected by the storm. "Well, there's some good folklore about the island, but that's not why you're going. Dr. Turner just started leasing this location for his therapy groups. This is our first retreat series here."

"He has other locations?" I asked, curious now about this program. If I could stay focused, the storm wouldn't freak me out as much.

"That's right. One up in Baltimore and another in the

mountains. He started these retreats after his wife passed away. He says they help him heal."

"I didn't realize he was a widower," I said.

Captain Leroy's gaze remained on the choppy water. "His wife died in a car accident. She was the love of his life, and he's never quite been the same. That's why he feels so strongly about helping other couples. He wants people to have a happy and fulfilling marriage, just like he did. He's made a lot of money on his books. He was a therapist in New York City for a while. His practice was thriving, for that matter. He gave it all up to start these retreats, though."

"It sounds like you know him well," I said.

"We met when I was working at a country club in Maryland. I knew both him and his wife. When he told me about these retreats and offered me a job, I couldn't say no. Now I run the boat, do some maintenance, and anything else the doctor asks me to do."

"Sounds like a good fit," Riley said.

Captain Leroy nodded. "It is. Dr. Turner is a good man. I've seen a lot of couples who've left these sessions changed. That makes it all even more worth it—seeing someone leave with hope where there was once hopelessness."

My interest spiked. Maybe there was more to this retreat than I'd initially assumed. A little more of my anxiety turned into excitement.

I sat back and felt the wind whip around me. As Riley and Leroy's conversation veered off into fishing again, I pulled out my cell phone and tried to send a text to Sierra. It wouldn't go through.

What? How was that possible? I mean, we weren't that far from civilization . . . were we?

"There's no service out here," Captain Leroy said.

"We've passed the point of no return."

"What?" There were actually places in the US with no phone service? In this day and age?

"It's true. Every once in a while, you can find a hot spot on the island where you might get patchy reception. But, overall, I wouldn't count on it."

This was going to be interesting, especially if I found myself in a situation where I desperately needed help.

And I always seemed to find myself in those kinds of situations.

CHAPTER 7

The storm passed, but now a heavy fog surrounded us as we pulled up to the pier at Bird's Nest Island. The low-lying clouds had come on quickly, beginning in the distance and then immersing us in their thickness. I could hardly see my hand in front of my face.

My nerves tightened as I stood and waited to disembark.

"Welcome to Cemetery—I mean, Bird's Nest Island," Leroy said.

"Wait—why did you say Cemetery Island?" I couldn't *not* ask that question because what I'd heard was too disturbing to ignore.

He shrugged, like it wasn't a big deal. "That's what the place used to be called. I wouldn't worry about it. Anyway, I'll bring your luggage up in a moment. I just talked to Dr. Turner on the radio and, he would like everyone to remain inside Blackbird Hall as a safety precaution until this fog passes."

Cemetery Island? Blackbird Hall? This whole place just seemed creepier and creepier by the moment. All I needed was a raven tapping at my window, playing mind games and chanting "nevermore!" Yeah, this place was Edgar Allen Poe weird, and I'd been here less than three minutes.

The Griffiths walked ahead of us, again not initiating the slightest bit of conversation. Riley and I followed silently behind.

A decent-size bluff rose in front of us, and we climbed a set of wooden stairs to reach the top. The fog only added to the eerie atmosphere I already felt about the place. The names, the people here, what had happened with Anna . . . all those things together nearly formed the start of a horror story in my mind.

As I glanced back at Leroy, I expected to see him gathering our luggage. Instead, he stood on the pier and stared at us.

My throat went dry. If I wasn't so determined, I would run far away from this island and retreat center now. There was no way off. No cell phone service. And a possible murderer.

Riley and I crested the top of the bluff and paused. I'd wanted to observe the island, but all I could see was fog. I didn't even see the Griffiths.

I squinted, trying to gather my bearings and at least figure out where to go from here. It was no use. We couldn't see a killer if he came running right toward us with a knife and a hand-painted welcome sign.

"What now?" I asked.

He sighed and glanced around. "I guess we keep walking until we either find someone or we find a building."

"You must be Riley and Gabby!" A woman appeared through the fog. She wore linen slacks, a navy-blue T-shirt, and clutched a clipboard in her hands. Her honey blonde hair was pulled back in a neat bun, and she had a large but thin build.

"Isn't this crazy?" she continued. "I don't know if I've ever seen the fog this thick. If we were in a cartoon we could cut a donut in the air and eat it, right?" She let out a nervous laugh.

"My thoughts exactly," I told her. "Scooby Doo would have a ball here. And possibly a bellyache."

The woman gave me a weird look, and I reminded

myself to appear cultured instead of *pop*-cultured. That was going to take some effort.

"Anyway, I'm Blaine, Dr. Turner's assistant. I saw the Griffiths had arrived, and assumed you were probably here as well."

"I'm Riley, and this is my wife, Gabby."

As Riley said those words, something twisted in my gut. If everything had stayed on schedule, we would have been married now. But a diabolical killer set on revenge had shot Riley only days before our wedding. That one tragedy had landed Riley in the hospital and in recovery for months afterward. Everything had changed.

One never knew when life would throw a curveball like that. I'd like to think I had accepted my circumstances as they were now, but I had my moments.

Like right now.

Hearing Riley call me his wife seemed so bittersweet.
Consider it pure joy . . .

"We're so glad to have you here," Blaine continued. "Let me show you to your accommodations. If you just follow the path, it will show you the way—in more ways than one." She laughed at her own psychology joke. "Anyway, Leroy will bring your things up in a minute. I just know you're going to love it here. We strive to make it as comfortable as possible for our guests."

Blaine was obviously well versed in PR and guest relations. She also probably knew everything going on at the place. She'd be a good resource for this investigation. I kept that thought in the back of my mind.

"Watch your step," Blaine said. "The island, of course, is mostly sand. Some say it started off as a sandbar. Anyway, the landscape shifts. Even though we grade this path quite often, little potholes, if you want to call them that, pop up frequently."

A wise man builds his house upon the rock.

The old song I'd sang as a child came to mind. At the moment, it didn't make me feel any better, though. I knew what happened to the house on the sand.

Just as Blaine said that, I stepped inadvertently in one of the "little potholes" she'd warned about. I lunged forward and grabbed Riley. I feared I might take him down with me, but, instead, strong hands wrapped around my waist.

My skin came alive at his touch. I was toast. Pure and simple toast, buttered up and cut into edible triangles.

I looked up at him, certain he'd see the battling emotions in my eyes. Certain he'd know I hadn't truly gotten over him. Except I still had my sunglasses on. Score!

Riley's lips parted like he might speak, but before he could, Blaine interrupted.

"I know it's awkward being here together." Blaine pressed her lips together in a frown. A compassionate frown, but still a frown. "All our couples feel that way. We hope to change that by the time you leave here."

With that proclamation, I backed away from Riley and quickly straightened my blouse.

I wanted to think of a witty comeback, but my mind drew a blank. It did that at the worst possible times.

A sound in the distance saved the day.

A faint cry for help.

It appeared this real-life version of Clue had already started.

CHAPTER 8

Instinctively, I started toward the sound, like a child drawn to the Pied Piper. Riley held me back.

"You don't know the terrain. You need to watch your step." His voice sounded firm and authoritative until he added a syrupy sweet "darling."

I wanted to argue, but he was right. The place *had* been called Cemetery Island. I didn't want to add my tombstone to what I assumed to be an already long list.

I slowed my steps. It was only then that I realized Blaine wasn't following us. Wasn't she concerned?

In fact, when I looked behind me, I didn't even see the woman. Was it because of the fog, or had she disappeared? A shiver captured my spine and didn't let go.

I heard the voice again. Someone had clearly called, "Help."

Riley and I hurried—carefully hurried, that is—toward the sound, my unease growing with each step.

You should have said no to this investigation. Should have said no.

I'd been in a lot of tricky situations, but this place was just spooky. I had a bad feeling in my gut about being here. Was there such a thing as a fear of islands? If so, I might have it.

Riley and I practically fell over two women who appeared on the path. One was Blaine. How had she gotten ahead of us so fast?

The other woman was heavy-set and probably in her mid-forties. She was a bleached blonde whose roots needed a touch up. She wore stone-washed jeans, the kind popular in the eighties, with Keds and a stained T-shirt. Was she part of the staff here also?

She lay on the ground holding her ankle. Her face scrunched with pain—narrowed eyes, rounded lips, veins bulging at her neck. In fact, her expression was almost comical. Or maybe I had a twisted sense of humor.

"I stepped on something, and my ankle twisted." She rocked back and forth.

"Dr. Turner asked everyone to stay inside." Blaine's voice was short and clipped. In other words, annoyed.

"But I just needed some fresh air. You know how it is. I feel suffocated—in more ways than one." The woman had a way of speaking that indicated she was perhaps from the country. Her teeth were also a mess—stained, crooked, and partially missing.

She couldn't possibly be a guest here.

"Ms. Daniels, we need to get you inside," Blaine continued. "We can take a look at your ankle there."

Ms. Daniels? I remembered what Brad had said about her. She was one-half of the redneck couple.

"You must be the new lab rats," Ms. Daniels said instead, looking us up and down. "You look about like the rest of them."

"Like the rest of them?" I asked, the words spilling out. I pictured myself with pointy ears, piercing eyes, and whiskers.

"The rest of the clients here. Hoity-toity. I keep hoping for someone normal like us beneath all that fancy exterior. That's not going to happen, is it?"

Score! I looked like I fit in. That was a near miracle. And I didn't look like a rat. Double score.

"Ms. Daniels, please. Mr. and Mrs. St. Thomas just got here. There's no need to greet them like this." Blaine shifted awkwardly as she glared down at Ms. Daniels, who still grasped her ankle and rocked back and forth.

The woman waved one hand, chipped red nail polish blurring through the air. "Oh, I didn't mean it like that. You know me. I speak my mind. That's one of the reasons my husband, Bo, and I are here. Apparently, I can't keep my trap shut." She cackled.

Note to self: Don't cackle at your own jokes. It sounds weird.

"Anyway, can someone help me get all two hundred pounds of me off this ground?" she continued. "It's harder than it used to be."

Riley crouched toward her. "Do you think you can put any weight on your ankle?"

"Probably not. But if I had a big, strapping man to help me, I'm sure I could make it to Blackbird Hall." She fluttered her eyelashes at Riley.

Was she really flirting with Riley when he was supposedly my husband? That was about as classless as a Sunday school dropout.

"I don't know if I fit the strapping part of that equation, but I'll do what I can to help." He reached under her shoulders and gently pulled her to her feet.

She winced as she stood. Her arms went around Riley, and I saw a gleam appear in her eyes.

Without wanting to, I scowled.

"Angelina," Blaine warned, glancing at Angelina's fingers sprawled across Riley's midsection. She'd dropped using the woman's proper name, so she must be getting upset. "How about if I go get your husband for you?"

"That big old lug? No, thank you. This gentleman is helping just fine." She patted Riley's chest and grinned.

You had to be kidding me. Who did stuff like this? My claws were starting to come out. It didn't matter that Riley wasn't really my husband. She didn't know that.

"I can help support your weight on the other side," I finally said, my teeth clenched.

Angelina Daniels shook her head and nudged closer to Riley. "Oh no. I think he's doing a fine job by himself. But, Blaine, you should have this path checked out. It's a lawsuit waiting to happen."

My fumes only increased. Was this woman looking for a reason to file a personal injury claim? Was she *that* kind of person?

As she stepped away, I looked down.

I gasped at what I saw on the path where Angelina had fallen.

It was a bony hand reaching from the grave.

Desperate for my help.

***

"This place is cursed. I knew it!" Angelina shrieked.

I ignored her and instead bent down for a closer look. "I'm no expert, but I think this is old."

"We've had some storms here lately. Maybe the shifting sands led to an old grave being uncovered," Blaine said.

"Hence the name Cemetery Island?" I questioned as another strong wind swept around me.

"Bird's Nest Island has a much better ring to it, doesn't

it?" Blaine said with a weak laugh. "The birds love this place."

So do dead people, apparently.

I tried to sound more clueless than I actually was as I responded. "I think in situations like these, you're supposed to call the medical examiner. He or she will come to investigate. No one should touch these in the meantime."

Riley chuckled and put his free arm around my shoulders. "That's my wife. Always reading mystery novels. She sounds like she's done this before, doesn't she?"

I cringed and removed his arm. I was just playing a role, I told myself. It had nothing to do with how my body responded to him. How every part of me seemed to come alive.

But the real issue right now was that I needed to act more clueless and less like a former medical legal death investigator.

"I'll call the sheriff and get someone to come out," Blaine said, her face pale. "That sounds like a good idea."

"I'll get Angelina somewhere she can sit down," Riley said. "Gabby, will you be okay out here?"

I nodded, practically wanting to do cartwheels. Nothing sounded better than being alone with this skeleton for a few minutes. "Yes. Someone should stay with these bones."

I glanced in the distance as they lumbered down the trail. A large stone building appeared out of the fog. It almost looked like a castle: imposing, eerie, with walls that could tell tales of days from the past.

But I wasn't nearly as interested in the building as I was this hand. I desperately wanted to brush away the granules of sand and see what else I could find. But instead of disturbing the scene, I simply leaned in closer.

There was nothing left on the bones, which indicated they had been there for a while. The phalanges almost looked brittle as they reached from the ground. They were dry and yellow with age.

At once, I wondered what had happened to this person. Had he or she received a decent burial that had somehow been unearthed? Or was this person left here by someone who didn't want to be discovered? Just what kind of secrets did this island hold?

"I was told to come out here and relieve you."

I jumped at the gruff voice. When I looked up, I saw a man I hadn't met before. He wore a black outfit, the kind chefs wore on cooking shows, and had chin-length dark hair that had been heavily gelled away from his face. He was probably in his mid-twenties. The nasty-looking scar across his cheek made me wonder about his history.

I quickly stood and brushed the sand from my jeans. *Play it cool, Gabby. Play it cool.* "I don't mind staying."

The man stared at me, his eyes absent of any emotion. "Don't be ridiculous. You're a guest here. You should go get comfortable. I'll wait for the authorities to arrive."

I offered my hand, trying to buy some more time. "I'm Gabby."

He didn't extend his hand in return. He only nodded and crossed his arms. "I'm Steve." He barely moved his lips as he said his name.

"I really don't mind staying. You look like you have other things you need to be doing." I pointed to his uniform. "Kitcheny types of things."

"I'm a food artist," he seethed.

"Of course. I was going to say that next."

"I was told to do this, so I will." He said the words with that I'm-an-angry-bird expression.

I wanted to argue, but I knew that would only look

suspicious. Any normal guest wouldn't want to wait here with a dead body. With reluctance, I took one last glance at the hand—the one reaching out for my help—and stepped away.

But the image of those bones wouldn't leave my thoughts.

CHAPTER 9

As soon as I stepped inside Blackbird Hall, the fancy decorations made me feel uncomfortable. There were antiques, distinguished-looking paintings of people I didn't recognize, and a baby grand piano, with oriental rugs, mahogany wood paneling, and the overwhelming scent of lemon. Other surfaces featured dainty teacups, collectable figurines, and expensive vases—that's *vauzes*, with a snooty French accent and not vases that rhymes with cases.

I felt like I'd stepped into a museum.

If there was anywhere my klutzy side would emerge, it was here, where there were so many valuables to break.

Riley knelt beside Angelina, who sprawled in a stiff-looking chair near an intricate wooden staircase beyond the entryway. She was still whining about her ankle and staring at Riley like he was her knight in shining armor.

"Gabby." Riley stood. "Is everything okay?"

I nodded. "Someone named Steve who works here is waiting for the authorities to arrive."

Blaine appeared from down the hallway. "I just called the sheriff's office, and they're going to come out. They might be a few hours because of this storm. But they're coming."

Angelina grabbed Riley's arm. "Honey child, I just need something to squeeze right now. Can I use that solid arm of yours? The pain in my ankle is about to knock me over and brand me as the cutest corpse this side of the Chesapeake."

I mentally rolled my eyes.

Based on the look Blaine gave me, it hadn't been mental. Oops.

I decided I'd had enough of Angelina's antics.

"Could you point me to my room?" I asked.

"Of course." Blaine looked away from Angelina with disdain. "It's right up this stairway and down the hallway. Suite 222. The third door on the right. Your suitcase should be in your room. However, dinner will be at five, and we ask that you arrive promptly. We have a full evening planned, and we don't want you to miss even a minute." She handed me the key.

"I would hate to do that," I muttered. I glanced at Riley. "I'll see you at five."

He looked up, a strange emotion in his eyes. I couldn't read it. Was he worried? Desperate to get away from Angelina?

It wasn't my problem. That's what I told myself, at least.

I wandered up the stairway and down the hallway, just as Blaine had instructed. There were at least three floors in the building, I noted. Everything was rather boxy, narrow, and dark. There was a serious lack of windows, and when the lemony scent faded, the building had a musty undertone.

I found Suite 222, but hesitated a moment before twisting the handle and stepping inside. I blinked in surprise at what I saw there. It was a small living area, complete with two couches, two chairs, and a table. There were no windows or TV.

An open door across the room revealed a bathroom. Two doors on either side appeared to be bedrooms. I had to share this space with someone? Wasn't that just peachy? But it would be a great way to keep an eye on everyone, so I couldn't complain.

I peered in the first bedroom and spotted my suitcase

on one of the beds. However, based on the cosmetics and other luggage already in the room, it appeared someone else was also staying in this room. Really? At a place this nice?

I'd have to address that later. Right now, I wanted to freshen up before dinner. I had to dress to impress, after all.

I popped up my suitcase and paused.

I knew my things may have shifted some in transport. That was to be expected.

But what surprised me was the fact that my clothes actually looked neater than I'd left them. I could accept them looking messier. But neater? No way.

There was only one way that would have happened.

Someone had gone through my things.

***

I finally found the dining hall after wandering aimlessly around the building for nearly twenty minutes. Apparently, everyone else was already there because I hadn't passed another soul. I tried to follow my nose and the scent of sizzling fat, but I encountered lots of dark, twisting hallways in the process.

Haunted mansion came to mind. I didn't see any eerie suits of armor, however, but I did find some model ships behind big, glass display cases. There were no paintings with moving eyes, but there were a lot of elegant portraits of people from decades past. I hadn't ruled out finding a bookcase that turned to reveal a secret passage, though. If there was ever a time in my life I might experience a building with something like that, it would be here.

Finally, I found the others. They were seated at tables for four in a richly decorated dining hall with walls of deep burgundy and floors of dark-brown wood. Linen tablecloths, atmosphere-setting candles, and clanking of silverware on porcelain completed the scene. I'd practically just stepped into a five-star restaurant. At least in here there were some windows. Finally!

Before looking for Riley, my gaze wandered to the windows. Even though it was raining outside, I could see people wearing yellow slickers in the area the skeleton had been found. A large tent had been set up. No doubt, law enforcement, with the medical examiner, were trying to figure out how long that skeleton had been there and how to best preserve it.

After a moment of perusal, I finally spotted Riley sitting a table with a couple I hadn't seen or met yet. Thank goodness, he wasn't sitting with the Griffiths or Bo and Angelina Daniels. I'd already had my fill of them, and I'd just arrived.

This was going to be a long weekend, at least if I based it on the first two hours.

"Gabby." Riley stood and pulled out my chair. "I was beginning to think you'd changed your mind."

"Not yet, but it's not too late." I was just playing along with our character roles, I told myself. It was coming a little too easily.

"Gabby, this is Jim and Ginger Wagnor. They're from Maryland."

I glanced at the couple. The woman in particular caught my attention. She was exquisite. Her features were perfect and pert, with high cheekbones and a nose that was just slightly upturned. Her dark hair curled gently around her face. The man, on the other hand, was probably twenty pounds overweight. He had only a fringe of hair and sagging jowls.

They appeared severely mismatched. Had Ginger married him for his money? Or was I giving in to too many stereotypes during my brief stay here?

I nodded as I placed a napkin in my lap. "Nice to meet you both."

"They were telling me how their time here has really strengthened their marriage," Riley continued.

I smiled, momentarily distracted by a server who placed some artfully arranged chicken, zucchini, and brown rice in front of me. The rice was in a perfect molded circle, the chicken drizzled with some kind of glaze, and a confetti of parsley surrounded all of it.

"That's great to hear. I hope we're able to say the same thing . . . at least, I hope that most of the time."

Ginger laughed nervously. "You're so fortunate that you were able to get in, especially since the session had already started. You do realize there's a waiting list."

I shook my head. "No, I had no idea. I guess we are fortunate, even when it doesn't feel like it."

Riley gave me a strange look. Maybe I was playing up our problems too much.

"I was surprised a spot opened up as well," Riley said, wiping his mouth with a silky napkin.

"Dr. Turner is the best," Jim said. "He's truly revitalized so many marriages. He's a miracle worker."

Jim and Ginger exchanged a look. They certainly seemed happier than either of the other two couples I'd met. Just like Brad had said.

I placed my napkin in my lap and raised my fork. "What do the two of you do for a living?"

"I'm very fortunate to be able to stay at home," Ginger said.

"With your children?"

"We don't have any kids. I keep the house straight and cook. You know, more of a traditional housewife's role. I wouldn't have it any other way." She glowed up at her husband.

I figured these people would be rich enough to hire help, but maybe not. "I see."

"Jim here is into real estate. Most people call him a tycoon, for that matter," she continued. "He works long hours and has to travel a lot. I just want to offer him a safe place to relax. He needs that after all the stress he encounters at work. It's the least I can do to make sure his clothes are pressed and he's well fed."

Wow. I was so out of my league here. I couldn't see myself being happy doing what she did. Did that make me a bad person? I'd never really encountered these questions before because I'd always been single and, as a result, I'd had to work in order to make ends meet. The idea of simply staying home had never crossed my mind nor been an option.

"That's . . . that's great." I didn't sound convincing.

"How about you?" Ginger asked, taking a dainty bite of her chicken.

I remembered my cover story. "I . . . uh . . . I also stay at home."

Her eyes lit. "So you understand where I'm coming from? It's always so refreshing to meet like-minded people. There's just nothing like a clean house and an organized home to give a person peace of mind."

"My thoughts exactly." I remembered the laundry piled up on my bed, the dishes I'd intended on washing, and my cluttered cabinets. I may clean other people's houses for a living, but when it came to keeping my own place straight, I was a failure of epic proportions. "We're practically living the same life here. You and me, we're cut from the same cloth. Birds of a feather. Two peas in a pod."

Again, I was going a little overboard here. Riley nudged

me under the table, and I forced a smile.

Ginger leaned closer. "Mrs. Griffith over there stays at home, but not like I do. She is a socialite, through and through. She goes to the spa a few times per week, shops, and has lunch with her friends. Her kids are being raised by nannies."

"Sounds very Park Ave." Like I had any idea. I could relate more to Skid Row.

"And then there's Mrs. Daniels," Ginger continued, obviously prone to gossip.

I kept in mind that those who gossiped about others would also gossip about me. However, this could only help my investigation at this point, so I didn't discourage it.

"Rumor has it she works at a gas station," Ginger continued.

"I see." I tried not to say too much. I figured it was safer that way. Safe was good, right? I had no problem with Angelina working a blue-collar job. I was simply curious about how the couple had gotten in.

"Anyway, what do you do, Riley?" Ginger took a sip from her water goblet and waited.

Jim glanced at Riley, his attention on the conversation. But only for a moment. Then his gaze scanned the room. Was he nervous? Was he looking for something or someone?

I couldn't be sure.

"I'm a lawyer," Riley said.

Ginger continued talking while we ate. She told us about redecorating their home, a vacation to the Grand Cayman she hoped to go on this summer, and what it would be like to own a private island. I just ate, listened, and nodded.

It was safer that way.

Halfway through dinner, my attention was drawn to a man who stormed through the room. Steve.

He stopped in front of Blaine, who stood in the doorway staring at her clipboard.

The woman gasped as she looked up at him. His sudden appearance had obviously startled her. "Steve, what are you doing?"

"We're out of propane again. How am I supposed to cook breakfast in the morning without any gas to light my stove? You want this to seem like a first-class joint? Then we gotta start making some changes."

Blaine looked around before offering what appeared to be a forced smile. "Is it really necessary to address this here and now?"

"It takes time to have the propane tank refilled, so, yes, it is. I can't do my job under these circumstances. My brown rice wasn't quite right tonight. Why? Because I was guarding a skeleton. Not in my job description."

"You're causing a scene, Steve." Blaine looked around, seemed to notice her audience, and nervously pulled a hair behind her ear.

"I take pride in my food, and I feel like I'm being hindered. You can understand my frustration."

"I'll take this up with you in the office. Understand?" Her voice took on a hard edge.

He stared at her another moment before nodding. "Whatever."

Ginger leaned toward me. "He's the chef here. He takes his job very seriously."

"I met him earlier. He prefers 'food artist' to 'someone who does kitcheny things.'"

"He also has some anger-management issues. We all try to stay away from him. Apparently, he used to be one of Dr. Turner's patients."

Just as I ate the last bite of my tiramisu, someone clanged his fork against a glass. I had to look twice because, for a moment, I was certain Mr. Rogers had made a guest appearance. The man had a slight build, a meek appearance, and he wore a cardigan. He and Fred Rogers could be twins.

"Welcome, welcome, everyone!" the man said, addressing the crowd. "I'm glad you all made it here safely. I'd like to welcome our new guests, Riley and Gabby St. Thomas. I hope you'll all make them feel like a part of the group. Riley and Gabby, I'm Dr. Turner."

I kept my chin up and offered what I hoped was a pleasant smile at everyone.

"I'd like to talk to the two of you privately a little later. But, now, it's time for our first session," Dr. Turner announced. "If you'd all follow me into the Therapy Lounge. You're in for a real treat tonight."

The Therapy Lounge? Interesting.

We followed him across the hall into a large room. It was dark inside, with electric candles lit around the perimeter. There were four couches and a woman doing what appeared to be some kind of yoga moves on the rug. What in the world was going on here?

Did I really want to find out? Because this seemed more painful than finding a killer.

CHAPTER 10

"Today we're going to practice cuddling techniques," Dr. Turner began from the front of the room.

Cuddling techniques? That meant I was going to have to touch Riley.

My stomach plunged as if I'd just gone down a rollercoaster hill. At sixty miles an hour. Without a safety harness.

Couldn't we have eased into this? I mean, I was kinda prepared to talk the talk. It would be easy sharing how I was disillusioned by my relationship with Riley. It wouldn't require that much imagination. Really, no imagination at all.

But cuddling?

Wow. Maybe this would be worse than I thought.

"With us today, we have professional cuddler Lilsa Spring," Dr. Turner continued.

Professional cuddler? He had to be joking. There was no such thing . . . right?

But, no, that would be too easy if he was joking. Lilsa sprang from the ground at that moment, one hundred pounds of lithe, cuddly perfection.

"I'm so glad I can be here with you tonight." She hugged herself as she spoke, swinging from side to side with girlish innocence. "I can't wait to teach you everything I know about cuddling and its importance. As humans, we're made to crave the touch and affection of others. This can be a powerful tool in marriage . . ."

The girl looked like she was just out of high school. And the lack of a ring on her finger led me to believe she probably wasn't married. This would be like someone who'd never walked a tight wire trying to tell me how to do it. No way. No chance. No how.

"We're going to start with what I like to call the Hibernating Bear."

I couldn't make eye contact with Riley because certainly he'd see my discomfort. I almost feigned a stomach virus. Maybe some female problems. No one ever questioned them.

"Now, I'd like you both to sit on the couch and wrap your arms around each other." Lilsa glided across the room, reminding me of a Disney princess on steroids. She looked so lovelorn and dreamy-eyed that I wanted to recite a Grimm fairytale—the ones without a happy ending—to her.

Hesitantly, I scooted closer to Riley. This couldn't possibly be really happening. But when I felt Riley's arm brush mine, the electricity that shot through me proved this was all too real.

This was an ex-fiancée's nightmare.

I turned toward Riley, again avoiding eye contact. Awkwardly, I put my arms around his waist, feeling my cheeks heat at the action.

In return, Riley's hands went to my waist.

At once, memories flashed into my mind. Memories of our first kiss. Memories of my yearning to spend forever by his side. Memories of the plans I'd once had for the rest of my life.

My sentimental side needed to die a quick death.

"Now I want the male to lie back against the couch. The female should flow with his leadership and lie back with him,"

Lilsa continued with a flourish of her arms. "Be sure to keep your arms around each other."

I was as stiff as a statue as Riley leaned back. My arms felt like cement. I hardly wanted to breathe. My neck might as well have a brace on it.

Even if we were married, going through this exercise in public would feel uncomfortable. I wasn't much for public displays of affection.

"Now, you two." Lilsa peered above us, her hands on her hips and shaking her head with adorable disapproval. "You're both adults and you're married. You belong to each other. Don't act like strangers."

I let out a shallow laugh and attempted to relax. It didn't work. "I'm out of my comfort zone here."

"Everyone needs to encourage this couple," Lilsa said, reprimand on her face.

I glanced at the other couples. They all looked awkward, except for Jim and Ginger, who actually looked like they were enjoying this. In fact, Ginger had a rather seductive look on her face and seemed lost in her husband's gaze.

"What are your names?" Lilsa continued, her high-pitched, baby-like voice grating on my nerves.

"Riley and Gabby," Riley said.

Why did he have to look at ease? He should be uncomfortable, just like me.

"Okay, everyone should encourage Riley and Gabby to be freer in expressing their affection for each other. I'm sure Dr. Turner will work with them as well. What do we want to say to them?"

"Marriage is good," everyone chanted around us. "Relationships are work. Our partners are worth it."

I cringed, feeling like I'd walked into a couples therapy

cult. How long had they all practiced in order to be able to recite that together? The creepiness factor doubled for me.

"You'll have the hang of that little ditty before you leave here," Dr. Turner said, appearing beside Lilsa and staring at Riley and I as we "cuddled." I might as well have been doing Heimlich with a grizzly bear.

I felt like I was touching fire, and I desperately wanted to pull away.

But I thought of the investigation. The greater good, I told myself. I had to do this so we could find answers. I tried to mentally block everything else. But dreams of forever didn't disappear easily like that.

Maybe in the process of being here I'd get over Riley. Could I be that lucky?

"We haven't done this in a very long time," Riley said. "So excuse us if we're awkward."

"We all were when we got here," Ginger called across the room. "There's nothing to be embarrassed about. We all came here with baggage and issues. Being here will expose all those things."

That was the last thing I wanted. I wanted to hide away all my feelings and pretend like they didn't exist.

"Exposing myself is not on my agenda," I mumbled.

Everyone froze and stared at me. I felt the air tightened around me.

My cheeks heated. "Exposing my *emotions*, that is."

"Now, move in a little closer, Gabby," Lilsa encouraged. "He won't bite."

Against my better instincts, I snuggled my head under Riley's chin. It had been there before—the spot where I could hear, almost feel, his heart beating beneath me. I breathed in his cologne, woodsy and leathery.

I was going to a dangerous place. Physically? Maybe. Emotionally? Definitely.

This trip had been much riskier than I'd anticipated, and now I was literally trapped.

As a loud rumble filled the air, I jumped, inadvertently pressing myself even closer to Riley.

"It's just thunder," Dr. Turner said. "Everyone relax. We do have some storms coming our way."

Great. I'd stepped out of my urban life and into the set of a gothic movie. Lovely.

The lights flickered above us, and I tensed, waiting for everything to go dark. It just seemed fitting for this moment and the scenario playing out around us.

"Maybe we should go on to our next move before we run out of time," Lilsa said. "I like to call this one the Marilyn Monroe."

Before she could explain to us exactly what that was, the room went black. Someone screamed. My hands tightened against Riley's shirt.

There could potentially be a killer here. I couldn't let myself forget that. Because this would be the perfect time for someone to strike.

Then it would be lights out forever for someone else in this room.

CHAPTER 11

"This is the perfect opportunity for us all to have a heart-to-heart talk." Dr. Turner's voice wafted through the darkness. "Our power supply is a bit delicate out here. But I'm sure it will be restored momentarily—much like our marriages. We just have to give everything time."

I heard movement, and then a flashlight popped on. I saw that Dr. Turner had pulled a chair into the center of the room. He sat facing us with some kind of book in his hand, like he might recite a bedtime story.

At the moment, I realized I was clinging to Riley. My hand gripped his shirt, my head nestled under his chin, and I was paralyzed in that position. My cheeks heated, and I drew back so quickly that the couch scooted back.

With that as an opening, I quickly scrambled away from Riley. I adjusted my shirt and tried to compose myself. Riley didn't look nearly as frazzled as I felt. In fact, he smiled as he sat up, something warm glimmering in his eyes.

How could he be so laid-back? Did he have any idea how all this was making me feel?

No, he probably didn't. He was a guy, after all. Most guys were clueless or at least they pretended to be. It seemed like they got the better end of the bargain in that regard.

"Has anyone seen Angelina?" a deep voice said in the distance.

I swung my head toward the person. It was Bo. Sure enough, the space on the couch beside him was empty.

I bristled. What could have happened to Angelina in that brief period of darkness? It didn't make sense.

Since no one else said anything, I decided to. "Did you hear her get up?"

"No, but I can't hear out of my left ear," Bo said. He was a large man with a barrel chest, a shaved head, and an earring in his left ear. He wore a beer T-shirt, baggy jeans, and scuffed tennis shoes.

"Did you feel anything?" Dr. Turner asked.

Bo shook his head. "No. She shot off of me like a cat out of the water when the lights went off. Then she was gone."

"Let's split up and look for her. But no one should go outside," Dr. Turner warned, his voice grim. "The fog is too thick."

"What if we find her just like Steve found Anna?" Ginger asked, her voice hushed and tinged with fear.

Jim gasped and grabbed her hand. "Don't talk like that, Ginger."

The snooty Griffiths remained icily quiet toward each other and toward everyone in the room. They looked like they couldn't care less and were just biding their time until they could leave.

I watched everything with a sad fascination. Of course, I hoped that Angelina was okay. But the dynamics in the room were soap opera worthy. And I had a front-row seat.

Dr. Turner found more flashlights, and we split into groups by couples, except for Bo who stayed in the room with Lilsa in case Angelina returned. Dr. Turner paired up with Blaine, and we each headed toward a different corridor of Blackbird Hall. Thankfully I'd familiarized myself with the place earlier when I'd gotten lost on the way to the dining room.

I wanted to grab Riley's arm so I wouldn't lose him. But I couldn't allow myself to do that. I had to keep my distance, no matter how much my instinct seemed to have the urge to operate differently. There could be no repeats of what happened earlier tonight.

"Someone went through my suitcase," I whispered to Riley instead.

"What?"

I nodded. "Everything was meticulously placed inside, which was not my doing. I guess your suitcase looked fine?"

"It did, but I *am* a meticulous packer. Why would someone go through your suitcase?"

"I don't know, but that's one more thing I need to find out." Only the beam of my flashlight lit the floor in front of us. The darkness here was overwhelming and frightening. I kept waiting for someone to jump out and send my nerves ratcheting into the stratosphere. "This place is nightmare inducing."

"I have to concur," Riley said.

It was strange because, in the past, Riley always seemed hesitant when I dove into investigations. He always tried to pull me back, but when he realized he couldn't, he would tag along as my protector or voice of reason.

But he seemed fully emerged in this mystery right now. He was taking the lead.

And this was a strange realization for me. What had changed after his brain injury? Something must have happened during his time at his parents' house in DC while he recovered.

I didn't know. But I had to admit that I kind of liked it.

I'd always wanted a partner in crime solving. I'd pulled quite a few people in with me over the years, but no one permanent. They'd all just been innocent bystanders or people who happened to be personally involved or held a stake in the investigation. Knowing someone had my back was comforting.

We headed to the second floor, where all the guests and most of the staff were staying while here. That's what Ginger had indicated earlier, at least.

"Angelina?" I called, knocking on a door.

There was no response on the other side, so I opened the door. A lodging area similar to the one where I was staying came into view.

"This is the men's area," Riley said.

That didn't stop me from wandering inside. "I'll take this room."

I pushed a bedroom door open and shined my flashlight in the space. There was no Angelina here. Despite that, I peeked in the closet. No one. Under the bed. Nothing.

Out of curiosity, I pulled open a dresser drawer. I didn't really expect to find anything of interest.

But then I saw a scarf.

A leopard-print scarf.

Just like the one Anna had been wearing in her photo.

CHAPTER 12

Just as Riley and I got back downstairs, the lights flickered on, and we ran into someone emerging from the bathroom.

Angelina.

"We've been looking for you," I muttered, wondering why the woman looked both relaxed and irritated.

"So I've heard." She continued walking, so we followed her back into the lounge.

The rest of the group was already there, but everyone became silent when Angelina walked in. Her ankle had been miraculously healed, it appeared.

Bo hurried toward her. "Where'd you go? We were worried about you, woman."

She scowled and held up a flashlight. "I went to grab this. I told you that before I left. You know I don't like being unprepared. If my Girl Scout troop knew, I'd be evicted as leader—and ain't nobody taking over that from me."

"You didn't tell me that you were leaving." Bo crossed his arms and scowled at his wife.

"I most certainly did. I said, I have to go empty my bladder—I was afraid I might pee myself right here if the lights stayed off too long. While I was out, I grabbed a flashlight. I guess I told you that in your mute ear."

Mute ear? Ears couldn't be mute, but I didn't bother to correct her.

Angelina stared at everyone, like we were the crazy, crass ones. "You all didn't have to get so worried. I'm a big girl, and I'm wearing my big girl panties." She said the last part with a cartoonish voice. Then she wiggled her hips as if she knew we all had an unwanted mental image, thanks to her word choice.

I attempted to poke out my mind's eye.

"Why didn't the people searching the first floor see you?" I asked.

Angelina shrugged. "I went up the back stairway. There's a window there, so I thought I could see better."

My gaze zeroed in on Atticus Griffith. Riley had informed me that I'd found the scarf in Atticus's drawer. Why did Atticus have Anna's scarf?

Dr. Turner cleared his throat. "I think we should call this a night. We should all get some rest and return bright and early tomorrow morning to begin fresh. You're dismissed for Bird's Nest Time, but be back to your rooms by nine. Sound good?"

Everyone began to disperse.

Except Riley and I.

Bird's Nest Time? What in the world was he talking about?

Dr. Turner seemed to sense our confusion and turned to address us. "I don't want to spend too much time sharing your story tonight. We prefer to do that as a group so we can all help each other. I did want to take the opportunity to say that we're thankful to have you here with us. Did you have any questions for me?"

"Is it always this exciting around here?" I rubbed my arms as goosebumps scattered across my skin like a minefield. I'd always said they popped up when fear had nowhere else to go.

"Not usually, but this past weekend was out of the

ordinary."

"Why's that?" Riley asked, moving closer to me.

Dr. Turner fidgeted. "The couple whose place you took met with an unfortunate tragedy. The wife took her own life, and that's shaken everyone up. But I think staying together through hardships like this is important. That's why I didn't cancel the rest of our sessions. We're going to use this experience to bring everyone closer together."

The doctor seemed to have a good explanation for everything, didn't he?

"That's terrible," I whispered.

He nodded. "I couldn't agree more. It's the antithesis of what I want to see happen here. In truth, it greatly concerns me, and I feared no one would want to come back. Thankfully, everyone saw her death for what it was—a terrible tragedy that we all want to avoid in our lives."

"I have one more question, Dr. Turner." I straightened my spine. "When I checked my suitcase in my room, it looked like someone had gone through my things. Do you know who would have done that?"

He pressed his lips together. "As a matter of fact, I do. I thought Blaine had told you. Leroy dropped your suitcase on the way up. It wasn't locked and your things tumbled out. He picked up everything and tried to neatly put them back inside. We apologize that it happened, and I'm sorry no one filled you in."

The explanation seemed logical enough . . . . I supposed. I was still bothered, though.

"Now," Dr. Turner brought his hands together. "Bird's Nest Time is what we call alone time at the end of each day. It's an opportunity for husbands and wives to talk about the day and air any of their problems with each other privately. We call it Bird's Nest Time because many birds mate for life. That's what we promote here also."

I nodded, not a fan of the cheesy, fowl-themed images his words evoked in my mind. I really hoped that one of his sessions wasn't about the birds and the bees. "I see. Is there anywhere in particular we're supposed to have Bird's Nest Time?"

"Wherever you would like. Wherever is private. But we do put a time limit on this interaction. We like to be structured here. Boundaries are good for all of us, both during our time here and for marriage in general."

"I understand," Riley said.

As we started to walk away, Dr. Turner called us back. We both paused and turned.

"I could sense that the two of you were highly uncomfortable with our cuddle time. I do hope you'll both give this process a chance. I know your marriage has probably weathered some difficult times. All marriages go through this. Just be open-minded."

Maybe the doctor was more insightful than I thought. On one hand, it had to be pretty easy to see how awkward Riley and I were with each other. But his advice for marriage was spot on. I'd never been married, but I'd seen plenty of bad marriages. I knew enough to understand it was better to stick together through tough times than to bail.

Like Riley had done on me when he decided we needed space during the middle of his recovery.

In the infamous words of Elsa, I had to let this go. Or even better, in the words of the Bible, I would consider this trial pure joy.

Pure joy.

***

"We better go find a 'bird's nest,'" I finally said after Dr. Turner walked away.

"Where should we go?" Riley whispered.

"I know what my vote is for. The widow's walk." And it wasn't because it was the best place to spy on people. Or maybe it was. "Although, the name has always seemed a bit morbid to me. Maybe I'll just call it The Tower."

"Can you imagine being a wife watching up there for your husband to return from being out to sea?" Riley gestured toward the bay.

"I can't. I would go crazy. Maybe patience isn't my thing."

"It was a hard profession. This sea has claimed many lives."

"Apparently, so has this island. I mean, really . . . Cemetery Island?"

Riley grimaced. "There are some things I wish I didn't know. That's one of them. This place doesn't seem so happy with a past like that."

"And don't forget the skeleton."

He raised his eyebrows. "How can I?"

"I wonder what the police have found out, if anything. They were still out there last time I checked."

We climbed two flights of stairs and reached the spiral staircase. Before we could take the first step, we heard voices drifting downward and froze.

Whoever was up there obviously hadn't heard us approach because their conversation continued. We stepped into the shadows and did the polite thing: We eavesdropped.

"I can't go on here after what happened to Anna. It's just not right," a woman said. "I'm scared."

"There's no reason to be scared," the man said. "We just have to watch each other's backs."

"But what if someone finds out about us?" The woman's voice cracked.

"They won't. Stop worrying so much, sweetheart."

"What about that new couple? They don't seem as self-absorbed as some of the others. If anyone notices what's going on, it will be them. We'll be ruined."

What? Were they talking about Riley and me?

"We'll just have to make sure that they don't find out our secret. Okay?" the man whispered.

The woman remained quiet until the conversation turned to plans for the future and other sappy subjects.

Riley gently pulled me away. We moved quickly, silently, down the hall, only speaking once we reached the library.

"That was Ginger and Jim, wasn't it?" I whispered.

"Sounds like there are definitely couples here who are hiding something. What do you think they were talking about?"

"Maybe they know something about Anna's death." I nibbled on my bottom lip in thought.

"We should see what we can discover individually. Maybe tonight back in our rooms will be a good time to casually bring up Anna in conversation. We need to find out if anyone had a grudge against her for some reason."

I nodded. "That sounds like a good plan. Someone here is hiding something."

"Then again, so are we."

I locked my gaze with his. "That's right. But we're not hiding something deadly."

***

Lo and behold, my roommate was Ginger. When I arrived, she had already changed into her nightgown—something silky and low cut—and was sitting on her bed filing her fingernails. She smiled when she spotted me, no sign of the distress I'd heard in her voice less than thirty minutes ago.

"We're rooming together, huh?" I asked, lowering myself onto my bed and taking my shoes off.

"I thought it was strange, also, but I guess some of the other rooms here are still under construction. Dr. Turner also said rooming with someone else will help to give us accountability and the chance to work on our relational skills outside of marriage."

"He has some interesting ideas."

"I think they're refreshing." She shrugged. "So, anyway, what do you think so far?"

I lowered myself onto my bed and crossed my legs under me. "I'm not sure yet. Is that a typical night?"

"There is no typical here." She let out a laugh. "Dr. Turner likes to keep us on our toes. He says when we can learn to live with the unexpected surprises and curveballs that life throws us then we can survive anything. Everything he says is an analogy to marriage. You'll discover that quickly."

"I've noticed already." I shifted, ready to get to the heart of why I was really here. Why waste time? "Look, I heard rumblings about the couple whose place we took. Is it true the woman died?"

"Anna Thorn?" Ginger frowned and put down her nail file. "She was one of the women going through this program. Super nice woman."

"What happened?"

She leaned closer, even though there was no one else in the room. "She overdosed. Steve, the cook, found her in the

80

boathouse."

I widened my eyes as if the news shocked me. "Really? That's horrible."

Ginger nodded grimly. "I know. I just can't believe the woman would take her own life. She just didn't seem like the type—not that there's a type, I mean."

"So, you're saying you don't think it was a suicide?"

Ginger suddenly straightened. "Oh, no. That's not what I'm saying. I mean, what else could have happened to her? It's not like you can make someone take pills, right? It's just sobering to have someone you know pass away like that."

I nodded. "I can imagine."

"Anyway, that's probably more than you wanted to hear. I don't want to give you a bad impression before you barely get started. I mean, I'm not saying that this program drove her to suicide or anything . . ."

Her uncomfortable laugh at the end made me wonder just that, though.

CHAPTER 13

I awoke early the next morning. I hadn't been able to sleep much because I had too many things running through my mind. No one else was stirring, so I bypassed the shower, pulled my hair into a ponytail, and headed outside to explore a little.

The air felt dewy as soon as I set foot out the front door. A slight fog still hung over the island, but nothing like yesterday. My gaze instantly went to the site where the skeleton had been discovered. To my surprise, the area had been cleared except for some yellow police tape staked around the gravesite.

I walked to the cliff's edge and looked down. There was a small indention in the ground where the body had been exhumed. Otherwise, I saw no sign of what had happened.

I wondered what the authorities had discovered about the body. My theory was, since this place was once called Cemetery Island, that the corpse was someone who'd died while traversing these waters many years ago. Though my mind usually jumped to foul play, I wasn't overly concerned right now. The find seemed more historical than nefarious.

With that settled in my mind, I pulled my sweatshirt closer and started my brisk walk. A crushed-oyster-shell path led around the perimeter of the island, so I decided to follow that.

Just breathing in the fresh air made my spirit feel

calmer and more at peace. I glanced around, getting my first real look at the place.

The island was small—it couldn't be more than twenty acres, if I had to guess. Blackbird Hall took up a majority of that space, but there were also a few outbuildings. A gazebo stood close to a bluff, with several wooden swings where people could enjoy the view. Some gnarled-looking trees grew on the edge of the bluff, their roots dangling precariously over the edge.

Okay, Lord. We're going to get through this together, right? I realize that being around Riley may be one of the biggest challenges I've faced recently. But I can do this. This will be a character-building experience.

It was usually the mystery or crime that had me on edge, but this time it was clearly being here with Riley. I'd just been getting some of my focus back when he'd swept back into my life like a Zamboni at a hockey game. Only, in my mind, a deranged lunatic was behind the wheel.

I'd give anything to be able to call my best friend, Sierra, and chat with her right now. But I couldn't exactly hop into my van and go have a little heart to heart with her before my sessions started today, nor could I call her. Or could I? On second thought, maybe I could find one of those magical spots where I could get a cell signal.

I stopped at the edge of the bluff and peered down. A fifteen-foot cliff with sandy dunes protected the island from the waves of the bay. At the bottom of the bluff lay a sandy beach littered with broken shells, seaweed, and even a horseshoe crab. On the opposite side of the island I'd noticed a rocky bulkhead and marsh grasses instead of sand.

If it weren't for the circumstances that brought me here, I could get used to a place like this.

My dad would love it here. He was a certified beach

bum, a former national champion surfer, and a cringe-worthy work in progress. We'd gone to the ocean often when I was young. My dad could catch some waves while I'd played on the shore and built sand castles. At once, the memories of my youth filled me.

I had few good memories of growing up in my dysfunctional home. The beach was one of them.

I thought about the couples here who were struggling with their marriages, and then I thought about my own parents. My mom had so many reasons not to be happy. She had to work, sometimes two jobs, in order to pay the bills. My brother had been kidnapped as a child, and my dad had fallen apart after that. He couldn't hold down a job for the life of him.

Yet my mom had stuck with him. It would have been easy for her to split, but she hadn't. She'd helped me form my mental image of what I wanted in a marriage some day. No, I didn't want the "worse" part of the vows, but they would happen. I felt like I'd been practicing for my entire life to weather the storms of the future.

I let out a deep breath, feeling more relaxed than I had been since I'd arrived here. I'd come to appreciate these moments of quiet reflection and prayer more and more as I'd grown in my Christian walk. They helped me feel grounded and somehow strengthened my core.

I turned my mind back to the investigation. I had so many questions. Like, what were Jim and Anna arguing over before she died? Who was outside last night in the rain? And if Anna had been murdered, who would want to kill her?

I had a lot of work to do here.

Shoving my hands in my pockets, I continued on my walk, pausing just long enough to watch the sun peak over the horizon. As I continued along the path, I decided to follow the stairway down to the beach. I glanced behind me one last time before I descended. I saw no one.

My feet hit the wet sand at the bottom. Seagulls were already out and soaring over the water. I started around the perimeter, pausing when I saw a building in the distance.

Could that be the boathouse?

My pulse sped. I knew I probably shouldn't do this at the risk of being caught and my cover revealed. But I hadn't seen anyone else, so what could it hurt to snoop a little?

I quickened my steps until I reached the weathered building. There was no real door, just an opening that I gladly stepped through. Inside was the pontoon boat we'd rode yesterday. Kayaks lined the edge, as well as life jackets. The scent of seawater drifted upward, strangely pleasant.

I squinted and tried to picture Anna here. I pictured her lying on one of the piers that lined the side.

Why would she have come here, of all places, to take those pills and die? Why not in her room? In the bathroom? Even on the shore?

The boathouse seemed like such an odd location for her to take her life.

But if she was murdered, the boathouse made more sense. Perhaps she'd come out here trying to escape. Had she tried to take this boat back to the mainland and get away from something? Or someone?

I shivered at the thought. I had a feeling this retreat center held more secrets than anyone cared to admit.

Just then I heard a footstep behind me. I quickly ducked against the wall. My chest heaved as I gasped in gulps of air. What if it was the killer returning? How would I explain being here?

I couldn't act suspicious, I reminded myself. Hiding at

the first sound of someone approaching would make people ask questions.

I pulled myself together and straightened my sweatshirt. Then I stepped out, determined to look clueless.

Steve, the angry cook, stopped in his tracks when he spotted me. He was wearing a black bodysuit and water shoes, not to mention his ever-present scowl.

"You're not supposed to be out there," he mumbled.

"Why not?" I asked.

"Because this island isn't safe." He pulled down a kayak.

I forced a laugh. "Don't be silly. We wouldn't have a retreat here if it wasn't safe."

"Listen, lady, I'm just saying there are a lot of ways someone like you could get hurt."

Was that a threat? He must have seen the question forming on my lips because he shook his head. "I just don't wanna see any more accidents or tragedies or whatever you want to call them."

"I was just getting some fresh air," I told him, watching as he prepared to board the boat. I pulled my phone from my pocket and held it up. "And checking for a signal on my cell phone."

"Too many strange things have happened here. That's all I'm saying." He raised his hands, as if offering surrender, before carefully climbing into his kayak.

"I hear you loud and clear." I took a step away.

"Ma'am?"

I turned and glanced at him, wondering what kind of wisdom he would espouse now. "Yes?"

"Good luck."

Good luck? Why would he say that? What a strange encounter.

My chills intensified.

It was probably getting close to the time when people would stir. My absence might be noticed, and I didn't want to draw any unnecessary attention to myself.

Today, I would be Gabby St. Thomas, wife of Riley St. Thomas. I'd be a housewife, immersed in the lifestyles of the affluent and desperate to work out a marriage on the rocks.

I drew in a deep breath and chanted, "I think I can, I think I can," as I chugged toward the lodge.

Or, maybe I should say, "Marriage is good. Relationships are work. Our partners are worth it."

***

As I got back to my room and began to get dressed in a "proper" outfit, I opened my dresser drawer to retrieve my mom's pearls. After all, they were the perfect finishing touch to my quest to look classy.

To my surprise, the drawer was empty.

I blinked, certain I was missing something.

Then, as if to prove I wasn't mistaken, I pulled the drawer out farther. I searched the empty corners, as if there was a hidden compartment somewhere.

The necklace wasn't there.

Okay, Gabby, think. Don't think worst-case scenarios. Don't think of devious explanations. Think logically.

With that thought in mind, I looked in the drawer below, thinking maybe I'd misplaced it while getting ready for bed.

It wasn't there, nor was it anywhere else—not the other drawers, not behind the dresser, not in my suitcase. I looked everywhere.

I sank onto my bed as my heart panged with a surprising grief. I wasn't overly sentimental, but that necklace had been special to me. It was one of the few heirlooms I had of my mom's. And now it was gone.

And why? Why would someone take it? Ginger had the other key to this room, but I couldn't imagine her as the culprit. It just didn't make any sense.

My steps felt heavier as I made my way down to the dining area. I spotted Riley sitting with the snooty Griffiths. I called out a polite "Good morning" before sitting down and taking a sip of coffee.

Before I could force any conversation, I glanced in the background as angry Steve stormed past, headed toward Blaine again. What was wrong this time? He'd only had a short kayaking trip, and I was surprised he'd had enough time to prepare breakfast.

I barely made out something he was saying about missing knives.

Missing knives? That sounded . . . disturbing.

I swallowed deeply, trying not to show any trepidation on my face.

"So, where are the two of you from?" I kept my cup perched daintily in my hands, raised near my lips. It just seemed like the sophisticated thing to do.

"The DC area," Atticus said, sounding bored.

It was the first time I'd heard him speak. His voice sounded strong and authoritative. But he still looked less than thrilled to be here.

"But we have a second home down in Palm Beach, and that's really where we prefer to spend our time," Farrah added.

"How does this island compare?" Riley asked.

She smirked. "It doesn't. I'm not the rugged, roughing it

kind of girl. I like my Starbucks and the ability to come and go. I keep expecting to see Gilligan and the rest of the crew appear here, telling us the tale of their fateful trip."

I smiled and began singing the theme song, jogging my elbow back and forth like a sailor with a mug of beer. When I saw everyone's strange expressions fixated on me, I realized I needed to stop. Now.

Thankfully, just then, a server placed a plate of fruit, cream cheese, and bagels on a table in front of me. Apparently, there was still no propane, which couldn't have made Stevie-weavie happy.

I hadn't had a chance to speak with Riley alone this morning yet. I wanted to tell him about my missing pearl necklace. I also wanted to ask him if he'd heard anything last night that might be helpful.

Right now Riley smelled freshly showered. His hair was still slightly wet, and he hadn't shaved, which gave him a little bit of a bad-boy edge. But not really. His eyes were still kind, and his smile was sincere. Besides, none of that mattered. I wasn't holding out hope that this relationship was going to ignite again. I'd be foolish if I did.

"Where are you two from?" Atticus asked. The question seemed forced, like it was said out of obligation.

The man obviously didn't want to be here. His wife didn't seem to want to be here either. So why *were* they here? I couldn't quite understand their motivation. And how did he get Anna's scarf?

"We live in Norfolk right now," Riley said.

The man turned his nose up. "I've been there before. I wish I could say it was a nice town, but why kid like that?"

Riley shrugged. "I think it's charming."

"Then again, you like this island also," Farrah retorted,

raising her coffee mug.

I swallowed back my disdain and continued eating. Thankfully, Dr. Turner appeared just then and clapped to get everyone's attention.

"We have an exciting day planned," he began. "I hope everyone likes the water because you'll be kayaking with your spouse."

Kayaking? That didn't sound too bad. I could definitely handle that.

"Everyone has thirty minutes to go get changed. We'll meet down by the docks for this adventure."

I stood just in time to hear Farrah say, "If I'm lucky, maybe my 'better half' will drown."

CHAPTER 14

I'd expected to see kayaks waiting down by the dock. Instead, we all boarded the pontoon boat with Captain Leroy. He took us back toward the mainland where four two-person kayaks waited on the shoreline. There were name cards on each of them.

"I don't like this," Ginger muttered. "I can't swim. Being on the island is hard enough, but being in the bay with only some plastic to protect me?" Ginger frowned and crossed her arms.

"You'll be okay," Jim said. "I'll make sure."

We were briefed in proper procedure, life-vested up, and told that we needed to make it back to the island by lunch. There were emergency radios aboard each boat, as well as bottles of water.

I hardly had time to get nervous about the task because all I could think about was having a chance to talk to Riley in private. Apparently, I'd be having plenty of time to talk to Riley in private because who knew exactly how long this paddling adventure would take.

None of the other couples looked excited either. Angelina and Bo were arguing about something, and Atticus and Farrah were giving each other the cold shoulder.

"Ladies first," Riley insisted. He held the boat right on the edge of the water with the paddle across the midsection, just as we'd been instructed.

I climbed into a bright-orange kayak, thankful it had what Leroy called an "open cockpit" as opposed to an enclosed skirt that would hold us each in. As Riley climbed in behind me, the kayak wobbled.

I held my breath, waiting to roll over into the water. The paddles prevented that from happening, though.

Atticus and Farrah weren't as fortunate. Their boat dumped them onto the shore. Farrah emerged from the shallow tide sputtering.

"I knew this was a bad idea," she muttered. "I don't know why I have to jump through all these stupid hoops."

"Grow up, Farrah. Let's just get this over with. Only two more weeks and we're done with this place, once and for all."

"I'd rather live the rest of my life cold and alone than continue with this atrocity of a marriage." She stood and stomped off toward the parking lot.

They were not a happy couple.

"You ready for this?" Riley asked.

"Ready as I'll ever be." I gripped my paddle and shoved it into the bay.

I sucked in a deep breath as I watched the ripples of water form around us. I wanted to pour out everything to Riley, but I had to make sure we were far enough away from the others before I did.

Angelina and Bo were still bickering several feet away. I doubted they'd hear anything over the sound of their own voices.

Ginger was actually letting Jim do all the paddling. She sat at the front of the boat and enjoyed the ride. They'd definitely hear our conversation, and, when Ginger did, she'd share it with everyone at the retreat center.

"You doing okay?"

I jumped. Riley had whispered the words in my ear. He'd been close enough that I'd felt his hot breath on my cheek, close enough that every inch of my skin lit up with fire.

I forced myself to nod. "Yeah, I'm doing just fine. Of course. More than fine."

"Good." His paddle slurped through the water.

We actually worked pretty well together. Surprisingly well. We got the rhythm of paddling and glided across the water. When I looked back, I was surprised at how far away from the shore we already were.

"What if we can't find the island?" I asked.

"We'll find it. Otherwise, we'll use the radio and Captain Leroy will pick us up."

"It sounds so easy when you say it that way."

"When you almost die, it kind of puts your worries into perspective."

My heart squeezed. Riley didn't talk much about the ordeal of what had happened to him. But I understood. I'd almost died also, just in a different way. Not because of a bullet through the brain, but because of long, drawn-out torture at the hands of a madman. I thanked God every day that I was still alive.

"I know you understand, Gabby," Riley said quietly, acknowledging my pain throughout all this.

I'd avoided hard conversations with him for a long time. At first it was because I didn't think he could handle them. He just needed to focus on recovery. Then his mother had informed me that every time we spoke it set him back further on his journey toward healing.

Life had been a confusing mess over these last several months. I'd like to think I was stronger for it.

Finally, we'd jetted a considerable distance from everyone else, past where the waves were breaking. The only creatures around us were the small schools of fish that swam past. In the distance, some dolphins raced in the sunlight. The sight was beautiful and peaceful.

The exertion from paddling and the snug life jacket helped keep me warm, although the water was still icy cold. It wouldn't warm up until June or July.

Out here, I felt comfortable talking to Riley. The only problem was that I couldn't look Riley in the eye as I spoke with him—not without tipping the boat over. Maybe it was better that way.

"Riley, my necklace is gone."

He didn't say anything for a minute. "What do you mean?"

"The pearl necklace I wore yesterday. It was my mom's. I put it in my drawer last night, and this morning it was gone."

"I'm sorry, Gabby. Why would someone steal your necklace?"

"That's what I've been wondering. I have no clue. It makes no sense."

"We'll get it back, Gabby. I promise."

I wasn't sure how he could promise that, but it did make me feel better.

"So, did you hear anything?" I asked.

"I'm rooming with Jack Frost. He's not very talkative, although he does seem to relax some when his wife isn't around."

That was interesting. And sad, I supposed. "And?"

"I asked him if it was always so crazy around here like it was last night. He doesn't seem prone to gossip, so I wasn't hopeful I'd get a lot out of him. He said he had an interesting

94

conversation with Jim last weekend after Anna was found."

"Oh really? Tell me more."

"He said that Jim's face went pale when he heard the news of Anna's death. Like, totally pale, as if their friendship went deeper than anyone knew. Back further than their time here at the retreat."

"That's interesting." Had there been something going on between Anna and Jim? Brad said he'd seen them arguing. "Did he say anything else about Anna?"

"Nothing."

I shook my head, finding a certain comfort in the rhythm of paddling. "I can't figure out why Atticus and Farrah are here. I mean, neither seems interested in working things out. It's almost like it was court ordered or something, but I can't think of any reason why something like that would happen."

"I'm not sure either," Riley said. "Usually at least one of the spouses would be pushing for something like this. It's perplexing."

I frowned, trying to store away all this information so that perhaps it would make sense eventually. "Well, I heard a couple of strange things. Ginger implied that this program had driven Anna to suicide."

"I'm not sure if I can see how that would happen. I mean, I know this is exhausting for people. Digging into emotions and motivations and failed expectations always is. But Dr. Turner does try to offer hope."

"I'm not saying I agree with that assessment either, but it's something to think about," I said.

"They didn't miss a beat here, did they? I mean, not even a week later and the program is still going."

I'd thought about that also. The continuation didn't

seem very compassionate. At the same time, I could see the importance of pushing ahead, just as Dr. Turner had explained. The situation was sticky, to say the least.

Just then, I noticed something at my feet. "There's some water at the bottom of our boat."

"Maybe some got in when we launched."

"Maybe." I kicked at the liquid. But it was weird that I hadn't noticed the water earlier when I'd readjusted my feet so my sneakers wouldn't get wet.

As I pulled my foot closer to my seat, something scraped my leg. Carefully, I reached under my seat, expecting to see a stick or some dried leaves. Instead, I pulled out a piece of paper.

"One second," I muttered to Riley. Despite the fact that we were in the middle of nowhere, surrounded by nothing but water, I put my paddle down across the kayak. I had to know what this was.

Carefully, I opened the square. Was this just a page from the owner's manual? A label that had been pulled off a life jacket?

In my gut, I knew it wasn't.

When I saw the handwritten words, my suspicion was confirmed.

CHAPTER 15

"Whoa," I whispered.

"What is it?" Riley leaned over my shoulder, and again my skin came alive at his nearness.

I quickly scanned the words, stopping by the name at the bottom "It's a letter from . . . Anna."

"What?" Riley's voice rose with surprise.

"She must have stuffed it in the kayak before she died. These boats were stored inside the boathouse."

"So you think it's another suicide note?"

The idea made me pause a moment. "I'm not sure."

"Well, what does it say?"

"It says: 'I have been a terrible wife. My husband didn't deserve to be treated the way I treated him. Instead of honoring my vows, I made a mockery of them. I cheated. I undermined his manhood. I didn't respect his role of leader in our house. I beg for forgiveness for the wrongs I've done and would like to start fresh. I come with an attitude of humility, sorrow, and brokenness.'"

"That doesn't make sense," Riley said. "If she wanted to start fresh, why would she kill herself?"

I thought about that for a moment. "I don't know. That's a good question. Brad said the police had her suicide note, right?"

"He did. Why leave two? Is this even a suicide note or

just some type of confessional?"

More questions filled my mind. "Whatever it is, why leave it in the kayak? Most people would leave it on their bed or even beside their body. That's the thing: Nothing about her committing suicide makes sense."

"I think we really might have a murder on our hands. The more I learn, the more that suspicion is confirmed."

I nodded. "I agree. And that only makes this island more dangerous."

"But there's something else more dangerous."

I cut a glance over my shoulder at Riley. "What's that?"

"The bay." He nodded at the kayak. "We're taking on water. I'm not sure how much longer we're going to stay afloat."

I swallowed hard as reality hit. We were sinking. In the middle of the bay. In April, when the water was still cold. "What are we going to do?"

"Let's paddle harder, faster. The closer we can get to land, the better."

I didn't have time to think. Instead, I quickly shoved the letter in my pocket. I wished I had time to preserve it, to protect it, but I didn't. Right now I had to think about survival.

I glanced around again as I grabbed my paddle. None of the other couples were nearby. Why was that? Were we that much faster? Or had we gotten lost out here in the sea of nothing?

I thrust my paddle deep into the water, trying to gain distance. Instead, I made the boat wobble.

"Fast but careful," Riley warned.

"I'm sitting in water now, Riley," I said, feeling the cold splash on my jeans, soaking through to my underwear.

"I'll paddle. You try to get the water out."

"How am I going to do that?"

"Your water bottle. It won't be fast, but maybe it will buy us some time."

It sounded like a better plan than the one I had. I balanced my paddle on the kayak, careful not to lose it, and began trying to scoop out the water.

How had this happened? Had someone not checked the boats before we were sent out on this incredibly long journey? Or had someone done this on purpose? Our names had been on this boat. With that knowledge, did someone sabotage us? Maybe Steve. He had been out at the boathouse this morning.

If so, why? Did they know who we were? Why we were here?

I had so many questions, but no real time to ponder any of them.

Instead, I worked hard, using my water bottle to collect as much liquid as possible.

As I bent down to scoop another container full, something on the side of the boat caught my eye.

A small prick in the side of the kayak was barely visible and almost looked like a nail hole.

It definitely hadn't come from aging or accident. Someone wanted this boat to sink.

"I think I see the island ahead!" It was barely a speck, but there was something on the horizon. I thought for sure it was Blackbird Hall.

Hope surged in me a moment. If we were to sink here, maybe we could make it to the shore.

That's when I remembered the radio we'd been given. Why hadn't I thought of that earlier? I'd been in reaction mode. "Riley, we can call for help!"

"Of course!"

I opened a little box at the front of the boat and pulled it out. I flicked the switch to ON but nothing happened.

What?

"Do you know how to use it?" Riley took another stroke and then another and another. We were moving at a nice clip . . . but would it be fast enough?

"I'm trying. I think the batteries are dead."

"You've got to be kidding," Riley muttered.

"I wish." I smacked it with my hands, but nothing happened. Realizing that more water was flooding inside the boat, I scrambled to open the back of the radio. When the cover finally popped off, I sucked in a quick breath.

"The batteries aren't dead," I said in disbelief. "There *are* no batteries."

"If I didn't know better, I'd think someone set us up."

I frowned. "I think they did. We're going to have to be careful. If we survive this kayak trip, at least."

The water reached my knees, and it kept coming in. The more water that filled the boat, the lower the boat sat in the water and the closer we became to being pulled under completely.

I gave up on the radio and began shoveling water again. I had to keep going because I really didn't want to swim back to the shore. I had a life preserver—if that hadn't also been compromised—but the chilly temperature of the bay would make it easy for hypothermia to kick in.

Of all the ways I'd seen myself dying, here in the bay while kayaking was not one of them.

No, I couldn't think like that. I just had to concentrate on getting the water out of the boat. And my other concern, next to dying, was the note. If it got wet, any of my potential evidence would be gone. I had no way of preserving it.

In the distance, the island became larger. It was definitely Bird's Nest Island. That was the good news.

The bad news was that no matter how fast Riley paddled, our safe place still looked really far away.

Lord, be with us. No matter how foolish this investigation may be, please show us Your favor. I beg You. Let me live through this trial so I can show my deepened character.

I prayed that prayer more often than I'd like to admit.

Splash, scoop, slosh.

Splash, scoop, slosh.

The sounds became a rhythm, one we needed to keep constant in order to get through this.

Something about it brought me comfort.

Until I realized the water was up to my waist.

"We're going under!"

He kept paddling. "Listen, even if we go under, we're going to be okay. We'll turn the kayak over and use it as a floatation device. We'll stick together and make it back to the shore. We'll be cold, but we can survive this. Okay?"

I nodded, continuing to scoop water. Riley always made me feel safe and like he was watching out for me. I craved that in my life.

I was falling back into my old patterns, wasn't I? I couldn't do that. I had to fight harder.

"You ready to do this, Gabby?"

I snapped back to reality. The land in the distance was probably a mile away. It was hard to guess. But at least we had a location to anchor us. We could do this.

"I'm ready," I finally said.

"Let's climb out. We can flip the kayak and use it to give us some buoyancy for as long as we can. It will help keep us from being completely immersed in the water."

"Are there sharks out here?" Last summer, a fifty-year-old man had lost his leg because of a shark attack in Virginia Beach. Why, oh, why, did I have to remember that now? My mental jukebox began playing the theme song from *Jaws*. I kept trying to switch tunes, but it didn't work.

"Sharks aren't going to mess with us," he said.

"How do you know?" I was already looking for fins circling us.

I straddled the kayak long enough to glance back at Riley. His eyes held assurance. He could always calm me like no one else could.

"I'm declaring that in faith." His firm statement comforted me.

That's right. Faith. I had to trust that God was in control right now.

With a touch of hesitance, I carefully placed my legs over the side. I gave Riley one last glance before propelling myself into the water. Icy-cold liquid surrounded me, so frigid that it took my breath away.

Riley followed behind me. We turned and grabbed the plastic boat. I pulled myself up as much as I could, desperate to stay warm.

"No matter what, we stick together, right?" Riley glanced at me, made sure I had eye contact and that I nodded. "Let's start swimming toward the shore."

"Aye-aye, Captain."

We began kicking. Our movements seemed slow, but at least we were moving. Moving gave me hope. As did Riley's muscles with his arms stretched taut over the kayak. Really, there was no one else I'd rather be stuck out here with.

"Look over there!" I pointed in the distance. It was a boat. Captain Leroy's maybe? "De boat! De boat!"

"What?"

I tried to shrug, but my life jacket concealed the action. *"Fantasy Island*, except with a boat instead of a plane."

"Well, at least you can maintain your sense of humor and your pop-culture references."

"Sometimes humor and pop-culture references are all you have. And God," I quickly added.

"Amen to that."

With urgency, I began waving my arms and yelling. Riley did also.

But the boat continued in the opposite direction. Water flew up behind the motor, and a steady hum filled the air.

"What's he doing?" I grumbled, frustration rising in me.

"Who knows?"

"He's going back to the shore for some reason. You'd think he'd look for the couples in the process in case something like this happened." I held on to the kayak and continued to kick my legs.

"You okay?" Riley asked.

I nodded, despite my chattering teeth. "Yeah, I'm fine."

"We had an interesting discussion in the men's suite last night. It was about roles in marriage."

"Oh yeah. What was so interesting?"

"Most of the guys here feel very strongly about women's roles and men's roles. Women do the housework and cooking. Men do the yard work and bring in a paycheck."

I knew what Riley was doing. He was trying to keep me distracted from thoughts of being surrounded by nothing but water. It was working. "And how do you feel about those things?"

"I feel like a husband and wife should be partners," he said. "Share the responsibilities. If you can replace your wife with a maid and cook, then there's a problem."

"Really?" His answer surprised me. I just saw him as having a more traditional viewpoint of those things.

"Why do you sound surprised? Did you think I was the type who wanted my woman barefoot and pregnant?"

"I'm not sure what I expected. I mean, we didn't really talk about stuff like that when we were . . ."

"Engaged?" he finished.

I wasn't sure why the words wouldn't leave my mouth. "That's right. Engaged." There. I'd said it.

"You don't have to be afraid to talk about it, Gabby."

"Afraid? Don't be ridiculous. I'm not afraid. It's just awkward, you know?"

"What's awkward about it?"

"Is this really the time to discuss it? I mean, shouldn't we concentrate on surviving?" I kicked my feet.

Just keep swimming.

Great. Now I was finding myself quoting Disney movies. I may have been previewing a few for my future godson or daughter.

But I couldn't stop thinking about what he'd said. Should it not be awkward? Was I missing something?

"Remember when we went paddle-boating that time at the park down the street from our apartment?" Riley asked.

"Of course, I remember that." I smiled.

It was a good memory. We'd just started dating. I'd thought I had a career ahead of me in forensics. And the future seemed bright.

So much had changed since then.

"I would like to talk to you about everything that happened over the past nine months some time," Riley said quietly.

"How about we sing 'Yellow Submarine' first?"

"What?"

I had no idea what I was talking about. Anything but what Riley wanted to chat about.

I shivered again. Shivered like I'd never shivered before. The reaction was so strong that my entire body shook uncontrollably. The water was just so cold that it zapped all my energy. My grip began slipping from the kayak, and I couldn't pull myself back up.

I had to focus, take my mind off my discomfort.

"Those were good times. But it's like they say . . ." My words began to fade as drowsiness overtook me.

"What do they say?" Riley asked.

What was I trying to say? I could hardly remember. "They say . . . all good things . . . must come to . . ."

"Gabby, are you okay?"

I couldn't answer. I knew the stark reality I was facing.

Hypothermia was setting in.

CHAPTER 16

"Gabby, I need you to stay with me," Riley said, a knot forming between his eyebrows.

"I'm numb. And cold. So cold." I felt like I was swimming in ice water. In the Arctic. After eating a popsicle.

My mind wanted to go to a happy place. A beach. In the Caribbean. With no clouds or breeze. Just searing UV rays burning my skin.

"Hold on to the kayak." He grabbed my arm and pulled me up higher, trying to get my upper extremities out of the water.

"It's no use." My words were a chattering mess. My body felt like it had taken on a mind of its own, and I had no control.

"Only a little bit farther. The Bible is full of stories that take place on or near the water. Think about Peter walking on water. If he did that through faith, then we can get to that island."

"He lost faith and sank."

"At least he stepped out. You've got this, Gabby."

But did I have it? I wasn't so sure.

That's when my foot hit something.

A shark? No, not a shark. This was something solid. Big. Expansive.

Land.

We'd reached land!

"Riley . . . the water . . . I can touch bottom."

We'd arrived just in time. The water was shallow for quite a ways until we reached the beach, but at least the end was in sight. I was already dreaming about a hot shower and coffee and . . . warmth. Just warmth. That was all I wanted.

Before I could say anything else, Riley swooped me into his arms. "I've got you from here, Gabby."

"You . . . don't . . . have to. I can . . . make it." But my words didn't sound believable, not even to my own ears.

"Let me help."

His chest felt solid beneath me. But I didn't have time to think about that, though. I had to concentrate on survival right now. My teeth chattered even more as the cold air hit my wet skin. My body trembled as it fought to get warm. Riley had to be cold. But he pushed through. He was my hero . . . again.

How many times had he saved my life now? I'd lost count.

"The kayak," I managed to say as he slogged through the water. "We should keep it for . . . evidence. The police might want . . . to see it."

"All I care about right now is getting you to safety. That trumps solving this mystery."

I held on to Riley and let him take charge. I was just grateful he was with me because I wasn't sure I would have been able to make it any farther. All of my She-Ra was fading.

My mind swam. I couldn't feel my hands. All I could hear was the slosh of water.

Finally, we reached the shore. The real shore. The sand. And I knew I was going to be okay.

***

I finished putting on some dry clothes and sat on my bed for a moment to decompress. I'd taken a long, hot shower then pulled on three shirts and four pairs of socks. I wanted to regain normal function, but I found myself climbing under the covers instead.

I just couldn't get warm.

Dr. Turner had wanted to take me to the hospital, but I'd insisted I would be fine. I hoped I was right.

Coffee and soup had been left on my nightstand. Blaine was probably responsible. She waited in the other room in case I needed her, but I didn't feel like talking to her now.

My hands were still trembling as I picked up the coffee and attempted to take a sip. It was no use. My hands wouldn't function the way I wanted.

Before I forgot, I grabbed my wet jeans. I reached into the pocket and pulled out the note I'd found from Anna.

What a soggy mess. The layers stuck together. The ink was smeared.

It was worthless.

Despite that, I tried to unfold it to let it dry. It was no use right now, though. With my hands shaking the way they were, I'd only end up doing more damage to the paper.

I frowned and placed the note in my suitcase—the dresser might be a better choice, but my pearls had disappeared from that location. This note had been my one solid piece of evidence, and now it was ruined.

Just as I put it away, someone knocked at the door. Before I could even say, "Come in," the door opened and Farrah stepped inside.

I couldn't even tell she'd been out on the water. She smelled clean, with a gentle perfume wafting around her as well as the scent of fresh shampoo.

"I hear you need to see a doctor," Farrah told me, setting a bag on the floor and pulling a chair closer to me.

"I do."

"I can help." She reached into her bag.

Was that a medical bag?

I stared at her a moment, feeling a bit speechless and perplexed. "You're a doctor?"

She shrugged and pulled a penlight out. "A pediatrician, but that doesn't really matter right now. How are you feeling? I heard you had quite the ordeal out there."

"We did. Who would have thought there was a hole in our kayak? Thankfully, we made good time before the boat started to sink."

"You'd think someone would check them out first," Farrah said with a frown and a shake of her head.

I got a good look at her. She had fine lines around her mouth and eyes. Maybe she was in her early fifties. Her gold jewelry and Ralph Lauren sweater gave her a certain finesse.

I remembered the way she stormed off before kayaking began. "Well, I'm glad you two made it in safely. No problems?"

"I gave up. Leroy came and picked us up."

So that's where he'd been going when he'd hurried past.

Farrah shone the light in my eyes. "You're very unfortunate, you know."

Had she said *unfortunate*? Yes. She had. "Why's that?"

"Because Jim and Ginger were supposed to have your kayak."

My back muscles tightened. "How do you know that?"

"I saw Jim switching the name cards before we got there."

Really? Why would he do that? Had he known the kayak was sabotaged?

"I'm just glad you're okay," Farrah continued.

I studied her a moment. A doctor? She hadn't struck me as the type, and I wasn't sure why exactly. I supposed it was because most people who were doctors and went through that much schooling didn't end their careers after getting married.

The mystery of Farrah Griffith deepened.

I paused as she listened to my heartbeat. "Why did you give up your career? You must miss it some. I mean, you have your doctor bag with you."

"I suppose I like to use my medical training whenever I can. It keeps my mind sharper."

"So why did you give it up then?" I repeated.

She shrugged again. "It's what the wives of men like Atticus Griffith do."

Now *that* was an intriguing statement. "Why?"

"The men consider it more of a symbol of their success if their wives experience lives of luxury. Atticus was charming and swept me off my feet. All that changed after we got married. I think there are other reasons men like Atticus act the way they do, but no one wants to admit it."

"Like what?"

"It traps us." She frowned and leaned back. "If the husband makes all the money, then it makes it hard for the women to leave. The men can cheat—and they usually do—and the women are powerless to do anything about it. We've been groomed to fully depend on them."

"That sounds horrible. I'm not recommending that you leave him, but you do have a career to fall back on. You don't have to be treated that way."

"Life as the wife of a powerful man is complicated. It's a

subculture within itself. All my social circles are connected with him. If I left him, I'd essentially be starting over. If you don't conform, you're shunned."

I was trying to understand. I really was. I mean, I'd watched *The Real Housewives* series. I knew how messed up people could be. "I know this is nosy, but neither you nor your husband seem to want to be here," I started. "So why are you putting yourself through this?"

Conversations could be the best way to find out information. I'd learned—sometimes the hard way—that people skills were essential in investigations.

She turned off her light and placed it back in her bag. "You're right. That is nosy. Truth be told, we promised my parents we would go through this program. My mom is dying of cancer, and this was her request. We're here, but we're going through the motions, I suppose. Neither of us really wants to work things out. We've already drawn up the divorce papers."

"I'm sorry to hear that."

She shrugged. "It is what it is. At least my mom will think she's done some good. She knows Dr. Turner personally, so we couldn't even fake coming here. She checks in with him. Of course, he can't say anything specifically about me or Atticus, but my mom always manages to get information out of him. If we didn't show up, she'd find out."

I nodded. "So, are the rest of the women here in the same boat you are?"

She twisted her lips in thought. "I shouldn't do that. My doctor says it will give me more wrinkles." She neutralized her expression. "Anyway, I don't know what to say. You're acting like this is a surprise to you. I thought your husband was some hotshot lawyer. You must understand."

My cheeks flushed. I'd forgotten my cover. How could I

have done that? I was just so fascinated by what she was saying.

"He is. We just . . . we believe that marriage is a partnership not a power play."

"Then hang on to him. Because, where I'm from, being a successful man means having control over your wife." She shook her head. "I've said too much."

I squeezed her arm. "Isn't that why you're here? So you can talk about these things?"

"Talking doesn't always change mind-sets, Gabby." She leaned back, seeming to come to her senses and putting on her ice-queen persona again. "You look like you're going to be fine."

"Did everyone else return?"

"I'm not sure. Angelina and Bo were arguing so much that they were practically going in circles. Ginger was letting Jim do all the paddling, so I'm not sure if they went faster or slower."

I thanked her before she headed downstairs. She sure had given me a lot to think about.

But the main thought lingering in my mind was that Farrah had been a doctor. That meant she would have extensive knowledge of prescription medications. Could she have had something to do with Anna's death?

CHAPTER 17

Dr. Turner approached Riley and me during dinner. I almost hated to not give my full attention to my grilled tuna, arugula, and risotto. Steve lacked many things—like a good personality—but he was a great cook.

Dr. Turner took a seat across from us, his arms resting on the table and his parakeet-yellow cardigan spotless. "I've been very concerned since I heard what happened. How are you?"

I shrugged, stealing a glance at Riley. "Hanging in. Still shaken."

"I want you to know that your safety is of utmost importance to us," he continued. "We're looking into what happened."

"When you say 'we're,' who do you mean?" I asked.

"Leroy," Dr. Turner responded. "He's an experienced boatman, and he's working security for us."

I nodded, not really satisfied with his answer.

"You know there was a hole in the bottom of the boat. We'd been reassured the equipment was all checked over," Riley said. "Frankly, Dr. Turner, I'm a little concerned."

"Is something strange going on here on the island?" I asked. "I'm getting a bad vibe."

Something shifted in Dr. Turner's gaze. I couldn't be sure, but I thought the question made him nervous. "No, I want to assure you that there is not. Unfortunately, a lot of couples who come here are in a bad place emotionally. That can lead to some poor choices. Our sessions have a tendency to bring a lot of emotions to the surface."

"So that's why the woman died last weekend?" I asked.

Dr. Turner frowned and leaned closer. "She was already depressed, and she'd had a particularly painful session with her husband that evening. She seemed okay when she went to bed, though. No one expected her to sneak out and end her life."

"So you don't think the kayak incident is related?" Riley asked.

Dr. Turner's jaw went slack with confusion. "No. Why would it be? The kayak was an accident. Anna's death was a suicide."

I nodded slowly, trying to let his explanation sink in. He seemed to sense my hesitance.

He lowered his voice. "To be honest, I've been very concerned. With God's guidance, I want to help people heal. I don't want to make people hurt any more than they already do. Things like this can shut down my entire program. That's the last thing I want. God led me to start this couples retreat. As it says in Proverbs, 'In their hearts humans plan their course, but the Lord establishes their steps.'"

"I didn't realize it was Christian based," I said.

"It's not overtly Christian. But the principles and foundation are all there. I take the Bible very seriously, as I do my calling."

"We appreciate that," Riley said. He reached over and grabbed my hand. "Faith is the only thing that will get us through this rough patch."

I swallowed hard, reminding myself he was just playing a role. Nothing more.

***

"Men and women have very specific roles to play in a marriage," Dr. Turner said, pacing in front of the group during our evening session.

We were back in the Therapy Lounge. The lights were low again, classical musical played softly, and the couch where Riley and I sat seemed more and more comfortable as I became accustomed to Dr. Turner's methods.

At least I knew the basic principles of this program were grounded in a biblical foundation. That made me feel a little better.

"I'd like for you to turn to your spouse and tell them what your expectations are for them," Dr. Turner continued. "I know this may seem strange, but it's good to be able to get these notions out in the open instead of just living them out in the subtext of our lives. Expectations can be healthy. So turn to your spouse right now and chat. I'll give you a few minutes."

I pulled a burgundy, tasseled pillow over my chest and hugged it for a moment as I turned toward Riley. That familiar awkwardness flopped around in my gut again. How were we supposed to talk about this exactly? It just seemed weird.

Besides, even though we'd bonded earlier—you know, when we'd almost died—I was starting to feel the urge to run and get away from this place. To get away from Riley, specifically. I'd started warming up to him again and setting him on that platform in my mind, the one where he could do no harm.

The truth of the matter was that he'd done too much harm. He'd broken my heart, which was on the mend. The last thing I needed was for it to be crushed again. I didn't want to be set back any further than I already was.

"Who wants to start?" Riley's arm was stretched across the back of the couch, and he leaned back casually, as if he were watching his favorite movie.

I wanted to see some sweat or something to let me know this was as stressful for him as it was for me. I was obviously going to be disappointed.

"You start," I said a little too quickly.

He shrugged and nodded, both slowly and uncertainly. "Okay, my expectations of our marriage. I expect commitment, I suppose. Friendship and support are always good. I expect you to have my back, even when you don't want to."

"That's it?"

He nodded. "That's it. Your turn."

"I expect for you not to break my heart." The words flowed from a place of truth, and I couldn't seem to stop them. "I expect you to be there for me through thick and thin. I expect you to choose me over your family."

Something flashed in his eyes. Surprise. Concern. A call to action. "Gabby—"

"I see you're both getting down to the nitty-gritty." Dr. Turner stood above us, nodding approvingly. "Good. Honesty is very important in relationships. Sometimes, the things that couples bring up during this session are formed because of past resentment caused by their spouse. That's what I'd like for you to talk about next. Gabby, why don't you start off that conversation. Continue from what you were just saying."

I scowled. I didn't want to talk about any of this. But it was obvious that Dr. Turner was paying attention, so it would be hard to avoid.

My shoulders felt stiff and my lungs wooden. "I think you're supposed to protect your spouse and do your best not to hurt her. Because hurting the person you love should never be on the agenda. You fight to make sure that doesn't happen because that's what it means to love someone."

Something soft yet painful glimmered in Riley's gaze. "But sometimes you have to choose the lesser of two evils. Maybe you think your loved one has hurt you on purpose. But maybe they're just trying to protect you from something that could be even more devastating."

"What's that mean?" My voice rose in pitch, and my words flew out. My emotions were getting the best of me. I was supposed to be acting, but I knew I wasn't.

"It means that I know God has a calling on your life, and I'd never want to come between you and your purpose."

"Why would it have to be one or the other?" Exasperation tinged my voice now. All this cryptic code talk was making me crazy.

"Gabby—"

Dr. Turner paced away then addressed the group. "Now that we've talked about expectations, I'd like to get practical. Tell your spouse one way they can put an action to the expectation. What does that expectation look like when lived out in your everyday life?"

I hugged my pillow even tighter as my jaw clenched. "You go first."

What was I even doing here? I'd told myself I would keep my distance. Maybe this *was* my way of keeping my distance. I had to bring up the hard stuff. I knew it would put a wall between us. Bringing these things to the surface was the best way to keep me from getting too close to Riley.

Riley rubbed his jaw a moment, suddenly not looking so laid-back. "What my expectation looks like: Being patient. Not rushing me. Trusting my decisions."

His answers hadn't required that much thought. Maybe he'd already had these things on his mind? I wasn't sure.

"Your turn," he said.

"Staying when you want to run. Not trying to be a martyr. Not giving mixed signals."

The two of us stared at each other for a moment.

Just then, Ginger stood and ran out of the room in tears.

What was going on? At least her drama had taken the attention off of me.

Sometimes that was all a girl could ask for, especially when her heart was on the line.

CHAPTER 18

When the session ended and Angelina and Farrah went back to their rooms, I lingered behind. Blaine had led a women-only time while Dr. Turner had taken the men aside.

I needed to talk to Blaine. As Dr. Turner's right-hand woman, she knew how things worked behind the scenes. Maybe she had some insight for me.

And I knew just how to start this conversation.

"Is everything okay?" Blaine asked, gathering up some papers she'd spread on the floor.

Notes, I realized. Almost like cue cards for our talk tonight.

"I'm doing okay. Except for one thing. My pearls are missing."

Blaine blinked, as if she hadn't heard me correctly. "Your pearls?"

I nodded. "They're one of the only things I have left that belonged to my mom. I put them in my dresser when I went to bed last night. By the time I came back from my morning walk, they were gone."

She hugged her papers to her chest. "Did you check everywhere?"

I nodded. "I did. More than once."

She frowned. "That's so strange. I can't imagine anyone here stealing."

I lowered my voice. "How about that cook guy? Steve? I heard he used to be one of Dr. Turner's patients. Someone said he has anger-management issues."

"He is a hothead, but he's not a thief." She stared into the distance and shook her head. "I don't know. I'll keep my ears open and talk to a few people. Until then, I think we should keep this quiet. Everyone's still shaken by a series of unfortunate events."

"You mean Anna?"

Blaine pressed her lips together before sighing. "I wasn't sure if you'd heard or not."

"I did, and that's incredibly sad."

"It's torn Dr. Turner apart. He cares about everyone here so much."

"Have you worked for him long?" I asked, desperate to keep her talking.

"A little more than a year. Best year ever. I worked managing a hotel before this. I'd much rather see lives transformed than to make travelers comfortable on their journey. At least, I feel like my work here has lasting implications."

"I can see that."

Just then, someone knocked at the door. Dr. Turner stood there. He offered a weary smile. "I thought I'd let you know that I'm headed back to the mainland for the night."

"Is everything okay, Dr. Turner?" Blaine's body instantly tensed as if she was concerned.

He nodded, but the circles under his eyes seemed more pronounced than they did earlier. "The police want me to come in at my earliest convenience. Now's the only time I've had today, and the detective said the late hour was fine."

"Is it about . . . ?"

"The skeleton Angelina stumbled upon. I think the authorities are going to want to explore the island a bit more. I want to double-check and see if there are any updates on Anna, as well. Mr. Robbins wants me to be there with him."

"Mr. Robbins?" I asked.

Dr. Turner glanced my way, a new emotion in his eyes. "The man who owns the island, of course."

"You mean Mr. Robinson?" I said.

His earlier look of exhaustion was replaced with a different emotion—relief? Justification? Had Dr. Turner been testing me? Or had it been an honest mistake?

"Yes, of course." He let out a feeble laugh. "My mind doesn't work quite the way it used to." He turned to his assistant. "You can handle things here?"

Blaine straightened her shoulders. "Of course."

Dr. Turner nodded. "Okay, then. Good night, Blaine, Gabby."

I took that as my opening to head to my room. I hoped Ginger would be there so I could talk to her again as well. I said good night and hurried upstairs.

As I walked into the room, I saw Ginger lying in bed.

I guessed I'd have to wait until tomorrow to chat with her.

In the meantime, now that my hands weren't trembling, I needed to check out that letter Anna had written. I opened my suitcase to retrieve it.

The letter was gone.

***

The only sound in the room was the heat kicking on and off. The cleaning ladies had been in here since dinner because the scent of lemon was still strong. I'd tossed and turned for what felt like hours—probably because it *was* hours.

As I lay against the silky sheets, unable to find sleep, all I could think about was Anna's note.

The only people who knew about it were Riley and me. I hadn't told another soul.

So who had taken it? And why?

A new concern began to grow in my gut. What if someone knew who I was? What if he or she knew I was investigating Anna's death? If my cover was blown, I would never get any answers.

I stared across the room, trying to figure out if Ginger was awake. Her chest rose and fell evenly as she lay in bed. Looking at her now, you couldn't tell she had a worry in the world.

Was she truly sleeping? I had no idea. I only knew that I hadn't seen her since the meeting when she'd run out. What had her fight with Jim been about? The two of them seemed the happiest of all the couples here. But things were rarely what they seemed.

Even with me.

I tried to act unaffected by Riley, but I really wasn't. The more I was around him, the more confused I became.

I was grateful we hadn't had any Bird's Nest time this evening. I really didn't want any more one-on-one time with Riley right now. I had too many things I feared might slip from my lips.

I'd tried so hard to pretend like Riley's rejection of me hadn't hurt. I'd tried so hard to pretend that I was stronger than that. But the truth was, a lot of hurt had been compounded in my soul. Eventually, it was all going to spill out. I only hoped that didn't happen here at the retreat center in front of an audience.

I'd distracted myself pretty well with my investigations and with Garrett.

I pressed my head farther into my pillow, unable to find sleep as I wrestled with my thoughts.

Garrett . . . I wondered how he was doing. He'd become a good friend to me. I'd wondered for a while if maybe he was the one I should be with. I still thought so at times. However, he'd gone on a trip to Africa, and we'd agreed to think about our relationship while he was gone.

Was he like those men Farrah had spoken to me about? The ones who were charming in the dating process and controlling after marriage. I just couldn't see it.

A movement caught my ear. I froze and listened closely.

Sheets rustled. A bed squeaked. A door opened.

Ginger had gotten up, I realized. I pulled my eyes open and saw that it was 2:30 in the morning. Where in the world was she going?

The bathroom, I realized. She was probably just going to the bathroom.

So I waited. And waited.

But Ginger didn't return.

She'd been gone long enough that I was both curious and worried, especially after she'd been so emotional earlier. She'd just seemed so happy up until that point. What exactly had she and Jim discussed that had upset her so much?

Best-case scenario was that maybe she was paying a late-night visit to her husband. It was the worst-case scenario that dragged me out of bed, though.

I wanted to make sure she was okay, especially with everything going on around here lately.

She wasn't in our suite. I quietly walked down the

second floor hallway. Everything was quiet. Since most of the suite doors were locked, I decided to stick with the common areas first.

I didn't see Ginger on the second floor. Spontaneously, I climbed to the third floor. I checked the rooms there—the workout room, the entertainment room, a storage room.

No one.

Out of curiosity, I climbed onto the widow's walk.

My throat went dry as I reached the top.

The area was empty—that was the good news.

But what I saw there made me pause. Binoculars and an ink pen had been left on the window seat, as if someone had been taking notes.

Was someone using this area to spy on someone else?

The thought left me unsettled.

After a moment of brief hesitation, I picked up the binoculars and put them to my eyes. I had a bird's eye view of the island. Bird's eye view? Great. I'd been listening to Dr. Turner too long.

In the dark it was hard to see, but the moonlight illuminated the waves in the distance.

On the rocky side of the island, I saw a light. What was that?

It was a boat, I realized. What in the world was a boat doing out in the bay in the middle of the night?

I tried to adjust the binoculars, but I couldn't make out any details. The night was too dark.

I moved to the other side of the island, curious if there were any more boats headed this way.

That's when I saw movement on the bluff.

Someone was out there.

I squinted, wishing I could make out some details. But it

was just too dark

Was that Ginger? Who else would it be?

What I saw next sucked the breath out of me.

The person jerked. Then he or she was gone.

It was hard to tell, but it almost looked like someone else was on that bluff.

Had that person pushed the other over the edge?

***

I burst through the outside door and ran toward the bluff before I could fully realize what I was doing. I was exposing myself and possibly blowing my cover.

None of that mattered at the moment.

All that mattered was finding the whoever fell and helping him or her.

I could really use my cell phone right now. As it was, I had no way of calling 911. Of reaching out for help. Of even contacting Riley for backup.

It was just me, a sandy bluff, and a potential killer.

I paused on the lawn and gathered my bearings. Everything appeared calm outside.

I didn't see any sign of life or of a killer.

If I'd thought ahead, I would have brought a flashlight, but I hadn't. I'd only reacted.

I reached the edge of the bluff and sucked in a breath. A woman with shadowed features lay below me. Was she still alive? I had to find out.

I scrambled down the steps, nearly tripping over my own feet. I looked over my shoulder, tense at the thought of a killer watching me and trying to stop me. Finally, my feet hit the sand. I sprinted across the beach.

Ginger lay in front of me, unmoving. I put my hand to her throat.

There was a pulse! She was still alive!

But I didn't know for how long. I had to get Farrah.

As I turned to rush back, I collided with someone.

I stifled a scream as I looked up.

It was Steve.

CHAPTER 19

"What happened?" he demanded. Perspiration beaded across his forehead like he'd been exerting himself.

Pushing a woman off a bluff might have been a workout for the island's resident chef.

"I . . . I don't know. I just looked outside. I saw her go over and rushed to help."

"Go. Call for help."

"No, I'll stay with her. You go." I feared he might finish what he'd started while I was gone.

When he looked up at me, the darkness in his gaze made me cringe. "You're wasting time. Every minute that passes, she's closer to dying."

He had a point. I took one last glance at Ginger and started toward the stairs. I hoped I wasn't making a huge mistake, though.

What had Steve been doing out here? Was he the one who'd been arguing with Ginger?

Moving quickly, I hurried back inside, up the stairs, and pounded on Farrah's door. "Farrah, Ginger needs you. She's hurt. Angelina, find a phone. Call for help. This is going to be more than we can handle on our own. Okay?"

Farrah flung open the door, her eyes hazy with sleep. "I'm on my way." She grabbed her medical bag.

By the time we all ran out into the hallway, the men had

stirred.

Riley was the first person I saw.

"What's going on?" He reached for me.

I didn't have time for that. I had to keep moving. "It's Ginger. She fell off the bluff and needs help."

His eyes widened. "I'll get Dr. Turner."

I nodded and continued jogging beside Farrah.

"What happened?" Farrah asked, her iciness replaced with an urgency.

I quickly considered my words. "I'm not sure. She's not conscious, but she still has a heartbeat."

"Is anything broken?"

"I don't know. As soon as I realized she was alive, I ran to get you. I knew she probably didn't have much time."

"Smart thinking."

We jogged across the stiff grass to the stairway leading to the beach. We took the steps by twos to the bottom.

Ginger still lay there. Steve knelt beside her.

"It's about time," he muttered. "I think she's on death's doorstep."

Now I just had to pray that she'd be all right.

***

"Can you explain exactly how you found her?" A detective with the Northampton County Sheriff's Department stared at me. The thirty-something man had a square face, short hair, and leathery skin. He'd introduced himself as Detective Hanson, and I was pretty sure I had more experience with murders than he did. I'd seen a lot in my twenty-nine years, but I couldn't be cocky here.

I wished it weren't so dark because I wanted to see the

man's eyes. But I couldn't. It was the middle of the night, and the almost total black was unnerving.

I started to speak but, in my moment of hesitation, I heard Jim wailing. Voices murmuring. Waves crashing.

Tragedy had turned people's lives upside down. Yet life continued on. The rest of the guests had gathered near the building to watch with a certain grimness in their gazes. Meanwhile, Ginger had been carried away by helicopter to a hospital on the Eastern Shore.

I prayed she would be all right. That was the most important thing.

Despite my priorities, I still swallowed hard. I'd have to tell the police what I saw. I might blow my cover and any chance I had to find the answers.

"Ma'am?"

I came back to reality. "It was dark. I couldn't sleep so I went up to the widow's walk. I thought I saw two people out here."

"Two people?"

I nodded.

"You knew one of them was Ginger Wagnor?" He cocked an eyebrow. Even in the dark I could see that.

I shrugged. "Well, we're rooming together, and she got out of bed. I think everyone else was accounted for, so I assumed it was Ginger."

"Did she seem distressed?"

"Would you be distressed if someone was about to push you over the edge?" I pressed my lips together, regretting my words as soon as they left my lips. But as I watched the other officers set up lights near the bluff, there were so many things I would tell them to do differently. They were trampling potential evidence and footprints—things that could prove a second person's presence.

"Excuse me?" Detective Hanson's hand went to his hip.

I shook my head and ran a hand through my hair, trying not to be too sassy right now. "I'm sorry. It's just that I thought I saw a man arguing with her. I think he pushed her. And those officers over there shouldn't be walking in that area. You need to take photographs first and look for trace evidence."

"A few too many episodes of CSI, Mrs. St. Thomas?"

I swallowed, wanting desperately to blurt the truth. My pride was trying to claw its way out like a baby alligator fighting out of its shell. "I suppose."

"Everyone thinks they can be a detective. Leave the police work to us, though. Now, could you make out any details on this potential second person?" His voice was humorless, annoyed, and impatient.

I shook my head again, glancing back at Riley. He stood with the rest of the crowd on the lawn in front of Blackbird Lodge. His body language clearly displayed concern—in his hunched shoulders, his folded arms, and his heavy expression.

I desperately wanted to talk to him. He was the only person I could be real with, and that was saying a lot considering he was my ex-fiancé. "I have no clue what the other person may have looked like. It was so dark outside."

"So dark that you couldn't really see?"

I knew exactly what he was getting at. He was trying to catch me in my assumptions and show me the error of my ways. "I could see well enough to have the impression that two figures were out there."

He stared at me another moment, still seeming annoyed. It was evident in the way he tapped his foot and his short, clipped words. Either way, I'd gotten on his bad side.

"Are you sure your eyes weren't playing tricks on you?"

The baby alligator inside me was turning into a full-fledged komodo dragon. A hungry, annoyed one at that. "How am I supposed to answer that?"

"Are you sure this other person pushed her?"

"I'm not sure of anything! She jerked as if she was being shoved, and the next instant she was gone." My voice rose, though I tried to tamp it down. He was treating me like an idiot, at best; a suspect, at worst.

"So maybe it was an accident?" He shifted his weight from one foot to another as he waited for my answer.

"Whether it was an accident or not, someone here knows something." My frustration was getting the best of me, and I was close to raising a fist in the air and stating my own version of the Declaration of Independence. "You need to find this person and question him. He has the answers."

"You sound like you've done this before." He chuckled. The man actually had the nerve to laugh right in my face.

I let out a sigh now. Then sucked in a deep breath. Tried to get a grip. "You're wasting time in here with me. I've told you what I know."

"No one left this island, ma'am. If this was an attempted murder, all our suspects are right here."

"For your sake, I hope you're right."

He scowled now. "Your attitude is a bit off-putting."

"I'm not trying to be off-putting. I just feel like I'm the only one who sees any urgency here. There could be a potential killer on this island." I had to calm down, but it was so hard.

"Or it could have been an accident. We don't want to jump to conclusions and scare anyone."

I shook my head and threw my shoulders back, realizing I'd spoken my piece and could do nothing else. "Of course."

If anything, I'd put the detective on edge, and he

seemed suspicious of me.

That wasn't good.

I had to tread carefully.

When Ginger awoke—and I prayed she would awake—she could tell us exactly what happened.

Dear Lord, watch over us all. Be with Ginger and Jim and the rest of us who are stranded on this island with a killer.

CHAPTER 20

"What a first weekend, huh?" Riley asked once we were safely in his car the next morning.

"There's one thing I know for sure after this session." I watched Leroy glide away in the pontoon boat. A surprising sense of relief filled me at the thought of getting away from that retreat center.

"What's that?" Riley asked.

"Bird's Nest Island is the place where fun goes to die."

Riley twisted his head in agreement. "I can't argue that."

Dr. Turner had sent everyone home early on Sunday, with the exception of Jim, who'd left Saturday night to go to the hospital with Ginger. It had been a long night. We'd been awake almost all evening. Everyone had been questioned. As far as I could ascertain, no one had any answers, just shock.

At least I'd have some time to clear my head during the week before I had to go back again on Friday. Would anyone else want to return? I had my doubts.

"What do you say we stop by and visit Jason Sparrow while we're up here?" I asked Riley as he put his car in reverse. Jason Sparrow was the man with whom Anna had an affair.

"I'm game. Brad said he worked up at the marina in Onancock, right?"

I nodded. "It would be worth a chat with him. However,

I have to say, if these two incidents—Anna and Ginger—are connected, I have a hard time seeing how Jason would be connected with both women."

"Maybe he can offer some insight into Anna," Riley said. "Collecting information is always helpful."

Spoken like a true lawyer. I nodded. They were always *so* practical.

We hit Onancock a few minutes later and easily found the marina. Riley and I strolled toward the sun-drenched docks and found a little shack with an "Information" sign above it. We asked for Jason Sparrow, and the woman nodded toward a huge yacht in the distance. A man was rolling rope on the pier and didn't bother to look up as we approached.

I observed him for a moment. The man looked to be in his mid-thirties. He was tanned, with neat clothing and short brown hair. He had purposeful-looking scruff that was manicured and groomed. The man obviously prided himself in the way he looked.

Someone who knew so much about boats could have easily traveled to Bird's Nest Island to meet with Anna one night, maybe for a secret rendezvous that turned ugly. Had Ginger seen something—leading to someone trying to kill her to keep the silence?

"Jason Sparrow?" I called, purposefully keeping my sunglasses on to conceal my gaze. All those secret service men were making more and more sense to me. Their sunglasses were simple but brilliant.

He barely glanced up and, instead, continued to work. He either had a great work ethic, had no manners, or both. "Yes?"

"I was wondering if we could ask you a few questions." The sun and warmer temperatures today were nice, except the heat seemed to enhance the scents of the bay. I couldn't pinpoint which sea creature exactly I smelled, but it was probably a mix of fish, clams, and seaweed.

"And you are . . . ?"

"I'm Gabby, and this is Riley. We were friends with Anna Thorn."

He froze and finally looked up. "Anna? How do you know her?"

"We go way back," Riley said. "We're concerned about the way she died."

"I've been concerned also," Jason said, going back to work.

"We don't believe she committed suicide," I added.

"I don't either." Jason scowled, rolling the rope with more urgency now. "I think someone's getting away with murder."

Yes, the trip to visit him was definitely worth it. I wanted to hear his viewpoint. "Why do you think that?" I asked.

"Anna would have never killed herself. Never." He swung his head back-and-forth, his jaw clenched with anger.

"Do you have any theories about what happened?" Riley shifted and his elbow rubbed mine, sending an electrical wave through me.

Jason grimaced and stopped rolling the rope. He stood and wiped the sweat from his forehead using a white cloth from his pocket. "No good theories."

"We'll listen to bad ones," I said.

He stared over the water a moment, and I could sense his thoughts were churning like an ocean storm. Finally he glanced at us again. "You're a family friend, so you probably don't want to hear this. But I think her husband killed her."

I remembered the grief I'd seen in Brad's eyes. But on a

purely logical level, the man could easily be grieving over killing her just as much as he was grieving over her death. "Why would you think that?"

"She was going to leave him."

My jaw instantly tightened. Leave him? Was there anyone who was telling the truth on that island? I was beginning to doubt it.

CHAPTER 21

"We heard they were working things out, that she'd left you," I said, reserving my judgment for later. Again, I was thankful for my sunglasses. Otherwise, he would have seen my surprise.

"That's what she told people." Tears glimmered in Jason's eyes. But, beneath the tears, I glimpsed rage. "She was just tired of all the arguing, tired of trying to live under her husband's demanding expectations."

"Is that what she told you?" I clarified.

"In so many words. With me, she could be free to be who she really was." He ran his hand over his face. "She had fun. She laughed. I loved hearing her laugh. The sound was beautiful and free and contagious. She told me she never laughed with Brad."

"Was she really that unhappy with Brad?" I asked. Brad had painted a totally different picture of their relationship.

Jason seemed more than ready to talk now. "They never saw each other. They slept in separate bedrooms, took separate vacations. The worst part, she said, was that they stopped fighting even. That was when she realized that they'd both grown apathetic. That's when she knew what they had was over."

"One of them must have had hope," Riley said. "They were going to counseling."

"It was like being told you had terminal cancer but going through chemo anyway. I didn't get it, but I had to respect her choice."

"I thought you said she was going to leave him?" I asked.

"She was, but they had a pre-nup. If she left him, she'd lose everything. I told her it didn't matter. I didn't care about money. The last time we talked, she told me counseling had only confirmed what she already knew: Her marriage with Brad was done. She was supposed to tell him after the retreat was over."

I nodded, soaking all of that in. Jason had given me a lot to think about.

"Just one more question," I said. "Where were you on the night she died?"

He balked and shoved his finger in his chest. His nostrils flared with subdued outrage. "Where was I? I thought you were family friends. You sound like you're cops."

"We're friends who want answers," Riley said.

Jason scowled. "I was actually on a four-day fishing adventure in the Atlantic. You can ask anyone around here. I was gone. I couldn't have gotten back here if I wanted to."

As Riley and I started to walk back to his car, I caught a glimpse of someone pulling out of the parking lot.

I frowned. I couldn't be sure, but the woman looked an awful lot like Blaine Stewart.

***

"There's something strange happening on that island," I told Riley as the miles blurred past us. We were already on the Bay Bridge Tunnel, heading back toward Norfolk. We'd grabbed a fast-food lunch on our way out and gobbled it down in his car. Just for fun, I wanted to leave one stray French fry on the floor and see how long it took for Riley to clean it up.

I wouldn't do that, though. It would be immature. I was *never* immature.

I was grateful that I'd be getting some space from Riley in the very near future. Maybe I could distance myself and figure out exactly what was wrong with me, because right now I honestly felt like I needed some counseling. Maybe when this was over, I could talk to Dr. Turner.

"If it was a man, then that limits our options as to who did this," Riley continued. "There was only me, Atticus, Bo, Jim, Dr. Turner, the cook, and Captain Leroy. Our pool of suspects is pretty small yet exceedingly large at the same time."

I frowned. His words were true. The problem was that everyone either had motive, means, or opportunity. Who had all three?

I could rule out Dr. Turner. He was on the mainland last night and had just returned this morning.

"What about Atticus? Did he leave the room?"

Riley frowned. "I don't think so."

"Did you hear him stirring at all?"

"I didn't." A strange emotion lingered behind his words.

Why did I have the feeling there was something he wasn't telling me?

I moved on. "I did see a boat pull up on the other side of the island."

"What? You didn't tell me that. Why would a boat come to the island at that time of night?"

I shrugged, wiping some stray salt from my jeans. There *was* a fry down there—and I hadn't even left it on purpose. Begrudgingly, I picked it up and placed it in my paper sack with the rest of my trash. "I have no idea. The bay would be a perfect place for something illegal. Don't you think?"

"Absolutely. You know pirate stories abound in these parts. We've practically got Blackbeard's ghost living in our back yard on our side of the water. But that would be strange, right? I mean, if there was something going on, what are the chances that two of the women at the retreat center who are both from different areas had something to do with it?"

"That's a good point," I said. "It would be hard to find a tie-in. Unless both women happened to be wandering around at night and stumbled upon something they shouldn't."

"We're going to have a hard time proving that."

Yes, we would. I stared out the window, trying to formulate my thoughts. "Are we meeting with Brad again?"

"I promised to talk to him and give him an update. Why?"

"I just think it's interesting that his wife cheated on him. That would make him a good suspect, especially since she'd decided to leave him."

"But why would he hire us if he was guilty? That seems counterproductive."

"Unless that was exactly his point, almost like a slight-of-hand trick where he convinces us to look one way so no one will see what really happened." I sighed and shook my head. "I don't know. I'd like to do a little more research on the people at the retreat center. I should be able to do that now that I'll have Internet and cell phone service."

"It's funny how we learn to depend on those things, isn't it? I feel old saying this, but I remember a time when we didn't have Internet or cell phones."

"You do sound old," I teased. I instantly sobered. What was I doing? I couldn't flirt and tease.

Distance, Gabby, distance.

I cleared my throat, trying to regain my focus. "So, tell me about your new job, Riley. What are you up to?"

"I got a job at a law firm based in DC, but they're letting me work from down here. I'm doing things that require a lot of paperwork. I'll travel up to DC about once a week to meet with clients and the partners at the firm. But they've given me a lot of freedom, which was what I needed."

Freedom. I supposed that's what he'd needed from me also. My feelings of resentment returned like a ton of bricks being dropped on my chest.

"I'm glad it's worked out for you," I finally muttered.

"I finished therapy, and all my doctors say my recovery has gone beyond their expectations. I'm ready to get on with my life. I wasn't totally onboard with that temporary pause that had been handed me."

Temporary pause? Is that what he considered it? To me it felt like a U-turn. Or a free fall. It depended on the day you asked me.

We pulled to a stop in front of our apartment building, and I turned toward him. "I know we'll probably both get busy this week with our jobs and everything, so I just thought I'd let you know that I'll look into Ginger and Jim. I want to find out more about their backgrounds."

"I'll see what I can find out about Angelina and Bo, as well as Atticus and Farrah. We'll exchange notes sometime. How's that sound?"

My heart felt unreasonably heavy, and I wasn't sure why. But I forced myself to smile. "That sounds great. In the meantime, I've got to gear myself up for my new job."

"You're not nervous about it, are you?"

I thought a moment. My stomach had been churning all

day, and that could very well be why. I had my first training session the next day, and I had to make sure I was prepared. I had to make sure my boss didn't regret hiring me, or come to the conclusion I'd only gotten my job because of my connections. I felt like there was a lot at stake for me professionally.

"Yes, actually, I am."

"You're going to kill it, Gabby," he said. "I have no doubts."

I smiled at his assurance but flinched at his word choice. His confidence in me actually did make me feel better. "Thanks, Riley. That means a lot."

With that, I stepped out of the car, ready to continue on with life—even if it meant living across the hall from the man I'd been in love with at one time.

CHAPTER 22

After getting home, I checked my messages and emails, sketched out my plans for the week, and made a grocery list. My little apartment may not have been the prettiest place on earth, but it was home. Even with its thrift-store, hand-me-down furniture, there was still no place I'd rather be.

I'd just sat down at my dinette with a cup of coffee when someone knocked at my door. When this person entered without invitation, I knew exactly who it was: Sierra.

She looked ready to explode. My tiny Asian friend was all belly.

I stood, ready to help her, but she held up a hand to stop me. "I'm fine."

"How's my little niece or nephew doing?" I'd already decided I would be Aunt Gabby. I wasn't sure if Sierra and Chad had ever officially extended that invitation to me. But I'd taken it.

"Baby Davis is doing gymnastics in my belly. He or she is also using my kidney as a pillow."

"You're only four weeks away from your due date, right?"

"Right, but, really, the baby could come any time now and I'd be happy—as long as he or she is healthy, of course. I feel ready to burst, so I'm all for that."

"I can't believe you're going to be a mom soon." I

ushered her to an orange upright recliner that no longer reclined, trying to get her off her feet.

"Why does everyone treat me like I'm fragile?" Despite her protests, she sat down and propped her feet up on a wooden stool I pulled over.

"You need to be pampered right now."

She looked at me like she didn't believe me.

"Remember that time you found that pregnant dog wandering down Colley Avenue?"

She nodded.

"Remember how you took it in and took care of her until the babies were born? You wouldn't let her out of your sight."

"What's that have to do with me?"

I shrugged and leaned back on my couch. "I'm just saying that if the poor, little dog deserved that extra attention then so do you."

"You know how to speak my language." She sighed and let her head fall back against the chair. "Before I forget, Garrett stopped by the apartment yesterday."

I suddenly straightened, nearly spilling my coffee as panic raced through me. "What? He told me he wouldn't be back for another two weeks."

She shrugged, seeming exhausted even after such a subtle motion. "Well, he got back early."

"What did you tell him?" I held my breath, worst-case scenarios rushing through my mind.

"That you were at a couples retreat with Riley, of course."

I stared at her, horrified. My worst-case scenario had materialized.

Then I saw Sierra smile.

144

"Of course, I didn't tell him that," Sierra said, all teasing gone. "I said you were away doing an investigation. Then I tried to call you, but it wouldn't go through. He didn't call you himself because he wants to surprise you. But what kind of friend would I be if I kept that news to myself?"

"You're the best."

"I know." She arched her back before focusing her hyper-vigilant gaze on me. "Why beat around the bush? What I really want to know is about you and Riley. How was it? Awkward?"

"For the most part, I think we were able to remain professional with each other. Even better, we were able to avoid too many conversations."

"What aren't you telling me?" Her eyes narrowed as she studied me.

I frowned before deciding to plunge into the truth. "It's going to be really hard having him live across the hall from me again."

"Maybe this is a chance for you two to make things right between you." She pushed up her plastic-framed glasses higher on her nose.

"Make right how?" Was there a good answer for that? Because I couldn't see anything good coming from having a front-row seat here in my apartment to see him go out with other women and move on without me.

She rubbed her belly. "At least you could go back to being friends."

"You still think he's a jerk?"

"Jerk is a strong word. He went through a lot. So did you. I think experiences tore you both apart. And I just want to see you happy. I thought Garrett made you happy there for a while, but honestly you've seemed fine since he's been gone."

Her words caused me to pause. "What do you mean?"

She shrugged, still absently rubbing her belly. "I mean, when I'm away from Chad I miss him terribly. He's all I think about. I didn't see that in you while Garrett was away."

I let her words sink in. She had a point. But I had a million excuses to explain all that. I was independent. Busy. Out of town. Concentrating on my new job. Were any of my reasons valid?

No, they weren't. Because throughout all those excuses, whom had I missed? Riley. "Garrett's a great guy."

He was wealthy, so wealthy that when my apartment building had come up for sale, he'd purchased it so I wouldn't have to move out. He'd been there for me, even through some of my not-so-flattering moments. There was nothing not to like about him.

"So what are you going to tell Garrett when you see him again?" Sierra asked quietly.

I thought about it a moment before letting out a sigh. "I don't know. I wasn't expecting to have to talk to him yet. I'm going to have to pray about this."

"I see."

"And I have so much going on right now. I've got my first training session tomorrow."

"Chad has a couple of jobs he needs some help with also, if you're available."

I'd seen his emails and planned on helping some. My new job was only part-time, which allowed time for crime-scene cleaning as well as some P.I. jobs. I wasn't a professional P.I., not by any means. But I'd had enough people contact me with little side investigations that I felt comfortable taking on the work. And I had worked as a medical legal death investigator for a whopping two months, so I had that professional experience.

"I think I should be able to help," I told her. "But I'll talk to Chad a little later to find out exactly what he's thinking."

"Speaking of which, he told me to give you this." She reached into the bag at her feet and handed me a shirt.

I held it up and smiled. It was a new work T-shirt with "Squeaky Clean Restoration Services" across it. We'd adjusted the name as time went on, but I thought this newest wording was a winner. "I love it."

"Well, I guess I should go." She tried to stand but could hardly push herself out of the chair. Before she could argue, I helped her to her feet.

"Don't forget: Your baby shower is next Wednesday."

"I haven't forgotten. I thought you might have."

"Me?" I pointed to myself in mock horror. "I could never forget such a thing."

But I did have to get on the ball. I was in charge.

It looked like my schedule was filling up quickly.

Good. Maybe that would keep my thoughts off Riley, Garrett, and murder.

Oh my.

***

That evening, after I'd reviewed all my notes for my training presentation and finalized some plans for the baby shower, I stared at the phone, wondering whether or not I should call Garrett and admit that Sierra had spilled the beans. But the truth was I didn't know what to say to him. He'd given me time to think about our relationship, and I needed to give him an answer. Considering the fact that I knew somewhere deep inside me that my feelings for Riley hadn't died yet, I didn't know if continuing our relationship was a good idea or not.

At gut level, I knew the answer. But I also didn't want to throw away a potentially great relationship with Garrett just because my ex-fiancé was living across the hall again.

I let out a sigh and decided to avoid the issue for a little longer. But if I really did care about Garrett, I would be rushing to see him right now, wouldn't I? I wouldn't be able to wait, especially since he'd been gone for so long.

Instead of dwelling on this, I sat at my computer and did an Internet search for Ginger Wagnor in Maryland. To my surprise, nothing came up.

Nothing? That *never* happened in this day and age. Everyone had some kind of digital presence.

I leaned back and tapped my finger against the desk. "Okay, let's try you, Jim Wagnor."

Thousands of results for the name appeared. I narrowed it to Baltimore and clicked through a few of the new results until I found an article on the Jim Wagnor from the retreat. I only knew for sure because of his picture.

I paused halfway through reading it.

According to this newspaper profile on the man, his wife's name was Jill, not Ginger. Was Ginger a middle name and Jill a proper name?

A picture appeared. Jill Wagnor looked nothing like Ginger Wagnor. They were definitely two different people.

I quickly scrolled back up to see the date on the article. Sure enough, it was written just six months ago.

Jim and Jill appeared to have been happily married for twenty years. They had three kids.

This was *the* Jim Wagnor. That was clearly his picture, career listing, and hometown.

"You've got to be kidding me." I shook my head. "Okay, let's do another Internet search here."

I typed in "Jill Wagnor," halfway expecting an obituary to pop up for her.

But, no. There was no obituary. In fact, just last week Jill Wagnor had been at a gala event with . . . Jim. Their picture showed them happy together with their arms around each other. The caption referred to them as husband and wife.

What was going on here?

I had an inkling, but I didn't want to believe someone would be that bold and obnoxious as to bring his *mistress* to a marriage retreat.

I leaned back in my chair and let that sink in.

That had to be it, though. There was no other explanation. Jim Wagnor had brought the woman he was having an affair with to the marriage retreat.

Someone had pushed her over the bluff.

As far as I was concerned, he was the most likely suspect. What if Anna had discovered that information and threatened to reveal it? Would that have been reason enough to kill her?

Maybe.

As soon as I got the chance, I needed to check this out.

Because I finally had my first decent suspect.

CHAPTER 23

I couldn't remember who'd said it was an irrefutable truth that when one thing in life worked out wonderfully well, something else in life went horribly wrong.

That felt like my life at the moment.

I'd just finished my first workshop with a police department about an hour from my home in Norfolk. I'd driven out to Franklin, Virginia, and worked with the officers there to show them how to use the new fingerprint-lifting equipment they'd ordered. Afterward I'd gone out with the police chief for lunch and had thoroughly enjoyed our interaction.

For the first time in a long time, I felt respected and like a professional among law enforcement.

I guessed that wasn't entirely true. I'd received an award a month or so ago for being a promising forensic investigator. I'd had newspaper articles written about some of the cases I'd solved, cases that had baffled the police. So I wasn't sure exactly why I felt like this, except that sometimes the professionals were the ones who didn't take me seriously. They thought I got in the way. And sometimes I did.

But for a moment today I'd felt like one of the gang. In fact, I'd had officers asking my advice about the best ways to lift fingerprints from various surfaces and the best kinds of dust to use in different situations. Answering their questions gave me an immense satisfaction. I was going to like my new job.

I was done with this training for today and headed back to Norfolk. I was headed a little farther than that, truth be told.

I hadn't been able to stop thinking about Ginger Wagnor—or whatever her last name was. I'd called the hospital, but, of course, there was no one there registered with that name.

Though it was a bit of a long haul and the tolls would cost me more than twenty bucks, I wanted to return to the Eastern Shore. I wanted to see Ginger, check her status, and find out if Jim was there. I might even want to talk to the police.

I felt a fire in my blood at the thought. Maybe I was finally getting somewhere.

As I came to a stop at a traffic light, my phone buzzed. I'd gotten a text from Garrett.

Yes, I might have texted him this morning instead of calling because I was feeling kind of wimpish.

Surprise. I'm back. Unfortunately, I have to go back to Cincinnati for a few days on business. I'm sorry we weren't able to see each other.

Relief filled me. Relief? What kind of a person was I? I should feel disappointed.

But my confusion was getting the best of me.

I quickly typed back:

Me 2. Let me know when U R back. I'll be out of town this weekend working on a new case. Leaving Friday.

Almost as soon as I sent that message, my phone rang.

It was Riley. After a second of hesitation, I answered. "Riley. What's going on?"

"I've been doing some research. I thought you might find a few things interesting. You up for meeting tonight?"

Drats! He'd caught me. "I was actually heading over to the Eastern Shore."

"Really? Why?"

"I want to check on Ginger and maybe talk to the police. I've discovered a few interesting things as well."

"Do you mind if I ride along with you?"

Kind of. "I figured you had to work."

"I have more flexible hours right now. When are you leaving?"

"I'm headed toward Norfolk from Franklin. I'm probably forty-five minutes away now."

"I can be back at the apartment by then."

I frowned. "Great. I'll swing by and pick you up."

I took several deep breaths as I threw my phone onto the seat beside me.

I could handle this. I'd handled it all weekend. Certainly I could handle a little drive across the water with Riley.

Despite that, my stomach was all twisty and knotty and uneasy.

Sometimes a girl had to face her challenges head on, though. At least, that's what I tried to tell myself.

***

My knuckles were white on the steering wheel as I headed across the Bay Bridge Tunnel with Riley beside me.

Strangely enough, he didn't seem uptight at all. In fact, he looked rather laid-back as he sat next to me munching on a granola bar and sipping some coffee. He'd gotten some java for me, as well.

Yes, something about him had changed. There had been a part of him that was uptight, and that seemed to be disappearing since his accident. Maybe it was like he said: Almost dying could put life into perspective.

"So, you want to go first or shall I?" He crumpled up his wrapper and stuffed it back into the plastic bag from the store.

We'd had the obligatory small talk the first twenty minutes of our trip. The weather. Work. Sierra and Chad's baby.

"You," I said easily. I took a deep breath, soaking in the warm sunshine that bathed the car and the road. It was a beautiful afternoon. I could handle this trip with Riley.

But as I glanced in my rearview mirror, my gut churned. Why did I have the strange feeling that someone was following us? I didn't see anyone suspicious behind us. But the feeling wouldn't leave me.

"Okay, I called Rae Gray up in Baltimore to see if she'd discovered anything about Anna's death," Riley said.

That was the reporter Brad had mentioned to us, the one who had disappeared. "And?"

"He's telling the truth when he said she's nowhere to be found. Her office said she was gone all week. Of course, they can't tell me too much. I did get her cell phone number, though. I tried to reach her, but her voicemail box is full. I couldn't even leave a message."

"So do you really think something could have happened to her as a result of investigating Anna's death?" I glanced in my mirror again. Just as before, there weren't any suspicious vehicles. My brain must be playing tricks on me.

"I have no idea. But it seems suspicious."

"I agree." I nodded, considering the possibility that

someone could be desperate enough to kill to keep a secret.

"Your turn."

I sucked in a deep breath before plunging ahead. I shared what I'd learned about Jim and Ginger whatever-her-last-name was.

"So Ginger is his . . . mistress?" Riley asked, his coffee frozen mid-sip. "Do people still use that word?"

"What else would she be?"

"I guess we're not the only couple there under false pretenses." Riley's jaw tensed as if he was deep in thought. It was a lot for anyone to take in.

"In my mind, that makes Jim the prime suspect. I mean, he has the most to lose. He's married. A divorce could take away his money or his children. Maybe he's desperate to keep this relationship quiet."

"Then why come to this retreat?"

I bit down before shaking my head. "I'm not sure. I've thought about that also. I figured maybe the retreat is so small they didn't feel threatened by being there."

"Even aside from that, why would a couple who's not married need to go to a retreat center for counseling? Most people end affairs. They don't seek therapy to make them work."

"All excellent points. Until we talk to either Ginger or her husba—her boyfriend, I guess we won't know for sure."

One more thought entered my mind. I'd seen that boat. What if Jim's wife—his real wife—had found out about the affair? What if she'd come to the island at night and somehow lured Ginger outside?

Stranger crimes of passion had been committed.

But I had to stop speculating. Right now, I needed to seek some answers.

CHAPTER 24

We reached the hospital, which was relatively small compared to most of the ones I'd been to—and, of course, the volunteer at the front desk told us that there was no one there by the name of Ginger Wagnor.

"Maybe Wagnor was her maiden name, not her legal name?" I said, leaning closer to the desk. "She was injured over on Bird's Nest Island—?"

"Bird's Nest Island?" she interrupted, her eyes narrowed in confusion.

"It used to be call Cemetery Island," Riley said.

Realization lit on the woman's face. "Oh yes. You mean the woman who went off the cliff?"

I nodded. "Yes, she's the one."

She pursed her lips contemplatively for a moment. "Let me see what I can find out. But I heard she's still not conscious, so I'm not sure how much visiting you're going to get in."

"I was hoping for better news." I frowned, honestly disappointed. I wanted her to be okay, and not just because I wanted answers.

"There's always hope." She tapped something in the computer and then pulled out a card, jotted a number there, and handed it to us. "She's in ICU. Maybe her family can give you an update."

Family? Did that mean someone was here with her?

Could we be that lucky?

Riley and I traveled down the hall, up the stairs, and found the ICU. A nurse disappeared inside just as we approached, so I grabbed the door, waited until the nurse vanished, and then slipped into the secure area. Moving quickly so we wouldn't be spotted, we found Ginger's room and ducked inside.

Ginger lay in the bed, with eyes closed and multiple tubes hooked up to her. The scent of rubbing alcohol or Lysol or some other universal hospital odor wafted up to me. The smell turned my stomach. I only had bad memories of hospitals— more and more of those bad memories as time went on.

I frowned as I gazed at Ginger. What had she gotten herself into? Why would someone feel so threatened by her that she'd been pushed to her death?

If I hadn't found her when I did, she probably would be dead by now.

Out of curiosity, I glanced to a white board on the wall across from the bed. There at the top of the board was her real name: Ginger Lambert. I stored that information in the back of my mind.

I looked back at Riley, noticing that he'd been quiet since we stepped inside. He looked pale, almost sickly white, for that matter. Concern ricocheted through me.

Instinctively I reached for him, my heart lurching into my throat. "Are you okay?"

He nodded toward Ginger, still looking shell-shocked. "Is that what I looked like?"

I rubbed my lips together, everything making sense. I glanced at Ginger. She looked nearly dead. Nothing about her screamed alive, nothing but the steady beat of the heart monitor.

"You looked worse," I whispered.

He swallowed hard, his Adam's apple bobbing up and down. "I've come far in the past nine months, Gabby."

"Considering you were on death's doorstep, I'd say definitely that you have." At once, memories of his time in the hospital began hitting me as well. Those were some rough days. I never wanted to relive anything like that again. Never. Nor would I ever wish it on anyone. The waiting. The not knowing. The uncertainty.

We exchanged a look that only two people who had experienced so much grief together could understand.

"How about we locate Jim?" I said softly. "We're not going to find out anything here."

We casually left Ginger's room, acting like we belonged there. No one even looked our way as their attention was drawn to another patient on the other side of the unit. Thank goodness.

As we emerged from the ICU and into the hallway, I walked a little closer to Riley, feeling some kind of nurturing need to comfort him. But that wasn't my place. Despite that fact, I wanted nothing more than to pull him into my arms.

We wandered down a few doors and found a waiting area. Sitting there in one of the seats was Jim. He was reading a magazine and talking on the phone.

I had to remind myself that we were undercover because my first instinct was to start questioning him. To admit my research. To lay everything out.

"I've got to go," he mumbled into the phone. He put it down and stood, extending his hand. "Riley. Gabby. I didn't expect to see you here."

"We don't live far away," Riley said. "We wanted to come check on you and Ginger."

157

Jim's face squeezed with pain. "I appreciate that. There's really been no change in her condition, though. She hasn't awakened from her fall yet."

"I'm so sorry to hear that," I said, nudging my hips against the wall. "Have the doctors said anything else?"

He shook his head. "It's all a guessing game right now. She has swelling on her brain. If that goes down, she could wake up and tell us what happened. If it doesn't . . . ?"

"Do the police have any idea what happened?" I asked.

"If they do, they haven't told me. One of the detectives came by here this morning to see if she was awake. He asked me if there was anyone she was having problems with. I told him no, not really. Besides, there were such a limited number of people on the island. We haven't been there long enough to make enemies."

I remembered my theory about Jim's wife. I remembered the boat I'd seen the night she died. Was there any kind of connection there?

I mean, the man had a good point. There was really no one on the island who would want Ginger dead . . . except maybe him.

Was I staring at a cold-blooded killer?

I observed the man for a moment. His eyes were bloodshot. The wrinkles around his mouth and eyes were more pronounced than before. Even his hair—the little he had— seemed a bit grayer.

This had taken a toll on him. Or had almost killing Ginger taken its toll? I had to keep an open mind here.

"Is there anything we can do for you, Jim?" Riley asked.

The man shook his head. "No, not really. Now I just play the waiting game."

"We'll keep Ginger in our prayers," Riley said.

"I appreciate it."

As we took a step away, he called to us again.

"You drove all the way up here just to check on Ginger?"

I nodded. "We did. We know how hard this must be on you."

"And you found Ginger without any problems once you got here?" He swallowed hard, his poker face nonexistent.

"Of course. We said we knew you from Bird's Nest Island, and she immediately knew who we were talking about."

A subtle relief washed over his features. He was still trying to keep his little affair a secret. I found it interesting that in the midst of worrying about whether she'd live or die he was attempting to protect his reputation. Had he told the police the truth about Ginger?

It made me not like him as much. Not that I liked him a ton in the first place.

I wasn't going to let him off the hook that easily.

"Why do you ask?" I tried to keep my voice innocent, but I wasn't sure if I'd succeeded or not.

"Someone stopped by earlier and asked for Ginger, but the nurse had trouble locating her. I was just wondering if the hospital had corrected their computer records yet."

I shrugged, realizing the ease by which he'd just lied to me. "I guess they have."

With a final wave, Riley and I exited the waiting area.

I was leaving with even more questions than I came with, though.

***

"That was interesting," Riley said when we got back in the van.

"Wasn't it?" I asked, cranking the engine. Today's weather was tepid, so I rolled down my window and let the fresh air waft through the van as we sat in the parking lot. "I just can't figure out what that man is thinking."

"He looked like he was grieving."

"But was he grieving over her condition or the fact that he didn't finish the job?" I hated to ask the question, but someone had to.

"That's a good point."

"If he's the type of man Farrah described to me then he probably uses his so-called business trips as an excuse for weekend rendezvous." Before I went anywhere, I had to get something off my mind. I grabbed some paper and a pen from my glove compartment, careful not to touch Riley in the process. Then I made my list of suspects and possible indications of guilt.

Atticus: strange text, Anna's scarf
Jim: argued with Anna, married to someone else
Brad: wife was going to leave him
Steve: anger issues, appeared moments after Ginger almost died
Farrah: former doctor who knows RX
Blaine: in Onancock
Jill: kill her husband's mistress?

I stared at the list and sighed.

"What's that?" Riley peered over my shoulder.

"I'm trying to sort out my thoughts. There are just too many people with either motive, means, or opportunity. I don't know if I've ever had so many potential suspects in an investigation, and none of them are really, truly standing out."

"Are you leaning toward anyone?"

"Maybe Jim. But my opinion is changing every hour, I think. I need a solid lead." I pointed to the last name on my list. "I'm also really curious about Jill Wagnor. Her husband was cheating on her. Maybe she wanted to put an end to the affair."

"But why would Jill Wagnor kill Anna . . . unless Anna happened to be in the wrong place at the wrong time." The idea hit me like lightning. It was my best theory yet.

"You mean that Jim's wife thought that Anna was actually Ginger and killed her by mistake?"

"Yep, that's it in a nutshell." I shrugged. "It's just a theory—and a complicated one at that. But if you look at Ginger and Anna's photos, they're similar. They were approximately the same size; they both had brown hair; and it was dark outside."

He bounced his head back and forth in thought. "It's an interesting one. I'm not sure how we would prove that."

I pressed my lips together a moment. "Me neither. Then there's Rae Gray. Is she somehow mixed up in this also? And there are my missing pearls. There are just so many angles here that I'm going crazy."

"It doesn't make sense. The pieces don't easily fit together."

Riley and I made a pretty good team, I realized. But I couldn't let myself get too attached here. There was too much water under the bridge, too much history between us.

I cranked the engine. "Let's swing by the sheriff's office. I want to ask a few questions."

"Whatever you say, Boss."

Boss? That was a new one.

And I kind of liked it.

CHAPTER 25

After I located the Northampton County Sheriff's Office using the map app on my phone, we pulled up to a small building. The good news was that I didn't see or sense anyone following me from the hospital to the sheriff's office. Maybe my paranoia had been working overtime earlier.

Inside, I asked the woman at the desk if I could speak with someone about the attempted homicide at Bird's Nest Island. While at the hospital, I'd pulled a jacket on over my Grayson Technologies polo. But here at the police station I thought it might serve me well to proudly display my employer's name. We were well-known in the law enforcement community, and I'd take whatever advantages I could get because I knew cops didn't easily trust outsiders—and they shouldn't.

A moment later, Riley and I were ushered back to speak with a detective. It was the same man I'd seen on the island on Saturday night—Detective Hanson. He sat at a cluttered desk, boasted a stained shirt, and had a jelly donut bleeding all over a napkin in front of him.

Recognition flashed in his eyes when he saw me. He wiped his hands and pointed to two seats in front of him. "Mr. and Mrs. St. Thomas. Have a seat."

I glanced at Riley, suddenly uncomfortable. I had to come clean about what we were really doing on the island and who we really were.

"Detective, before we start, there's something I need to tell you. My name is actually Gabby St. Claire and this is Riley Thomas. We're not married."

His eyes narrowed as he laced his hands across his midsection and leaned back to observe us. "Go on."

"We were hired to go undercover and investigate the death of Anna Thorn."

His lips twitched like he was amused. "So you're trained P.I.s?"

I shook my head, my gut indicating that this talk wouldn't go well. "No, we're not. I actually work for Grayson Technologies, and I previously worked for the Virginia medical examiner. I've got a few cases under my belt."

He nodded like he didn't care. I might as well have told him about an obscure friend who'd just gotten a scholarship or something else inconsequential to him.

"Anna Thorn's death was a suicide," he said.

"Her husband believes it wasn't," Riley said.

"The evidence is contrary to that. She left a note."

"She left two." I explained what I'd found.

Detective Hanson shifted in his seat and narrowed his eyes. "Sounds like another suicide note to me."

"Why would someone leave two suicide notes?" I asked. "And why leave one in a kayak? That's what doesn't make sense."

"Lots of things that people do don't make sense." The detective let out a slow sigh. "Now, what else can I do for you, Ms. St. Claire? I'm assuming you didn't come all the way here just to tell me these things."

I reminded myself to remain professional. "I know you're not allowed to talk about an active investigation, but I believe Anna's murder and the attempted murder of Ginger may be connected."

Detective Hanson pressed his lips together, not bothering to hide his annoyance. "All the evidence shows that Ginger accidentally fell. That island has a history of tragedy. Apparently, the tradition is continuing. That place is dangerous. I think the retreat center should be shut down, but what can I say? It's a free country. People can decide for themselves."

Heat climbed in me. He'd easily discounted what I had to say, and I didn't appreciate it. Why wasn't he listening? How could I get his attention? "But I saw someone out there with her."

"You *think* you saw someone. It was dark, Ms. St. Claire. We searched for footprints or any other evidence to prove what you said. We found none. It's only your word against the evidence."

My hackles were rising and quickly. "But I know what I saw. Besides, you and your guys weren't following protocol."

Riley put his hand on my forearm. He must have sensed my rising anger.

"Everyone at the retreat is accounted for," the detective said, still unaffected and bored.

"Unless someone is lying."

"Too bad you don't have that other note. Why were you keeping it yourself instead of turning it in to the police? Why didn't you bring it to me immediately?" Something glimmered in the man's eyes. Was he trying to get me riled up?

"I was going to but, as I said earlier, I had no means of getting in touch with the police while on the island. I was hoping to dry it out and then drop it by. But someone stole it, just like he stole my pearl necklace right out of my drawer."

"Let's talk about that again. Why would someone steal

it?"

I shrugged, biting back my sharp retorts. "Maybe there was a clue there. Maybe someone knew it made him look guilty."

"Maybe. But what I'm hearing is that you tampered with evidence." He raised his eyebrows, challenging me.

I let out a verbal grunt of frustration. My anger had risen and was about to spill over. It was never a pretty sight. I drew in a deep breath. "I wanted to dry it out. I wanted to tamper with it, but I didn't."

"This is all very interesting, Ms. St. Claire. But I don't think it means anything."

I leaned toward him, my voice tight—almost as tight as my muscles, which were wound up and ready to spring. "You're wrong, Detective. Something is going on, and I implore you to keep investigating."

He let out another sigh. "Ms. St. Claire, you really should leave these investigations to the professionals. You're looking for something that's not there. Remember, those who can't, teach."

My emotions finally exploded. "You're not seeing something that's staring right at you." I stared him down, not even trying to hide the challenge in my gaze. "Did you even know that Ginger's last name isn't Wagnor?"

"As a matter of fact, Jim told us all about it."

"You can't see how compelling that tidbit is?"

"This meeting is over." The detective stood and pointed toward the door.

I locked my jaw in place. So much for this shirt gaining me more respect. No, the detective thought I was a joke.

"Let's go, Gabby." Riley put his hand on my elbow and kept it there until we reached the van.

I was fuming inside. I wanted to scream. I wanted to shake the detective.

But I could do none of those things.

I remained quiet as I got into the van. As I pulled on my seatbelt. As I cranked the engine.

"Listen, there's a seafood restaurant a few miles from here," Riley said. "What do you say we grab a bite to eat?"

I nodded, not in the mood to argue anymore. "Sure, that sounds good. Then we can head back."

"I never realized you faced that kind of adversity, Gabby," Riley said quietly.

"It doesn't matter what I do or accomplish, I just feel like I'm always an outsider." I raised my hand before he felt sorry for me. "I mean, I get it. You can't have just anyone come in and tell you how to run an investigation. But I just feel so invisible."

"You have this new job. Maybe that tide is turning."

"Maybe."

But deep inside, I didn't know if that was the case at all. Especially as I remembered the detective's words: Those who can't, teach.

Before I could dwell on that any longer, I reached toward the center console to look at my list of suspects again. That's when I realized it was gone.

I exchanged a glance with Riley. Neither of us had taken it.

So who had?

CHAPTER 26

At the restaurant, Riley and I were able to grab seats outside on a deck overlooking the barrier islands that protected the peninsula from the Atlantic Ocean.

The seafood restaurant was located beside a wharf, and the scent of salty air saturated the area. In the distance, I could see the boats coming in and going out. People bragged about their catches of the day on the docks. Tourists loaded up a charter boat full of fishing rods and coolers. Marsh grass stretched into the water almost as far as the eye could see, and a channel marker with a large osprey nest on top sat within viewing distance.

Riley and I had already exhausted the possibilities of what had happened to that list. We had no other conclusions except that someone had taken it. Maybe my earlier intuition that we were being followed was correct. I recreated it and stuck it into my purse for safekeeping.

I played with one of the hushpuppies that had been set on our table by a tired-looking waitress. Finally, I gave up on eating and took a sip of water from the sweaty glass in front of me.

I could feel Riley watching me, and I hated the fact that I looked weak in front of him. I was supposed to look like everything was great and that I had my life under control. Wasn't that what everyone wanted when they were around their exes? The last thing they wanted was to show that life was hard or full of struggle.

"Have you ever heard that old hymn 'Trust and Obey'?" Riley leaned toward me with his elbow perched casually on the table.

I looked at him and blinked. This wasn't where I expected our conversation to go. "Of course. It's one of the classics."

He leaned closer. "I really think that song fits you, Gabby."

I nearly snorted, but then I realized he was serious. "Why would you say that?"

"No matter what happens, you push forward. No matter what kind of adversity you run into, you overcome it. You don't let anything get you down."

His words surprised me. But some kind of internal instinct rose in me, and I couldn't bring myself to be authentic in the moment. "Maybe my theme song should be 'Dust and Obey.' That more accurately sums up my life."

It was a lame joke, but humor and sarcasm had always been one of my defense mechanisms.

"What you're doing is important, whether it's crime-scene clean up or training forensic technicians or doing P.I. work on the side."

He was getting to me, and that fact made me uncomfortable. I had to get a grip here. I needed to just thank him and wiggle my way out of this conversation as quickly as possible. "I appreciate your encouragement, Riley. Maybe one day I'll actually arrive at some of my goals."

"I'm learning that you never really arrive. It seems like our goals are constantly changing. Once we get to where we thought we wanted to be, our perspective changes and we have to start again."

"Are you speaking from experience?"

He nodded. "Maybe. I mean, my life isn't what I thought it would be. I just have to make the best of it."

I wanted to ask him about us. About what he'd been thinking. About how he could have shut me out the way he did.

But I didn't.

Our conversation was halfway pleasant, so why ruin it by bringing up painful subjects? Or maybe I was afraid to face the truth. Maybe I was afraid to hear him say that he didn't care about me.

"You've been through a lot," I finally said.

"I had some really dark days." He let out a soft sigh and stared into the distance. The setting sun hit his face and baked it in an orange glow that was really quite lovely and atmospheric. However, the conversation was anything but glowing. No, it was gut-wrenching.

"Dark how?"

"Being stripped of most of my independence? It was hard. People treated me like a kid. They acted like I was incompetent. And it was difficult not knowing what the future held. I'd like to think I'd be okay whatever the outcome. But there was a part of me that didn't know how I would go on if I was unable to work or live independently. I did a lot of soul-searching."

I swallowed hard. My heart warmed as he opened up to me. I needed to hear about his life, I realized, whether I wanted to know all the details or not.

"That sounds difficult."

"Leaving Norfolk. Realizing the law firm I had poured my heart and soul into starting would probably never be resurrected again. You just never know what kind of curveballs you're going to get in life. But I do realize that I'm stronger for it all."

"You do seem different somehow. I haven't been able to put my finger on exactly how. But there's something."

He shrugged. "I am different. It would be crazy to think that I wasn't. I mean, at my core I suppose I'm the same. But my perspective has definitely changed."

"I see."

He cleared his throat. "You're probably wondering why I didn't hear anything on the night Ginger was pushed off the cliff. To tell you the truth, I've been taking sleeping pills."

"Sleeping pills?" I asked the question quietly. It wasn't really my business, but I needed to know.

He pressed his lips together a moment. "The nightmares are too much for me sometimes."

"I can imagine."

"I've worked to control and manage a lot of things. Nightmares are one thing I don't have much control over. My therapist says it's just my mind's way of dealing with everything."

"Most people would say it's pretty remarkable how far you've come. I bet your nightmares will fade with time."

"I think so too. In the meantime, it's good to be reminded of how far I've come." He stared at me a moment, his gaze intense. "How about you, Gabby?"

I had a feeling he would turn this talk into one about us. I couldn't let that happen.

Thankfully, just then, the waitress brought our food— flounder for me and crab cakes for Riley. As the savory aromas wafted upward, I thought maybe I could eat something.

And this would be the perfect time to talk more about the case. To talk about anything but us.

CHAPTER 27

"So, Jill Wagnor is off my suspect list now," I told Riley as we drove back to the marriage retreat on Friday.

I'd had a training session in Maryland on Thursday, so I'd swung past the Wagnor home. To my surprise, Jill had been home and seemed more than willing to talk. She'd informed me that she knew her husband wasn't faithful, but neither was she. They had an open relationship. Then she gave me the number of the man she'd been with the weekend Ginger had been pushed from the cliff.

I felt pretty confident she was innocent.

"Good detective work," Riley said.

Riley seemed to finally understand my perspective. That was something that had never happened before. Last year at this time, he always discouraged me about handling things on my own. Finally, he was seeing my point of view.

"While I was up that way, I also stopped by the newspaper office and asked to speak with Rae Gray," I continued.

"Smart thinking. And?"

"She wasn't in the office, and they're not sure when she'll be back. I left a message with the receptionist for her."

"I did some of my own research," Riley said.

"Did you?" He'd never sounded more appealing. For real.

"I did. You'll never believe what I found out. Ginger is a . . . um, for lack of a better word, a professional."

"A professional what? Home wrecker?" Wasn't I clever? I wanted to chuckle at my brilliance.

"Escort."

"What?" I nearly screeched. My snarky comment had been a little too close to the truth. "Now this really isn't making sense. Why would Jim bring a prostitute with him to the retreat center?"

"That's an excellent question. We might have to ask him that ourselves at some point. When we're willing to risk our cover."

This was going to take a while to process. "How in the world did you discover that?"

"I was talking to one of my father's friends who's made a fortune in real estate. I happened to mention Jim Wagnor. This man, my father's friend, has always had rather loose lips, so he willingly offered up the information that Jim was known for his, shall we say, liaisons."

"Tell me again what he told you." I just couldn't comprehend that information.

"Rumor has it that Jim Wagnor likes to pay for his companions. When I heard that, I started doing some research online. I found Ginger's picture on a popular website for escorts in the DC area. She goes by the name of Star Matthews."

"You can't make these things up, can you?" I shook my head. "What do we do with that information?"

"Maybe confront Jim? We just have to be careful because we don't want to blow our covers."

"Let's think about it, and between the two of us maybe we'll come up with something."

I picked up Dr. Turner's book, which was nestled

between our seats. The man had called Riley last night to make sure we planned on coming back. Apparently, the other couples were also feeling skittish about returning after the two tragedies that had occurred there. He assured us our safety was of the utmost importance and he was stepping up security on the island.

"You been reading this?" I asked.

Riley shrugged. "I've skimmed it. I thought I should at least do that in case it comes up during one of the sessions, you know?"

"Is it any good?"

"A lot of it is generic marriage advice. There are some good reminders, but nothing life-changing, I'd say. He emphasizes the importance of being committed and faithful and weathering the storms of life together."

"Sounds good enough."

"Yeah, I think Dr. Turner is a decent therapist. Why he leased this property and set up the therapy the way he did perplexes me. If these incidents continue, certainly he's going to have to shut down."

I stopped on one page and read some endorsements. *Dr. Turner revitalized our marriage—Sheila W. from Delaware. He raised a dead marriage back to life—Mark from Virginia. He changed my life—Tina from Pennsylvania.* "It looks like a lot of couples have been helped."

"There are some great testimonials in there. That's for sure. You can borrow it, if you'd like."

"I would like to take a look at it."

He put his hand across the back of the seat. It was a matter of convenience, I told myself. Not affection. So why were happy tingles dancing all over my skin?

"Are you ready for this weekend?" he asked.

"I'm not sure if we'll find any answers, especially if Jim isn't there. But I want to keep my eyes wide open. Because you never know what you might discover."

CHAPTER 28

After Riley and I each got settled on the island for the evening, I found Riley down in the lounge area. I nodded, trying to get him to come closer to me and away from the crowd.

"What it is it?" he asked.

My skin came alive at his nearness—which was the last thing I wanted. I forced myself to remain where I was and not to take a step back. But my throat ached as I replied. "I need you to be my wing man."

"You're going to hit on someone here?"

"What?" I questioned. "No, I just wanted to use a bird reference."

He smiled. "Should have known. What do you need?"

"I'm going to sneak into Steve's room while he's cooking dinner."

"What? Why would you do that?"

"Because as I was unpacking my things I started thinking about my mom's necklace again. I want it back, and he's my best suspect here."

"How would he get into your room?"

"He works here. I'm sure he could get his hands on the master key." I smiled sweetly as Blaine walked past. As soon as she was several feet away, I dropped the smile and turned back to Riley. "I want to do this. You don't have to help if you don't want to."

Riley stared at me a moment, his blue eyes intense. "I've got your back."

His words made my heart flutter. He was with me. We were in this together. That was a good feeling. A really good feeling.

We casually crept back upstairs. "How do you know where his room is?" Riley whispered.

"I saw him go in and out last week. I can only assume it was his room."

"What if it's locked?"

I pulled out a few tools. "Then I'll pick it."

"When did you learn to do that?"

"I've got skills. Didn't you know that?"

"You never cease to amaze me, Gabby."

I wondered what he'd think if he knew about my gun. I wouldn't mention that now. I'd brought it with me this weekend, and I'd tucked it between my mattress and box spring. There was too much weird stuff going on here. I had to take every precaution possible.

We paused outside Steve's door. Riley leaned against the wall to block anyone coming down the hallway. I turned the handle. Of course, it was locked. It would have been too easy otherwise.

Quickly, I pulled out my lock-picking kit. It was a hobby I'd picked up at my training with Grayson Technologies. One of the other trainees had done it in a past life, as he'd said, and he'd taught me in the evenings after official training was over. The skill would prove to be quite useful, it seemed.

It only took me a few tries before the lock mechanisms clicked. The lock released, and I opened the door.

Riley grabbed my arm before I slipped inside. "What do I do if someone comes?"

"Tie your shoe."

"And if it's Steve?"

"Feign a stomachache." Yeah, I'd come up with that off the top of my head. Maybe it wasn't the best idea. I mostly hoped Steve wouldn't come this way.

Moving quickly, I stepped into the room. After a moment of hesitation, I flipped on the light. A room that looked much like mine came into view.

I glanced around. Where did I even start?

If I were a thief, I supposed I'd stash my loot in the dresser. I pulled the first drawer open. Socks and underwear stared back.

I continued moving down the drawers, finding an assortment of clothes and toiletries, but no pearl necklace or letter from Anna.

Where else could he have put it?

There was a gold box on a bookshelf. Out of curiosity, I opened it. Inside there were . . . pictures?

I studied the photos a moment. They were all taken here on the island. Everyone attending the retreat center was featured in candid shots. Some were on the beach. Others were of us eating. There were even some of Brad and Anna.

Strange. Why would he take these? Why would he hide them? Did he go back to the mainland during the week to have these printed?

I glanced around the room. I certainly didn't see any computers or printers.

This was weird. Too weird.

Just then I heard a sound outside the door. Voices drifted from the area. Riley. Talking. Tying his shoe maybe?

I quickly flipped off the light and ducked into the closet. I held my breath and waited. Excuses for me being here rushed through my head. None of them sounded legitimate, except maybe that I'd been sleepwalking. But it was the middle of the day, so that didn't sound quite believable either.

My throat tightened as I waited. And waited. He was having a full-fledged conversation out there.

Finally, the voices faded.

I counted to ten before creeping from the closet and cracking the door open. Riley stood there alone.

"Coast clear?"

He nodded. "Just barely. Dr. Turner just happened to come past, but I followed your advice. I pulled out my cell phone and pretended to be looking for a signal."

"Better than my bathroom idea," I conceded as I stepped out.

I told him what I'd discovered. It appeared everyone on this island had some kind of secret. Whose secret included murder?

***

No one looked at ease when we gathered for dinner. Everyone seemed shifty, from the way they fidgeted to how their eyes darted around. Apparently, Dr. Turner had called each couple and convinced them to come back this weekend. Everyone was nervous, I realized, and I could understand why.

As we all sat down for some roast beef and mashed potatoes, Dr. Turner got our attention. He looked grim and not like his sunny, smiling self as he stood at the front of the room.

"Thank you all for coming this weekend. Rather than ignore everything that's happened here on the island, I wanted to take a moment and acknowledge the past." He rubbed his hands together as his gaze traveled to each person in the room.

"Let's be honest. We've seen some hard times here."

"That's an understatement," Angelina muttered under her breath.

"I want you all to know that hard times can make us stronger," Dr. Turner continued. "It can make our marriages stronger. That said, I thought you might want an update on things. Anna Thorn's death has been ruled a suicide. The police have closed the case, and Anna has been buried. May her soul rest in peace. Anna was very troubled, and she came here with a lot of problems. What happened was tragic."

"What about Ginger?" Farrah said. "What's the update on her?"

Dr. Turner nodded slowly and frowned. "Again, it's very unfortunate, but it appears she was taking a walk late at night. She was upset. And she walked off a cliff as a result. She remains in a coma. Our prayers are with her and Jim. This is why we ask residents not to venture outside at night. It's very dark here, and the terrain can be treacherous."

Interesting that he hadn't mentioned anything about foul play. Had the police not mentioned that I might have seen someone out there with her? Or was Dr. Turner just trying to make sure everyone remained calm? Was he more interested in his bottom line? I had no idea.

"What about the skeleton?" I asked, curious about that hand I'd seen reaching up from a sandy grave.

"Very interesting that you asked that." Dr. Turner smoothed his cardigan and seemed to relax slightly. "The body has been turned over to the state. The medical examiner believes the person found here on the island died more than one hundred years ago. Who knows what kind of history surrounds this person? She was a female. There's been some speculation that maybe she was associated with this lodge.

Maybe we'll never know."

"I know what happened," Angelina said.

Everyone's gaze swiveled toward her as we waited for her deduction. She seemed to love the limelight because she raised her chin, a new sparkle in her eyes. "This island is cursed. That's why all these bad things are happening here. That's the only explanation that makes any sense to me."

"Now, Angelina, we really don't believe in curses." Dr. Turner offered what appeared to be a tight smile.

"I heard what used to happen to the people who came here to vacation. They died also."

"Many of them drank too much and fell to their deaths. From what I understand, there was a mysterious poisoning incident as well. But what really closed this place down was the stock market crash. Everyone lost their money."

I shivered as I heard that story. Creepy.

Definitely creepy.

I didn't believe in curses either. But if I stayed here much longer, I might start.

CHAPTER 29

After dinner we all sat in the Therapy Lounge for the first evening session of the weekend.

"Tonight we're going to talk about the beginning stages of love," Dr. Turner started. "And to kick this off, I'd like for everyone to share the moment you first knew you were in love with your spouse."

My stomach dropped. How was I going to get out of this one? I immediately wanted to crawl out of my own skin and disappear, which, unfortunately, wasn't an option. Instead, I tried to focus on the other couples. Maybe, while watching their interactions, I'd have some insight into whether or not one of them was guilty of murder.

"I'll start," Angelina said. "I met Bo when he came over to repair the roof on my house. I thought he was the hottest hunk on the west side of town. I kept thinking of excuses for him to come back so I could see him more. I didn't think he'd ever get the hint."

Bo shrugged. "I thought she was pretty cute the first time I saw her. But she really won me over when she kept bringing me lemonade whenever I came over. That's when I asked her out. Besides, I knew she didn't have anything else on her house that needed fixing any more."

Telling that story seemed to draw the two of them closer because, for the first time since I'd seen them, they looked at each other like they were in love.

As Dr. Turner talked to them a moment, I saw Steve walking outside. He paused at the window and looked inside. His gaze met mine, and he scowled.

Did he know I'd discovered his pictures? I swallowed deeply at the thought.

"Farrah? Atticus?" Dr. Turner asked.

I turned back to the discussion, trying not to act suspicious. I stole one more glance outside. Steve continued walking toward the docks.

Steve had been Dr. Turner's patient at one time, I remembered. Was it strange that the therapist would hire his former client? I wasn't sure. But something about Steve made me uncomfortable.

"I took my daughter from my first marriage to see the doctor," Atticus was saying in the background. "She had pneumonia. I noticed the way Farrah treated her, and I thought she was the most beautiful woman I'd ever seen. As soon as my divorce was finalized, I stopped by her practice and pestered the lady at the front desk until Farrah came out. That was it."

"How about you, Farrah?"

She shrugged, her smile fading. "I'd always thought he was handsome—but married. That made him off limits. Then he showed up that day at my office, and he was so bold and confident. There was a whole waiting room full of people, but he didn't care. I was swept away."

My heart pounded out of control. Their stories were captivating and were obviously breaking down walls. I wanted to keep my walls erected and strong.

"Gabby and Riley?"

We glanced at each other. I drew in a deep breath, about to launch into some made-up story that I hadn't fully formed yet. But I was pretty sure I was going to base it on the Taylor Swift song "Love Story." Before I could start, Riley did.

"One of Gabby's friends had been accused of setting a building on fire. Long story short, I was able to tag along with her when she went over and sat with his grandkids. She played with them and really showed how much she cared. I knew at that moment there was something different about her. I could tell she was loyal and feisty, and I kept hoping I'd run into her again and find more excuses to spend time with her."

My heart warmed. It melted, in fact, into a gooey mess. His story was real. I could see it in his eyes. I had never asked him when he'd decided he wanted to marry me.

We'd broken up before that could happen.

But such fond memories filled me that I nearly forgot about all the bad stuff.

Nearly.

"Gabby?"

I nibbled on my bottom lip for a moment as everyone stared at me, waiting to hear my side.

"Riley's always been there right when I needed him. I was trapped in a garage once with a running car—long story—and I didn't have much hope of getting out. I would have died if Riley hadn't shown up. I knew after that moment he was a keeper."

He reached over and squeezed my hand.

I wanted to pull away. I felt like I'd been touched by fire. But I couldn't move. I sat there instead, feeling like I might drown in my own emotions.

"Very good," Dr. Turner said. "I think we've all gotten an excellent start to this weekend."

Maybe. But all I could think about was that my heart was treading dangerous waters.

CHAPTER 30

That night after everyone else was in bed, I decided to sneak up to the widow's walk. This time I brought Riley with me, mostly because he'd insisted. I really didn't want him here. Especially not since my emotions seemed to be spinning wildly out of control.

I couldn't admit it out loud yet, but I was still in love with Riley. I guess I always had been. And I had no idea what to do about it.

But he'd insisted on being nearby, especially after everything that had happened. And I couldn't blame him, nor did I want to end up as the next victim.

"What exactly are we looking for?" he whispered.

"I'm not sure. But I'm halfway expecting to see a raven driving me to the edge of madness while saying 'Nevermore.'"

"Poe reference? I like it."

"Well, I'm cultured like that. I'll be quoting Shakespeare next and humming Mozart."

We climbed the spiral staircase and, thankfully, found that the room up top was empty. I pulled my legs under me, trying to give Riley room to sit down also. He sat a little closer than I'd expected—close enough that I could feel his body heat and smell his cologne.

This could be romantic, I realized. Being up here, maybe with a cup of coffee and a warm blanket, having a heart-to-heart talk about the future and all the plans we'd like to make.

But not with Riley.

I had to stop myself.

"You think we'll see anything?" Riley glanced at me, the moonlight illuminating his eyes.

I just wanted to reach up and wipe a stray hair off his forehead. While I did that, I wanted my hand to linger at his cheek, to feel the scruff of his five o'clock shadow, to connect with him like I used to.

I looked away, coming back to the perfunctory conversation we were having. I had to downplay what my heart wanted to dramatize. My feelings had no place here.

"I can only hope we'll see something." I glanced around the space, trying to see if anything had changed. "There's one thing I don't see. The binoculars."

"This area appears to be getting a lot of use."

Silence fell. And this was real silence.

The silence at my apartment was filled with the sounds of cars honking and driving past, college kids partying, sirens going by, and even an occasional train. Out here, there was literally nothing to hear except the waves. And, right now, the windows blocked that sound.

I felt the strange need to fill the space with words.

"So, do you think anyone is on to us?" I glanced at Riley, my throat tightening again.

"Overall, no. The missing necklace and letter are the only things that give me pause. Even the kayak wasn't directed toward us, but at Jim and Ginger. I don't think anyone knows we're not really a married couple."

As he said the words, our gazes locked. I felt certain there was something he wanted to say, that something was being communicated between us without any words at all.

And was it just my imagination or were we leaning in closer to each other? Did I want that to happen? Did Riley?

My blood pumped with anticipation. But my brain was urging me to be cautious, reminding me of all my hurts, reciting my "Operation Protect My Heart" mantra.

Just then, something caught the corner of my eye. I quickly looked away, breaking the moment. There was a light in the distance.

I grabbed Riley's arm. "Look!"

Over the water I saw a boat puttering toward the shore. The watercraft stopped by the rocky shoreline and remained there. It was too dark to see if anyone was getting on or off.

I shook my head. "The question is: How does the boat tie in with what's been going on here?"

He nudged me. "Look, Gabby. The boat is leaving already. That was fast."

I stared out the window. Sure enough, the boat was pulling away from the island. Was it here just long enough to drop someone off? Because, otherwise, no one had time to do much damage. Just what was going on? I hated to say it, but I almost needed to be down there to truly find some answers.

Were these visits a nightly ritual? Would the ghost boat return again tomorrow night?

"Did you know why they call this Cemetery Island?" Riley asked.

"No idea." I also had no idea where he was going with this.

"I did some research at home this week. It's because there was no lighthouse on this island. Back in the old days—I'm talking the time of pirates—there were a lot of shipwrecks right off of these shores. That meant there were a lot of dead bodies that needed to be laid to rest."

"And this is where that happened?"

"That's the rumor."

"That doesn't really make me feel any better." I shivered.

"But it's interesting. There's a lot of history here in this area." He stared at me, something strange in his eyes.

Oh no. He didn't want to have a talk, did he? One of those talks where he told me he was sorry for hurting me and glad we were able to make things right between us so we could truly move on? He'd marry someone better suited to his upper-class attorney lifestyle. I'd move on and . . . well, maybe I'd even end up with Garrett. Who knew?

There were so many other things we could talk about. We could talk about the Therapy Lounge, about the emotions that had been stirred as we'd talked about first falling in love, about the painful reality that things would never be like they were.

But those discussions required a certain emotional investment I wasn't sure I wanted to make. It was better if I pretended that entire conversation hadn't happened earlier and simply moved on.

I had to concentrate on solving this mystery and finding some answers. Anything else, at this point, was futile.

"We should go," I blurted. "Before someone realizes we're gone."

He slowly nodded. "You're probably right."

I began climbing down the staircase. Just as I hit the last step, I heard someone behind me.

I twirled around, expecting the worst.

I twirled, expecting a killer.

CHAPTER 31

"Dr. Turner?" I asked. Had he overheard any of our conversation? I hoped not.

He regarded Riley and me, his gaze processing this discovery. "Is everything okay? You know the rules, correct?"

I nodded, probably a little too quickly. Before I could say anything, Riley's arm snaked around my waist, and he pulled me close.

"We should have told you before we came. Gabby has a problem with . . . sleepwalking," Riley said.

Sleepwalking? I resisted the urge to steal a glance at him.

"And you somehow heard her leave her room?" Dr. Turner asked, a knot between his eyes.

Mr. Rogers Takes a Late-Night Walk. He was only missing the striped flannel pajamas and a nightcap. Or did he wear a cardigan to bed?

"I admit the timing was uncanny," Riley said. "I heard someone in the hallway and peeked outside. It was a good thing I did."

I nodded. "I'm obviously awake now."

"And you didn't immediately go back to your rooms?" He sounded a bit like a crusty old schoolmarm.

"We were just talking, doctor," he said. "I know it's against the rules, but . . . I just miss having one-on-one time with my wife. And the widow's walk is so—"

"Romantic." I wrapped my arms around Riley's waist and fluttered my eyelashes.

Dr. Turner raised his eyebrows. "Well, I'm glad to see the two of you are reconnecting. That's the good news. The bad news is that we're all supposed to be quarantined in our rooms at night, not just because of our therapy-session guidelines, but because we don't want any more accidents. Two is enough. Two is too many, for that matter."

"Of course." I nodded, my cheeks heating.

"I trust the two of you will be going your separate ways? Not in life, but just for the evening."

I understood his implications and nodded. "We will."

"Very well, then. I'll see you in the morning."

When he disappeared, I turned to Riley and we exchanged a silent look.

"That was awkward," I whispered.

"But we covered it well—believably. He doesn't think we were snooping, just having a little romantic rendezvous."

"That's a crazy thought."

Riley stared at me. "Yeah, a crazy thought." His expression was impossible to read.

My throat tightened. I had to break this spell he had on me.

"Goodnight, Riley," I said.

"Goodnight, Gabby."

***

We all met outside the next morning after breakfast, dressed for something "sporty," as Dr. Turner had instructed. I could do sporty, though I chose to leave my snarky T-shirts at home in favor of something a little classier—a turquoise golf shirt my future stepmother had given me for Christmas. It normally wasn't my style, but it worked perfectly here with a parka over it.

Today was a little balmy. The sky was overcast, and the wind coming off the bay was strong.

"Anything new last night?" I whispered to Riley. We hadn't had a moment to talk during breakfast because we'd sat with Angelina and Bo, who, of course, had dominated the conversation.

The strange thing was that they weren't bickering like they had last weekend. In fact, they both had lovelorn looks in their eyes. Maybe this therapy was working for them.

"Just one thing. I decided to take some action last night. I pulled out Anna's scarf—the one we found in Atticus's things. When Atticus came into the room, I told him I'd found it on the floor."

"What did he say?" I whispered.

"He told me he found it in the hallway a couple of weeks ago. He knew it wasn't Farrah's, and Angelina and Ginger claimed it wasn't theirs either. He didn't know what else to do with it, so he stuck it in his dresser."

I frowned. "Do you think he was telling the truth?"

"He didn't act suspicious or guilty. And if he was trying to conceal something then, for such a smart man, he didn't hide the evidence very well."

"That's true."

"How about you? Anything new?"

I shook my head. "I was by myself. The other two ladies went to bed as soon as we got back last night.

Dr. Turner appeared ten minutes later wearing a floppy fisherman hat. *Mr. Rogers Goes Fishing*. "I have today's challenge for you. This will test you as a couple, but ultimately it can bring you closer together."

Great. Fishing?

"The couple who catches the most fish will earn a romantic dinner tonight. I hope that gives you some motivation. You get to choose your own fishing spot on the island, and, no, there are no instructions on how to do this. If you don't know how to fish yet, now is the time to learn."

Riley and I grabbed two poles and a tackle box, and we took a wooden set of stairs down to the pier. We sat there, our feet dangling over the edge in a way that made me think of a Norman Rockwell painting.

"You ever been fishing?" Riley asked.

"Only a few times with my dad. I never really got into it, though."

"I used to fish at the lake behind my house. It's kind of relaxing, actually."

Riley loaded some bait onto the hook and showed me how to cast the line. I tried myself, but my sinker landed only a few feet in front of me. "I think I'll stick to solving crimes," I mumbled.

"Don't give up. It's like this." He wrapped his arms around me from behind and grabbed the fishing rod.

My lungs froze at his nearness. It had been a long time. Well, at least since we were forced to cuddle last weekend, but that hardly counted. Warmth filled me at his closeness, and it made me crave even more.

Londonbeat's "I've Been Thinking About You" began playing in my head. My mental jukebox always knew just the right song to play, and it was hard to stop the music once it started.

He swung my rod back and launched the line into the

water. This time, it went out far enough that maybe I could catch something.

With that done, he released me. It seemed like he hesitated a moment, but I was probably just seeing what I wanted to see. I had no reason to believe he actually wanted to wrap his arms around me.

He grabbed his own line and cast it into the water. Then we both sat silently.

This would be the perfect time for him to bring up that talk he wanted to have—the one I'd desperately been trying to avoid. Movement at the top of the bluff caught my eye. It had almost been a slight glare, like the sun had caught something reflective. I glanced up, but I didn't see anyone. Had I been imagining things?

Leroy walked up at that moment.

"How's it going?" he asked, pausing beside us.

"No bites yet," Riley said.

He nodded slowly. "Give it time. You picked a good spot."

"You know a lot about fishing?" I asked.

He nodded. "I used to be a commercial fisherman."

"Really? But you gave it up to be a boat captain?"

"This old body just couldn't handle the workload anymore. I started chartering fishing boats, and that's where I met Dr. Turner. I heard he was looking for someone to help him, so I agreed. It's a great job for retirement."

I thought about the boat I'd seen at night. Captain Leroy would be the perfect person to ask about it. He seemed to know these waters better than anyone.

"Why would people go boating at night?" I asked, trying to sound casual. It didn't really work, though. I mean, the question was out of the blue.

"At night?" He grunted. "Night fishing can be popular. I suppose that's one reason. Or people who are partying. Unfortunately, drinking and boating don't go together, just like drinking and driving. Why do you ask?"

I shrugged. "Just wondering. I saw a boat out here one night when I couldn't sleep. I thought it was strange."

I'd probably said too much. As I looked in the distance, I saw a boat coming our way. I paused a moment. It almost looked like Blaine behind the wheel.

My eyes riveted on her. She was headed straight toward us, and she wasn't slowing down.

Then when I saw her expression. Fear.

Something was wrong.

CHAPTER 32

"Run!" Riley yelled.

We abandoned our fishing rods and began sprinting across the pier. Before we could reach the end, I felt the wood tremble at my feet.

Blaine had hit the dock!

I looked back just in time to see the boat was still coming, eating the pier board by board.

Only a few feet from us.

Riley grabbed my hand, and we dove onto the sand, pulling Leroy with us.

I held my breath, waiting to feel an impact. I anticipated feeling debris rain down on us. Expected the crash, the pain that would follow.

After a few seconds of nothing, I pulled my eyes open. I was still intact. So were Riley and Leroy, who sprawled in the sand beside me.

I jerked my gaze to the boat. It had stopped mere inches from us. Just a couple seconds difference and we could all be dead or seriously injured.

But I couldn't see Blaine through the rumpled pier and battered boat. Was she okay?

I scrambled to my feet, but Riley beat me to the boat. He boosted himself inside, threw some rubble into the water, and emerged with Blaine in his arms.

Leroy took her from Riley and laid her on the beach.

I crouched beside her, trying to determine how injured she was. She had blood on her forehead and blinked as if confused. But she was okay.

"Thank you," she whispered, her hand going to her cheek.

"What happened?" Leroy asked.

She shook her head. "I don't know what happened. I had to pick up a few supplies. One minute, I was heading back to the island. But the throttle got stuck. I couldn't slow down."

"We're just glad you're okay," I told her.

But I had to wonder whether the throttle getting stuck was an accident at all.

***

"And tonight's winners are . . . Riley and Gabby!" Dr. Turner announced. "Though they didn't officially catch any fish, no one did. And since they were able to rescue Blaine, it only seems fair that I declare them the winners."

I wasn't going to argue.

"Gabby, Riley, if you'll go get cleaned up, we have a meal planned for you outside on the deck attached to my private suite. Thank you all for your participation. I hope you all learned a little something about working together."

Back in my room, I put on a little black dress—*the* little black dress, for that matter. I only owned one. As I looked in the mirror, I smiled at what I saw. I'd straightened my unruly hair into smooth waves and donned some simple heels. It was a nice look. If I had my mom's pearls, it would be even better. I frowned at the thought.

I hadn't given up on finding them.

I glanced once more at my reflection. I'd worn this dress to a banquet with Riley once. I remembered the moment with fondness for a second. Swaying back and forth in his arms had been magical.

My smile disappeared. But those days were over. Why did I have to keep reminding myself of that? I wanted total and complete control of all my thoughts and emotions. Easier said than done, though. I might have an easier time getting Detective Hanson to respect me.

I flipped my light off and stepped out into the common room. I sucked in a breath at the darkness that greeted me before laughing at myself. I'd simply forgotten to turn the light on out there.

I was always reading too much into things.

I started to reach back into my room when a gloved hand covered my mouth. I fought back but another arm snaked around my midsection, locking my arms against my body.

I was powerless. I couldn't move. I couldn't even fight.

"You're not welcome here," a gravely voice whispered in my ear.

I struggled again, trying to escape from his grasp. I couldn't.

Did someone know who I was and what I was really doing here? Why else would this person confront me like this?

"I want you to leave and to mind your own business. Do you understand?"

I froze, not responding.

"I repeat: Do you understand?"

Finally, I nodded.

"Good girl," the man said.

The next instant, he shoved me back into my room and

slammed the door.

***

A few minutes later, I hurried downstairs and found Dr. Turner's room. I was still shaken.

I'd emerged from my room to find the man gone. I'd left the lights on, not daring to turn them off this time. But that didn't dispel my fear.

Someone knew who I was. Was I next on his list of people to knock off?

I'd have to dwell on that a little later. Right now, I had a dinner date with Riley.

Before I could knock at the door, it opened. Dr. Turner stood there. My throat squeezed for a second. Until he smiled. Mr. Rogers, I told myself. He's just Mr. Rogers, king of sweaters and loafers. There was nothing intimidating about the man.

"We've been waiting for you. Come on in."

I stepped into his room, instantly noting all the Bible verses on the walls. A huge display of the Ten Commandments took up an entire wall. I had no idea he was this religious.

Riley sat in the distance, out on a deck that overlooked the water. My heart sped at the sight of him. Some things would never change.

However, I had to be careful. This would be the perfect place for some sentimental talk about why he'd dumped me. I wasn't in the mood for that.

"Your food will be here shortly," Dr. Turner said. "Congratulations on winning today, and I hope you'll both take this time to really talk about the things that matter."

I nodded. "Of course."

As soon as he was gone, I turned to Riley and smiled. He

197

looked handsome. He'd put on a button-up shirt and rolled up the sleeves. I wasn't sure what it was about seeing a man's forearms that seemed so appealing and made my mouth go dry, but it was there and it was real.

"Riley . . . someone confronted me as I left my room," I started, venturing into safer territory.

"What?"

I told him what had happened.

He leaned toward me, his eyes wide and his voice soft with concern. "Are you okay?"

I nodded. "Yeah, I'm fine. Just shaken."

"There's no way anyone should have discovered who you are."

I shrugged. "Unless the police told someone. But why would they do that? My role in this investigation is the only reason I can fathom that the confrontation occurred."

Riley sighed and ran his hand through his hair. "I don't know. Maybe I shouldn't have pulled you into this."

My hand covered his. "I love being pulled into stuff like this."

As soon as I realized what I'd done, I pulled away quickly, feeling like I'd touched fire.

"If at any point you want to bail on me, just say the word and we're out of here."

I won't bail on you. I didn't say the words aloud, though.

"Gabby, maybe we should talk about the things that really matter." Riley lowered his voice, almost to an intimate level. "Just like Dr. Turner said."

I was reading too much into this, and I had to take the reins. I nodded. "Absolutely. Things that matter. Like Anna. Have you heard anything else about Anna?"

A wrinkle formed for just a second between his

eyebrows. He exhaled and nodded slowly. "As a matter of fact, yes. I did hear something."

My excitement spiked. "Please share."

"Apparently, as a part of the program on the weekend that Anna died, all the participants were instructed to write a letter. They had to write about all the ways they'd wronged their spouses."

"Ouch." That's a tough pill to swallow. Most people wanted to bury their mistakes, not acknowledge and take responsibility for them.

He took a sip of his water. "Yeah, that would be tough on more than one level. But, anyway, I started thinking about that letter Anna wrote that you found in the kayak."

"You think it wasn't the second part of a suicide note but that it was part of this therapy?"

He nodded. "It's a theory, at least."

I contemplated it a moment, picking at a crusty roll on my plate. "You could be onto something. I mean, it would make sense when I think back on everything she wrote. But, still, why the kayak?"

"I don't know."

A server came in with two plates of food at that moment. Oysters.

I'd never been a really big fan, and it must have shown on my face.

"Try them. They're good, and the bay is known for its oysters," the server said.

I nodded, not wanting to be rude. "Maybe I will. Are these from the Eastern Shore?"

"Of course. We serve local whenever possible."

As he left, I glanced out again at the water.

"I didn't realize that Dr. Turner was staying on the first

199

floor," I said, determined to avoid any uncomfortable conversations.

And to eat any oysters.

Riley gobbled one down and placed the shell back on the plate. "I heard he has bad knees so I guess that makes sense. Plus, this was the innkeeper's quarters so it's more spacious."

"This place must have been grand at one time."

"And now it's being restored. I love it when that happens." As he said the words, his knee brushed mine beneath the table and sent electricity through my veins.

There was something in his gaze that took my breath away. Again, though, I was reading too much into things. There was no hidden meaning in his words. He wasn't hinting at our past or future relationship. He was just making conversation.

That's what I had to remind myself for the rest of dinner.

Because there was no romance here. This was a business arrangement. When this investigation was over, both of us would resume our normal lives. Riley would get on with his life, and I would get on with mine. I simply had to accept that reality.

And that was all.

I stood, suddenly feeling like I needed a breather. I left the table on the deck and began wandering the bookshelves in Dr. Turner's room. He had a lot of great self-help books, along with some interesting articles that may have been left from the original lodge.

"What are you doing?" Riley appeared behind me. A little too close. But I wasn't complaining.

"Just being nosy, I suppose. Look at these pictures." I picked up one of some men and women grinning in front of the lodge. The black-and-white photo looked old. Could one of these women have ended up the skeleton that time had uncovered? I set the photo back down.

As I reached for an antique-looking *vauze*, I heard something click. I froze a moment.

What was that?

Riley heard it too. I could see it in his eyes as I looked up at him.

That's when I realized that the *vauze* wasn't budging. It was almost hinged on one side. How strange was that?

"Look at this, Gabby." Riley had moved toward the other end of the bookcase.

With a surge of excitement, I joined him, anxious to see what he'd discovered.

To my surprise, the bookcase had jutted out.

Was this a secret passage?

CHAPTER 33

The wall rotated out. Riley shoved it some more, and finally a room on the other side was revealed.

I glanced at Riley, our eyes sharing the same excitement. This place really did have a secret passage!

I was a little too excited for my own good. But all my Nancy Drew fantasies as a child had involved something like this.

"I'll go first," Riley said. He slid between the wall and the bookcase. I followed behind him. We stepped inside another suite.

This was one more along the lines of Dr. Turner's digs: large and fancy. How interesting.

"Whose room is this?" Riley asked.

"As far as I know, Dr. Turner is the only person staying down here." I stepped farther inside the room. "It doesn't look like anyone is using this room."

"This lodge is quite charming. A murky history, dead bodies, secret passages. What more could you want?"

"My thoughts exactly."

"I was being funny," he added.

"Sure you were." I ran my hand across a bookcase before pulling open the closet door. It was empty, just as I'd suspected.

"We probably don't have much time, Gabby." Riley

stuck his head back into Dr. Turner's room. "Who knows when someone will come to get us for whatever evening activity has been planned."

"I just want to look a few more places." I went to the dresser and pulled the first drawer open. I blinked at what I saw there.

My mother's pearls, the letter from Anna, and Steve's kitchen knives.

***

"Yesterday, we talked about the moment you first fell in love," Dr. Turner started. "Today, we're going in the opposite direction. I had you all write letters a couple of weeks ago. Tonight we're going to talk about what you wrote. I want you all to share how your spouse has hurt you and what that's done to your life."

Oh great. Another uncomfortable conversation. And in front of an audience.

As usual, the mood had been set. There were electric candles, soft classical music, and that ever-present scent of lemon furniture polish. The moon glinted softly outside through the windows.

I tried to avoid thinking about it. Instead, I thought about my mom's pearls, which were now safely tucked into my pocket, along with Anna's letter. It had dried wet, so I doubted it could be salvaged at this point. But still—I had the letter, and I would give it to the police.

Who would have left those things in that room? Why?

It just didn't make sense.

Riley and I had managed to get back into Dr. Turner's suite in the nick of time. We'd clicked the wall back in place and assumed a relaxed position just as the server came with dessert: chocolate cake with mascarpone cream.

My thoughts volleyed from there to a plan that was developing in my mind. A plan for how to catch a killer.

And it would take place tonight.

Really, one of the only solid pieces of evidence I had and a surefire way of finding answers was catching someone in the act. I'd seen a boat near the island several times at night after everyone was in bed.

If I wanted to either confirm or disregard my suspicions, then I needed to be more proactive.

As the plan simmered in my mind, I came back to the present. I glanced around the room, trying to figure out what I'd missed as I'd been plotting.

Farrah was already crying before she even spoke. She shared with the group about when she first realized Atticus loved his job more than her. Atticus shared that it came when Farrah no longer tried to understand him and his hard work to give her whatever she wanted.

Angelina talked about Bo buying a sports car when they could barely make their mortgage. Bo talked about how Angelina always put him down in public.

Then all eyes were on Riley and me. I'd already formulated my story. I would talk about Riley and I drifting away. How we'd changed since we got married and how it was never more apparent than while at a friend's birthday party. It was far from the truth, which was what I needed.

"You go first," Riley said.

I opened my mouth, about to dive into the fake birthday-party story. Instead, the words, "You hurt me" escaped.

"What?" Riley squinted, almost as if he'd been slapped.

Tears filled my eyes. "You hurt me. I gave you my heart. I trusted you, and you trampled over me without regard."

The words seemed to shock me just as much as they shocked everyone else. All my buried emotions started to bubble to the surface. It had been bound to happen sometime.

"Gabby . . ." His eyes were soft, compassionate.

That look always dispelled my anger. But I'd already put my true feelings out there. I couldn't snatch them back now, nor could I leave them without explanation. Unfortunately, we had an audience for this conversation. And instead of using a cover story, I was telling the truth.

"Nothing you say can change what happened," I continued.

"I was broken, Gabby." He grabbed my hand. "I hardly wanted to live with myself. I know you don't believe me when I say that I left because I loved you, but, at that time, that's exactly what I was thinking. In retrospect, I can see where it was a dumb idea."

"You actually left her?" Angelina gasped. "I knew we had problems, but Bo never left me when the going got tough."

"It wasn't like that," Riley started, exasperation staining his voice.

"Then what was it like?" Dr. Turner crossed his legs and gave us his full, undivided attention.

All eyes in the room riveted on Riley. I almost felt sorry for him, but I was powerless to correct this now.

Riley sighed, long and heavy. "I had a brain injury, and my recovery became my life. The more my pain and frustration grew, the more my vision became cloudy until I couldn't see clearly anymore. I ended up moving back home with my parents."

Angelina snickered, at least having the respect to cover

her mouth. "You moved in with your mommy?"

Riley cut her a sharp look and frowned. "It's complicated. Honestly, I didn't want Gabby to turn her whole life upside down in order to take care of me."

"She's your wife, though," Farrah said. It was the most passion I'd seen in her eyes since we'd started this marriage retreat. Unfortunately, it was directed at Riley and me instead of her husband. "That's what spouses do."

"I also didn't want her to see me in that state." He grimaced as he said that last part. His hand brushed over his face, and the agony inside him was obvious.

"Did you think she'd see you as less of a man?" Dr. Turner asked.

I squeezed my eyes shut, suddenly realizing what a bad idea it was to have this conversation. It wasn't meant to be had in a group like this, especially not since everyone had jumped in to contribute their opinions.

"Being in the place I was in was humiliating. I learned a lot in the process. There are things I would have changed if I could now. But hindsight is always twenty-twenty, right?" Riley's voice had lost a lot of its liveliness. In fact, this conversation looked downright painful for him.

I wanted desperately to reach over and touch his back. To smooth his tight muscles. To tell him everything would be okay.

I could do none of those things, though.

I had to keep my distance. Keep things superficial. Take my emotions out of this equation.

"Gabby, how did this make you feel?" Dr. Turner turned toward me.

I rubbed my neck, wishing my muscles didn't feel achy. But it was the same way I'd felt when I'd learned my mom had cancer. I was grieving in my own way for all the things I'd lost.

"It made me feel like I wasn't enough." My voice sounded raspy, clear evidence of the turmoil I felt inside. "I felt like I wasn't good enough. I felt rejected—again. All the men in my life have let me down, and I added Riley to that list."

Maybe I'd been too honest. Maybe I should have tamped down what I'd said. Most likely, I shouldn't have said it at all. But again, for some reason, the truth insisted on pouring from my lips.

Riley's gaze was so intense on mine that I wanted to cry. But I somehow managed to hold myself together.

"Riley, what do you have to say to that?" Dr. Turner said.

You could have heard a pin drop in the room. It was that quiet. Everyone watched us like we were on an episode of VH1's *Couple's Therapy*. This was one time I didn't want to be the center of attention, though.

Riley swallowed hard, his Adam's apple bobbing up then down again. "I never wanted to hurt you. I only wanted what was best for you. Sometimes I don't feel like I'll ever be able to make things right."

"Gabby?" Dr. Turner said, his voice solemn.

That did it. A tear escaped and drizzled down my face. "I don't know either."

"And here I thought the two of you were the only normal ones here." Angelina snorted, pulling us out of the moment. "I guess we all have our problems, don't we?"

"Yes, we do," Dr. Turner said. "We're all human, and that makes us imperfect. I think we've covered enough here tonight. Why don't you all have some time to yourselves before we call lights out?"

Riley and I having time to ourselves was the last thing I

needed. I didn't think I could handle talking about this anymore. And this look in his eyes just made it all more confusing. It made me want to turn to mush and fall into his arms. Either that or slap him. Neither option was appealing.

"Dr. Turner?"

We all stopped and turned toward Steve.

"Yes, Steve?"

"Has anyone seen Blaine?"

We glanced at each other and shook our heads.

"No, not since dinner," Dr. Turner said. "What's wrong?"

"She wanted the staff to meet with her about some improvements she'd like to see. However, she didn't show up. I've got stuff to do."

I immediately tensed. Oh no. Not Blaine. What had happened now?

CHAPTER 34

I gripped my flashlight as I walked outside along the oyster-shell pathway. The night had grown quite brisk, and I shivered as I gulped in a deep breath of frosty air. We'd split into teams to look for Blaine, and somehow Riley and I had convinced Dr. Turner to let us search outside. He'd urged caution but agreed.

My gut churned with anxiety. Where could Blaine be? No one would be able to deny something odd was going on if three things happened at this retreat center.

The silence between Riley and me was downright uncomfortable. I wanted to do whatever it took to avoid it.

"Gabby—" he started.

"This is probably the worst time ever to talk about what happened back there," I rushed before he could go any further. "I guess I played my role a little too well."

That's right. Pretend this is all part of our cover.

I knew he'd never believe it.

"That's because you were telling the truth," he said quietly.

I focused on the path ahead. "It doesn't matter, Riley. That's all water under the bridge, as the saying goes." Before I could talk about it any more, I pointed to a maintenance shed in the distance. "There's a wheelbarrow against the door. I don't remember seeing it there before."

He frowned, hesitated a moment. "Let's check it out.

But I'd really like to finish this conversation later."

I decided not to confirm or deny his request. With any luck, he'd forget about it or we wouldn't have the opportunity to talk about things. Except luck was rarely on my side.

Right now, I was going to concentrate on Blaine.

We reached the shed and pulled the wheelbarrow from in front of the entrance. When we pulled the door open and shined our flashlights inside, I spotted someone curled in the corner.

It was Blaine.

I crouched beside her. "Are you okay?"

She nodded, obviously frazzled. "I came out here to get a hammer and nails. I've been waiting for someone to fix a rickety table in the Therapy Lounge, but I decided to just do it myself. When I stepped inside, someone pushed me and slammed the door. I gave up yelling for help about fifteen minutes ago."

"Let's get you inside," Riley said. "Can you walk?"

She nodded. "Yeah, I can walk. Thank you."

Despite what she said, Riley and I walked on either side of her until we entered the hall and lowered her onto a bench in the entryway. After I yelled for help, I studied Blaine a moment.

There were cut marks on her arm. How had that happened? Had someone hurt her?

Blaine followed my gaze down to her cuts. She pulled her arms closer, as if trying to disguise her injuries. "It's nothing. I was just trying to get out. I thought I could prop myself up and get to a high window. I cut myself on the cinder blocks on the way down."

"Are you okay?" Farrah asked. "Maybe I can put something on those cuts."

Blaine shook her head, suddenly not looking so

composed. "No, I'm fine. Thank you. I think I'll just go take a shower and get ready for bed. If you'll excuse me."

Though she'd insisted she wanted to be alone, I followed her anyway. She stopped outside her door and turned to me. "I know you're worried, but I'm okay."

"But first the boat crashed and then this . . ."

She licked her lips. "I've thought of that also. You think I'm going to be the next person to get hurt?"

"That appears to be the case. You can't deny that something suspicious is going on here."

"As far as the boat, it was my fault. I didn't know what I was doing. I'm not sure what happened tonight, though. Maybe there's someone here that resents my position with Dr. Turner."

"What do you mean?"

She shrugged. "The doctor pays well. I'm his right-hand woman. There are plenty of other people who'd like to do my job."

"Like Steve?"

She shrugged again. "I'm not naming names. Now, if you'll excuse me. I really would like a shower."

Just as she stepped into her room, I called her again. She paused.

"Blaine, I saw you in Onancock a couple of weeks ago. Do you go there often?"

She swallowed hard. "As a matter of fact, I do. My sister has a gift shop there."

I nodded. Her explanation made sense.

But nothing else on this island did.

CHAPTER 35

Riley and I stepped outside later that night while everyone else slept. A blustery wind swept against the building, sending sand in our faces.

"Feels like a storm's brewing," Riley said, looking toward the horizon.

Just as he said the words, lightning flashed in the distance.

"You got that right."

"Where should we go to keep a lookout? You have any ideas?

"I want to go down by that rocky shoreline. The boat that keeps coming and going could provide some answers. There's only one way to find out exactly what's going on."

"And if we come face-to-face with a killer?"

I swallowed hard. I hadn't thought of that. We had no cell phone service so we couldn't call for help. No one would hear me if I screamed.

"Then we get tough," I said. "And I have my gun."

"You have a gun?"

I shrugged. "You're not the only one who was affected by Scum."

Scum was the name of the serial killer who'd nearly ended Riley's life. He'd nearly ended mine as well. The memories were still painful, and they hit me at the oddest times, inducing nightmares that didn't allow me to sleep.

But not many people knew that. No one could understand.

No one but Riley, and we hadn't really talked about it. In fact, instead of allowing the incident to draw us closer, it had pushed us further apart.

"I know it was hard on you also, Gabby," Riley said. "I'm sorry I wasn't there for you."

Well, at least he'd put that out there. His plea for forgiveness left me speechless. I wanted to say, "It's okay," but it wasn't okay. Nothing was okay, and that was becoming more and more obvious the more time we spent together.

"Well, life happens, right?" It was the best I could come up with.

"Don't try to brush it off." He grabbed my arm and planted himself firmly in front of me until I looked at him.

My hair, once smooth, now whipped around me in the wind. Lightning cracked the sky, illuminating his face. The sight took my breath away. There was a new intensity to his gaze.

I could have been imagining things, but he seemed to be leaning closer to me. I could feel the pull between us. The tension—it could push us away or draw us together in a heartbeat.

Which direction would this moment go?

"Gabby," he whispered. His hand brushed my jaw.

I couldn't let this happen. I couldn't go down this rabbit hole again. Even if everything in me cried out to get closer, to reminisce old times, to feel connected again.

At that moment, a light in the distance caught the corner of my eye.

"Get down!" I pulled him toward the ground before we were spotted.

We tumbled into the prickly grass beneath us.

"There's the boat." I pointed. "We've got to get to the stairs and go down to the beach," I whispered. "It's the only way we'll figure this out."

"I agree. Let's go."

Staying low, we made it to the steps. We crept down them until our feet hit the sand at the bottom. We ducked behind one of the large rocks that formed a natural bulkhead and waited as the boat came closer.

I could hear two men talking. I tried to make out what they were saying, but it was nearly impossible with the wind and the approaching storm. Thunder rumbled overhead.

Any minute now, the sky was going to burst.

"Can you understand them?" I asked.

"All I heard was 'Be quiet.'"

Another odd sound filled the air. It was almost a scraping, a shuffling, but it was filled with occasional loud clinks and plops. It sounded like someone was dropping something into the water and then pulling it back up a few minutes later.

I couldn't put together what was happening. It just didn't make sense.

At that moment, I spotted someone else coming down the stairway. The footsteps were loud and heavy, but I couldn't make out whom they belonged to.

I nudged Riley and nodded toward the figure. We slipped deeper into the shadows. Concealing ourselves could be the difference between life and death right now. I wasn't sure what exactly we were in the middle of.

As lightning lit the sky again, I recognized the figure rambling across the sand.

Captain Leroy.

Was he involved in all this?

I heard a yell and another loud plop. From my position behind the rocks, it appeared that a man jumped out of the boat and waded through the water toward Captain Leroy.

Was this it? The big moment when we'd finally get some answers?

As I waited to see what would play out, suddenly lights illuminated the area. Over a bullhorn, a deep voice rang out. "This is the Virginia Marine Police. Everyone, put your hands up."

CHAPTER 36

I watched as Leroy and the man he was meeting raised their hands in the air.

Two other boats pulled up, and police officers appeared on the shoreline, surrounding the men.

The man in the water—the one from the boat—didn't even ask why they were there. He just looked resigned and maybe angry, with his hunched shoulders and flared nostrils.

Had the marine police been investigating him for the death of Anna and the attempted death of Ginger? I couldn't remember exactly, but I thought they primarily checked fishing licenses and boating permits.

"You're under arrest for the illegal poaching of oysters from the Chesapeake," the officer said through the bullhorn.

Again, there was no argument from anyone.

That must mean they were guilty.

Illegal poaching of oysters? What? I didn't even realize that was a crime, nor that a person could be arrested for doing so.

The men talked while the police examined the boat. I supposed that was the sounds we'd heard. They'd been harvesting oysters.

Who would have thought?

I tried to stay still, but legs were beginning to ache from crouching low. The rocks were uncomfortable and hard beneath

CHRISTY BARRITT

me—huge boulders filled with smaller stones and pebbles. Sharp crags dug into my skin.

"Someone else is coming," Riley whispered, crouching lower beside me.

I glanced at the steps leading to the beach and saw Dr. Turner descend. He wore his infamous cardigan and loafers. His hair, normally neat and in place, flew like a kite in the wind. *Mr. Rogers Guest Stars on* Cops.

"What's going on down here?" he asked. "Leroy? Are you involved in this?"

Leroy didn't say anything. He just looked the other way.

At that moment, I tried to readjust my position before I fell over. But my plan backfired. I lost my balance and fell backward. My hand hit a rock, which sent several stones cascading downward. It wasn't my best moment.

"Is there someone back there?" a voice called out.

I froze when I realized the light was pointed at me.

With a frown, I rose to my feet, my hands in the air. Riley followed suit.

"Gabby? Riley?" Dr. Turner asked. Disappointment saturated his voice.

We stepped out, trying not to make things worse.

"What are you doing out here?" he continued. Then realization dawned across his features. "Sleepwalking."

"She appears lucid now," an officer said.

"We were kind of stuck down here once all this happened," Riley said. "We were scared, so we hid."

"You two certainly have a knack for being in the wrong place at the wrong time," Dr. Turner said. "Why do I have a feeling there's more to this story?"

I started to object when Riley cut in. "We do. It's Gabby, actually. She's a little on the nosy side."

"I can see how this would affect your marriage, but we'll have to save that for another conversation," Dr. Turner said.

I waited for Riley to deny it, but he didn't. Not that we were really married. But, really?

I didn't have time to think about it at the moment. One angry-looking marine officer was waiting to hear our explanation as well.

***

Dr. Turner had asked to meet with Riley and me the next morning. This was after a short church service in the "chapel" at the lodge. We hadn't had one last week after what had happened with Ginger. Everyone was too weary after being awake all night talking to the police. Dr. Turner presided over today's Sunday morning gathering, after informing us that he was also an ordained minister.

We stayed behind, and I fully expected to receive a lecture. I was tense all over as I waited for him to begin. Riley and I sat on an uncomfortable pew that was covered in burgundy. Dr. Turner sat in front of us.

Mr. Rogers Goes to Church.

For a moment, I felt like we were two high schoolers who'd been caught making out under the bleachers. Only we hadn't been making out. Or around any bleachers.

"First, I thought I'd give you an update," Dr. Turner started. "Apparently, some fishermen Leroy knew had been paying him a percentage of their profits in return for his silence. Those watermen knew that the oysters being cultivated on the shores of this island were protected."

"Protected?" I clarified.

"The oyster population in the bay had been steeply declining in recent years. Watermen can only harvest a certain amount of oysters at certain times of the year. These men knew exactly what they were doing. They were making thousands of dollars from their crimes."

"That's horrible," I said. Sierra would have a field day with this. The animal lover would fight to the death to protect any living creature from being mistreated. Even oysters.

Dr. Turner nodded, his head looking heavy as it moved up and down. "I agree. Leroy admitted that he was suspicious you were on to him. He said you were constantly in the wrong place at the wrong time."

"I see." I touched my throat.

"He said something about a confrontation he had with you last night?"

I nodded, realizing he had been the one who threatened me in my room last night. I must have tipped him off and made him nervous when I informed him about the boats I'd seen at night on the water. "Someone told me to go home. It was dark. I couldn't see his face."

"I apologize that happened to you on this island. He was obviously getting desperate. He would like to fully retire, but he just hasn't had the money. He took the easy way out."

My heart softened toward the man. He must have been the person I'd seen outside that first night I was here. He'd been working with the poachers even then. "I see."

Dr. Turner let out a sigh. "I worry about the things happening here. I want to heal, not harm. I'm afraid I'm failing."

"I can see a difference in the couples here, Dr. Turner," I told him. "Don't lose hope. Not yet."

"I appreciate your kind words. I hope you're including yourself and Riley in that equation."

"Will you fire Leroy?"

"I believe in second chances, Gabby. I hope with some help and counseling that he'll be able to turn from his ways."

"That's generous of you."

"People have been generous to me in the past. I try to pass that along to others." Dr. Turner paused for long enough to lean closer. "You want to know why I started doing this? I started as a psychotherapist, but I decided to specialize in marriage counseling. My own wife was killed by a hit-and-run driver. We had a beautiful marriage, and I want the same for other people."

"I'm so sorry to hear about what happened," I told him.

"I think I'm really beginning to see what the root of your problems are," he continued. "It's your nosiness, Gabby."

My jaw literally seemed to come unhinged. "What was that?"

"Nosiness can lead to a multitude of sins."

"Oh, so this is all about me? The disintegration of our relationship has nothing to do with him?" Outrage lined my voice, and I didn't even try to hide it. It took all of my willpower not to charge out of the pew and throttle someone.

"Men like to feel that they're first priority," Dr. Turner explained.

"He was first priority! He always has been."

Dr. Turner didn't look convinced. "Riley, what do you say to that?"

He swallowed hard, a surprising seriousness in his gaze. "There have been times when I wonder if I can even compete with your curiosity."

My mouth dropped open again. Could this get any more absurd? "What?"

"Let him talk, Gabby," Dr. Turner encouraged.

Riley nodded. "I mean, I think that's your first love."

"Nosiness?" Dr. Turner asked, his eyes crinkling.

Riley nodded. "Getting in other people's business. Injecting yourself into situations uninvited. Having no concern for your own safety."

I stood this time, unable to resist the impulse. "I knew it! You don't support me, and you never have! That's what this all boils down to, isn't it?"

"Calm down, Gabby," Dr. Turner instructed, lowering his hand toward the ground like he was performing a magic trick.

I wouldn't be that easily manipulated.

"It's not like you're nosy for a living, but I can understand what you're saying," Dr. Turner said. "You don't feel like he supports who you are. Is that correct?"

I stared at Riley, my gaze no doubt sending daggers into him. With that message clearly communicated, I sat back down, feeling much colder now than I did before.

"Exactly. I'm not nosy for a living. That's a ridiculous thought." I cleared my throat. "I suppose I just embarrass him when I'm a little too pushy sometimes."

"You could never embarrass me, Gabby." He said the words softly, gently.

"Then what is it?" I asked, my voice still edgy.

"In the past, I guess I just never felt like we were partners, you know? I felt like you got in trouble, and I tried to get you out of trouble."

"Many couples experience that," Dr. Turner said. "It's how you handle stress that makes the difference."

"I never meant to be a nuisance," I told him. "And, believe me, my entire life I've felt like I've encountered people who don't accept me as I am."

"Having people accept you for who you are doesn't

mean that you close the door to change and growth," Dr. Turner said.

"I guess what I'm trying to say is that I'm different now, Gabby. So are you." Riley sounded so sincere, so intense. But there was an underlying message he was trying to get across. I just wasn't sure what. Or I didn't want to know.

"What would you like to see from Gabby, Riley?"

"I love her spirit," he started, leaning toward me casually. "I want her to keep being who she is. I think I just needed a wake-up call to get me away from all these expectations that people have put on me for my entire life. I've always been taught to fit a mold, but I feel like my purpose has changed."

"The person you married is rarely the person you eventually are married to," Dr. Turner said. "We all change. It's a part of life. You just have to learn to grow together. It's important that we don't look to someone else when we realize the gravity of those changes. Your curiosity hasn't led you to anyone else, has it, Gabby?"

I blinked, stunned at his questions. "You mean, have I cheated?"

"Well, yes, I suppose that is what I'm asking."

"No, I haven't cheated." But as soon as the words left my mouth, I thought about Garrett.

But Riley and I had broken up. So going out with Garrett wasn't cheating. I had nothing to feel guilty about.

"Riley, your gaze is telling a different story," Dr. Turner said. "You feel like she has been unfaithful."

"Maybe deep down inside I thought our relationship meant more to her," he said quietly.

I flexed my jaw trying to keep my emotions at bay. It wasn't working well, though. My emotions raged inside me with hurricane-force winds. "That's not fair."

"I thought I just wanted you to be happy. But maybe the truth is that I'm selfish, and I can't imagine my future with anyone but you."

"How about you, Gabby? What would you like to see from Riley?"

I stared at Riley, my words gone. Had he been acting earlier? Or was he speaking the truth?

My head spun while my heart squeezed and released. Squeezed and released. Squeezed and released.

"Gabby?" Dr. Turner continued.

I pulled my gaze away from Riley, trying to come back to reality. "Commitment. That's what I want. Our relationship has an ebb and flow that hasn't always been healthy. We had—have issues. It's time to face the truth."

"I agree," Riley said.

"Great. You both agree on something," Dr. Turner said. "I think we've gotten a good start here, Riley and Gabby. I'd like to talk about this again more next weekend, and I have some very specific homework for the two of you this week. I want you two to write down everything you love about the other person. Can you do that?"

Begrudgingly, I nodded. "Of course."

"Yes," Riley said.

"Wonderful. Now, we have one more session until it's time to leave for the weekend. I have a new captain coming to take you back to the mainland."

Captain Leroy might be gone. But there was still a killer out there.

CHAPTER 37

I'd felt the tension between Riley and me since we'd almost kissed last night and since our "session" with Dr. Turner this morning. We hadn't had time to talk about anything, and, truth be told, I didn't want to talk about it. There was no need to dig up the demons from the past. We'd both had a moment of lapsed judgment. They happened, but I tried to avoid stuff like that overall.

That's why, when my boss called me to talk about my assignments for the week, I was more than happy to fill the drive home with that conversation rather than one with Riley. In fact, our phone call lasted nearly an hour, which worked out perfectly for me. I may have even drawn it out, talking about barbecue and baseball and dream vacations.

But then the time came when we pulled up to our apartment complex. I knew there would be an opportunity as we said goodbye, and the thought made my stomach clench.

I climbed out before any deep talks could be initiated and grabbed my suitcase from his popped-open trunk.

"Well, it looks like we have another weekend behind us."

He nodded stiffly. "That's right. At least we can rule out Captain Leroy."

"That means our pool of suspects is only getting smaller and smaller. That's the good news." My voice sounded falsely cheerful.

"Gabby, I really think we should talk," Riley said as we stood on the front stoop.

This was it. The moment I was dreading.

Suddenly, the door beside us burst open. "Gabby!"

The lump in my throat nearly choked me a moment. My eyes had to be deceiving me.

Please?

Finally, I croaked, "Garrett?"

It was definitely him. Tall and lean and with undeniable swagger. Though he also had dark hair like Riley, his good looks were far more exotic. His hair had a touch of curl, his eyes had a touch of naughty, and his smile seemed to indicate that he could own the world if he chose to.

Before I realized what was happening, he pulled me into his arms and swung me in a circle. His familiar scent— sandalwood, I'd always guessed—filled my senses.

"I couldn't wait another second to see you."

"You're back here. I just can't believe it." I was stunned. More than stunned. I was stupefied.

"Sierra told me you'd be home this evening."

I'd seen a couple of missed calls from Sierra. Perhaps I shouldn't have ignored them. But if the baby was coming, she'd promised to send a SOS text to inform me, and I hadn't gotten one of those. I figured I'd been safe to wait.

I pulled my hair behind my ear, suddenly feeling self-conscious. "Right. We're just getting back from an investigation we were hired to take part in."

It was only then that Garrett's gaze fell on Riley. Some of his earlier gusto slipped from his gaze.

"Riley." He nodded woodenly.

"Garrett." Riley regarded him.

Tension as thick as the fog around Bird's Nest Island fell between all of us.

"I'll let you two talk," Riley finally said. "I'll catch up with you later, Gabby."

Garrett watched him walk away before turning back to me. When he saw me, a huge grin stretched across his face. "You look great. The weeks have been good to you"

I nodded. "I guess you could say that. I have a new job. I'm moving in the right direction."

"That's great."

"You look great also," I told him.

"I can't wait to tell you about Africa." He practically glowed.

"I can't wait to hear about it."

He shifted and took a fleeting glance toward the door where Riley had disappeared. "I realize you just returned, but do you have time tonight? I just hate that it's taken this long to see you, especially considering I've been back for a week."

"I can do something tonight," I said, despite the fact that I really just wanted a hot shower and time to decompress.

"Great." He grabbed my suitcase, and we started upstairs. "There's a new restaurant some of my colleagues have been raving about. I thought we might go there. It's got oysters that are out of this world."

Oysters? Argh. He had no idea.

"Sure. Let me just get freshened up."

***

An hour later, Garrett and I were seated at a window table overlooking the bay. It seemed ironic to be here. The basic landscape was the same. The basic food was the same. Yet so

CHRISTY BARRITT

much was different. The location, the company, my feelings.

Garrett Mercer was a great guy. Anyone would say so. He was handsome and generous and kind. A world changer. A most eligible bachelor. A dream come true.

"So how are you?" He leaned toward me and took my hand.

Earlier, I'd felt like I was betraying Garrett by being at the marriage retreat with Riley. Now I felt like I was betraying Riley by being with Garrett. *Gabby Goes to Royal Messville.*

What exactly did it say about me that I kept giving titles to portions of my life, as if I was living in various sitcom episodes?

"I'm doing well, Garrett." I told him about a conference I'd gone to a few weeks ago in Oklahoma, meeting my future stepbrother for the first time, and starting my new job. I talked about Sierra and the baby and a new coffee flavor I thought he should try out.

"It's amazing what can happen in your life in a few short months, isn't it?"

"That's the truth," I told him, an uncomfortable feeling of dread in my stomach.

Our food came. I'd bypassed the oysters again, especially knowing now what I did about them. Instead I'd gotten some grilled wahoo, steamed vegetables, and brown rice.

After we prayed and as I raised my fork, I turned the conversation on Garrett. "Please, tell me all about your trip."

A fire seemed to ignite in his gaze. Passion—that's what it was.

"There's so much to say. I loved it over there, Gabby. I've been to Africa before, but this trip was different somehow. Something stirred in my heart."

227

"Tell me more." I honestly wanted to know. He was doing good work over there, leaving an impact that would last for years.

He told me stories about the children he'd met, the villages he'd visited, and the ways people had let him into their lives. He told me about interesting foods he'd tried and about trips to the market and how kids entertained themselves with rocks and sticks.

"I'm going to be spending more time over there. I want to oversee the operations more."

His announcement surprised me, even threw me off kilter. "But what about your coffee business here?"

"I'll still oversee that as well. But I want to be more hands-on. Life is too short to just sit behind a desk all the time and push paper."

"I'll have to agree to that."

His gaze latched onto mine. "I want you to come with me, Gabby."

Suddenly, I lost my appetite. I put my fork down mid-bite and stared at him, waiting to hear "just kidding!"

"What?" I had to have heard him incorrectly.

But the earnestness in his eyes told me I hadn't.

He leaned closer. "You would love it over there. It would change your life. I could see us doing good work together."

I leaned back, hitting the chair behind me a little too hard. "I don't know what to say. I'm flattered."

"Say yes." His eyes implored me. There was a promise of adventure there, of every day being different, of the chance to be satisfied.

"It's not that easy." My throat ached as I said the words.

"It could be."

"As tempting as it sounds, my life is here. I just got a new job. My interest is in the field of forensics. I know I would love it over there. But I feel my place is here."

His smile dimmed. "Is it because of Riley?"

I totally abandoned my food now. At least I'd had the chance to down about half of it before we got to this point in our conversation. I was downright uncomfortable and wished I could teleport myself to a happy place. "There's nothing between Riley and me."

He didn't break his gaze. "My assistant said Riley moved back and stopped subletting his apartment."

I nodded curtly. "He did. I found out while I was in Oklahoma."

He put his fork down also, his food forgotten. "And you're working on an investigation together?"

"That's correct. But it's purely professional."

He tilted his head, questions swirling in his eyes. "Do you really believe that?"

I nodded, maybe more adamantly than necessary. "I really do. We're done. Over. History."

"I'm not so sure."

I swiped my hand through the air, indicating my decision was final. "Well, I am. I'm determined to be the bigger person and prove that we can still be friends, though."

He stared another moment longer. When he glanced down, I knew the conversation was turning yet again. "I see. So what does this mean for us, Gabby? You've had three months to think."

A physical pain twisted my heart. "I can't fit into your life, Garrett." My voice cracked as I said the words. "I think that's obvious. We're different people going in different directions. There's no part of me that feels led to go to Africa long-term."

"I see." He placed his napkin in lap. "I guess this is it then?"

Tears rushed to my eyes. Why was this so hard? Why did chapters have to come to an end? I supposed the only way to avoid that was to never take any risks. "Life's a Dance" by John Michael Montgomery began playing in the soundtrack of my mind. "You've meant so much to me, Garrett."

"You've meant a lot to me also, Gabby. It's going to take me a while to process this, to be honest. I was hoping you would have a different answer." His eyes lost their light, their hopefulness.

I hated myself for making him hurt.

"There's a part of me that wishes I did too."

He stood and dropped some money on the table. "What do you say we call this a night then?"

My heart was in my throat as I nodded. "I guess that's a good idea."

I prayed I wasn't making the biggest mistake of my life.

CHAPTER 38

I spent the beginning part of week avoiding Riley. I figured as long as I kept busy, I wouldn't have to talk to him. We wouldn't have to rehash any of our revealing conversations from last weekend. There wouldn't have to be any awkward moments.

I'd also replayed my conversation with Garrett a million times. I'd had a certain measure of security knowing he'd been there for me. Now I really was going at life solo. My two best friends, Sierra and Chad, were married and expecting a baby. My dad was getting remarried. My brother had started a new business.

Meanwhile, everything that had happened at the retreat center was weighing on me heavily. I really wanted to provide some answers to Brad. Riley and I were supposed to meet with him before we left for the retreat on Friday. He needed some closure.

With a sigh, I glanced at my watch. Sierra's baby shower was supposed to start in thirty minutes, and I was hosting it at the coffeehouse across the street from my place.

Called The Grounds, it was my little home away from home. I was friends with the pink-haired, pierced like a pincushion owner Sharon, and she'd been more than open to hosting the event there. The place was lovely, with wooden floors and glossy oak tables and sweet, heavenly scents that seemed to saturate the very walls.

Sierra had insisted that her party be for men and women. That meant that nearly everyone from the apartment complex would be there. As far as I knew, Riley wouldn't.

"You ready for this?" Sharon asked, placing a tiered cupcake holder full of culinary delights on the counter. Sharon had even worked with me to make sure everything was vegan, since that was really important to Sierra. I would have never managed that on my own.

"Brownies?" I asked.

"Acorn brownies," she said with a smile.

Sierra was infamous for once making brownies out of acorns and then feeding them to all her friends without any sort of heads-up.

"You seem different, Gabby," Sharon said, pausing and leaning against the counter. "I've noticed it the past few times I've seen you."

I pressed my lips together, feeling rather reflective and burdened with thought. "I guess I am different. Life can do that to you sometimes. I'm not the same person as I was last year at this time."

"Does it have anything to do with him?" She nodded toward the door.

My throat went dry as Riley walked toward the coffee shop. He was coming. Argh.

"I guess he's been a part of it. I'd be lying if I denied it."

"That's one thing I've always loved about you. You call it like you see it."

"I try to." Although I had learned to hold my tongue more as the years went on. Not every thought that passed through my mind needed to be voiced out loud. That required some self-control, an attribute that only came with effort.

"You got this, Tiger." She nudged me forward.

I plastered on a smile and stepped toward my ex-fiancé. "Riley. I didn't realize you were coming."

He looked great in his low-slung jeans and a blue T-shirt that clung to his muscles. His hair glistened, shower-fresh, and I could only imagine what he smelled like right now.

"I wouldn't miss it." He offered that sincere smile that always got to me.

Thankfully, more people flooded in so we didn't have to force any conversation.

I let people mingle as they arrived, not wanting to rush into any of the candy-bar-in-a-diaper type of games I'd planned. I stood back and watched Riley a moment. He easily talked to everyone, looking happy and at ease. He seemed to genuinely be doing well.

Good for him.

Just at that moment, he caught me staring. I wanted to look away, but instead I smiled sheepishly and waved. He seemed to take that as a cue. He finished his conversation with our neighbor Bill McCormick and approached me. The smile left his face as he got closer, though.

"It's great to see everyone. It feels like old times."

I forced a nod, immediately sensing the tension between us. "Doesn't it?" *Except in old times we were supposed to spend the rest of our lives together.*

He glanced over at Sierra and Chad. Sierra rubbed her belly, and Chad leaned down to say something animated to the baby. It was a beautiful sight.

"I'm really happy for Chad and Sierra," Riley said, following my gaze. "They really seem to have their lives together now, don't they?"

"They do." At least a few people in my life did. Maybe I'd put myself on that list one day.

Riley cleared his throat and shifted awkwardly. "How's Garrett?"

"He seems great. He's going back to Africa."

Riley blinked as if processing that information. "I'm sure that will be hard on your relationship."

Was he fishing for more information or trying to get a read on my feelings? I wasn't sure. "We're just friends. Our lives aren't going in the same direction." I cut a sharp glance at him. "And I was always very hesitant about ever dating him, FYI."

"You don't have to explain. I was out of line to bring it up." He shifted, signaling a change in conversation. "By the way, I think I know what that text Atticus got was about."

"Really? What?"

"On the news this morning it said something about Griffith Technologies. One of the programmers there left and went with another company. He took some of the product designs with him, and now there's a big lawsuit starting. As soon as I heard that, I thought of that text. I'd bet anything that's what it's about."

I nodded and let that sink in. "I guess that makes sense."

Riley glanced at his watch. "I hate to run, but I just wanted to make an appearance and drop off my gift."

"Hot date?" I wanted to smack myself for asking the question.

"Mixed martial arts class."

I raised my eyebrows. "Since when?"

"Since I decided to take back control of my life." He offered a half-shrug, half-nod.

"I'll see you on Friday morning?"

I nodded. "Sounds good."

***

On Thursday morning, I had to do a training session . . . where else? On the Eastern Shore for the Northampton County Sheriff's Department. I wondered if Detective Hanson would be there. Could I possibly be that lucky?

I was going to do my job and not worry about proving myself to anyone. After all, I was a professional. Before I left, I picked up Dr. Turner's book, trying to shut out all the voices inside my head. Emotions could certainly make a mess of people.

The man really did have some sage advice. His counsel was peppered with Bible verses, but not so overwhelmingly that people who weren't believers should be offended. Of course, some would be upset at any mention of God or the Bible.

He told stories about his late wife that made her sound like a saint and stressed the importance of sticking with your partner through thick and thin.

He'd definitely spoken the truth into my life, even if I didn't like it. In fact, I almost found myself craving his advice.

Just as I grabbed my supplies, my phone rang. I didn't recognize the number, but I did realize the Maryland area code.

"This is Gabby," I answered.

"Gabby. It's Rae Gray from the *Baltimore Enquirer*. I got your message."

The reporter Brad had mentioned. She was finally getting back with me! And she wasn't dead! Two for two.

"Thanks for giving me a call. We were worried something happened to you."

"Happened to me? My uncle died. I was in Wisconsin for his funeral. I like to keep private things private so that's why no one at the office told you what was going on. Now, how can I help you?"

"Brad Thorn told me he contacted you about his wife's death."

"That's correct. I thought it was interesting, and I planned to look into what happened. Then my uncle died."

"Any reason why his wife's death interested you?"

"I've had my suspicions about the retreat center, especially after I heard what happened to Khloe Wescott."

"Khloe Wescott?" I hated being clueless, but that's exactly what I was at the moment.

"The woman who died at another retreat run by Dr. Turner."

"What?" Had I heard correctly?

"I figured you knew."

"I had no idea." How had that detail slipped past?

"She was a mess. Had cheated on her husband five or six times. Started drinking too much. Had done some irresponsible things. I guess people weren't surprised she died after living the way she did."

"How did she die?"

"A heart attack."

I bit down for a moment. A heart attack didn't exactly fit my overall theory that something shady was going on. Yet I couldn't dismiss it either. "You should know that another woman fell off a cliff last weekend. She's on life support right now."

"Now, that's just crazy. How can anyone deny something is going on?"

"That's my exact question. Do you have any theories about what had happened to either Anna or Khloe?"

"Well, I've been trying to connect the dots. There are only so many people who were at both of the retreat centers.

At first I thought about Dr. Turner. I mean, he's the connector, right? But I looked into his background, and I even talked to him once, and he seemed sincerely upset about what had happened. There were only two other people at both of the retreat centers."

"Who were they?"

"Blaine Stewart and Steve Anderson."

"Well, we can rule Blaine out. She almost died when someone tampered with her boat."

"I wouldn't be so quick to rule her out."

"Why in the world would she do something like this?" I asked, trying to picture Blaine as a murderer.

"Because I discovered she used to be one of Dr. Turner's patients. Of course, her official diagnosis is confidential, but I talked to some people who used to know her. Apparently, she suffers with some kind of obsessive disorder."

"Do you know how that disorder manifests itself?" Really, what she'd said could mean so many things and take on various forms. I needed more details.

"From what I hear, she's basically delusional with attachment disorders."

"Any idea how that plays out in her life?"

"No, but it makes her a suspect to me."

CHAPTER 39

I decided to stop by the hospital to check on Jim and Ginger before heading home. Plus, I had a few questions for him. I wasn't sure if he would be there but I decided to chance it.

To my delight and surprise, he sat in the waiting room. He had his laptop out and a phone on the table and empty coffee cups littered the floor around him. He looked awful, with circles under his eyes, and his forehead appeared especially shiny.

He straightened when he saw me. "Gabby?"

"I just happened to be in town."

"Really?"

I nodded. "For work."

"I didn't think you worked."

Oh, yeah. My cover. "It's a long story. I wanted to check on Ginger."

The light left his eyes. "There haven't been any changes. I wish I had something different to tell you, but I don't."

"Have you been at the hospital this whole time?"

He shrugged "When I can. I set up my mobile office here. It's easier this way."

I sat down beside him and handed him the cup of coffee I'd bought. He looked eternally grateful and took a sip—more like a gulp, actually.

"Can I ask you a question, Jim?"

He shrugged. "Sure."

"Why were you and Ginger arguing on the night she fell off the cliff? I haven't been able to stop thinking about it."

His cheeks turned red. "It was nothing really."

"I know you two aren't married, Jim."

His face went pale. "How did you know that?"

"I put it together when the receptionist said Ginger had a different last name. Everything started to make sense."

His shoulders slumped. "It's true. It was Ginger's idea to come to the retreat center. She wanted our relationship to be the best it could possibly be."

"Even though you aren't married to each other?"

He nodded. "I know it sounds crazy. The truth is that I love her."

"I don't understand. I'm not advocating you leave your wife. Not by any means. But most people would do that and marry the other woman."

"That's actually what we were fighting about. She'd always been happy with our relationship before, just the way it stood. But that day at the retreat center, something changed. She said she wanted more. She wanted me to leave Jill and marry her. I told her I couldn't."

"Why not? Again, not that I'd ever advocate that."

"Jill and I have our whole lives wrapped up in each other. Our kids, our careers, our social circles. It just wasn't going to happen. Besides, I've brokered several land deals for the military. Some top-secret stuff that I had to sign a confidentiality agreement on before doing the work. If my affair became public, someone could blackmail me. That wouldn't make the government very happy."

I didn't exactly know what to think about that. "I see. Can I ask another question?"

"Are you always this nosy?"

"It's one of the problems Riley and I face."

"I can see why. I don't think I'm going to be able to stop you from asking these questions, am I?"

"Probably not. I heard you and Anna also had an argument on the night before she died. May I ask what it was about?"

"How did you find that out?" He shook his head and let out a long sigh. "Never mind. I don't want to know. Truth is, Anna knew Jill from living in the DC-Baltimore area. She knew that Ginger wasn't my wife and confronted me about it."

"What did you tell her?"

"I told her the truth. I told her what I just told you. Besides, Jill knows about Ginger. We have a very open relationship, and we're both okay with that."

That confirmed what Jill told me earlier. "I'm not even going to try to understand that."

"You don't have to. Just understand this: I would never hurt Ginger. Never."

***

Detective Hanson was involved in my training session. And I may or may not have put him on the spot a few times when I threw out an especially difficult forensic question. And I also may or may not have felt an immense satisfaction when he didn't know the answer.

I supposed that was immature of me and that I should feel ashamed. But I didn't. I wasn't sure what that said about me.

At the end of my presentation, as I packed up my things and prepared to leave, he called me.

I continued putting away the samples in a blood-testing kit. I tried not to show the satisfaction in my eyes. "Yes?"

He frowned beside me. "Listen, sorry I gave you a hard time earlier. What I said was true: Everyone thinks he or she can be a detective. But I didn't give you the respect I should have."

"I appreciate that," I told him, honestly surprised at his apology.

"I thought I'd let you know we are taking these investigations seriously. However, Anna Thorn did appear to die at her own hands, and we have no evidence to prove anyone pushed Ginger. There was no unusual bruising or even footprints to verify your story."

"What would you say if I told you there was another woman who died at another one of Dr. Turner's retreats?" I paused and crossed my arms.

"Really?" His lips pulled down in a deep frown.

I nodded. "That's one of the problems in police work: different departments in different cities not sharing information. This other death looked like a natural one—a heart attack. But some people suspect that might not be true."

He thought for a moment before shaking his head. "So Dr. Turner is guilty? Is that what you think?"

"No, he can't be. When Ginger fell, Dr. Turner had gone back to the mainland. He wasn't even on the island. But I do have at least one other suspect whom I think you'll find very interesting."

I told him about Blaine and her past history, as well as Steve the cook.

"Motive?" he asked.

I had his full attention. His gaze burned into me. Thank goodness someone was finally taking me seriously. This was about more than me proving myself. This was about justice for

Anna and Ginger and Khloe.

I let out a long breath at his question. That was where I was struggling also. There was no clear-cut motive I could pinpoint. "That's a harder one. I don't want to think this is all the result of a deranged killer. But part of me thinks this is just some sicko getting his kicks out of killing women."

He pulled his lips back in an expression that clearly showed reservation. "I'll see what I can find out. If you find out anything else, please let me know."

I nodded, picking up the last of the rubber gloves I'd brought. "I will."

"Thanks again, Gabby."

Sometimes thank you was all a girl wanted to hear.

CHAPTER 40

I tried to pretend that it wasn't awkward to sit beside Riley as we drove back to the marriage retreat center the next day. But it was, especially when considering all the unspoken conversations that lingered between us like beasts waiting to devour their prey.

The only possible safe conversation was to talk about the investigation. Apparently, Riley agreed because he jumped in before I could.

"I heard an update today." Riley glanced at me. Heaviness weighed down his words. "I wasn't going to tell you now, because I know you have a lot on your mind. But the more I think about it, the more I realize you'd want to know ASAP."

Curiosity pulsed in my blood. I had to tell him about my conversation with Rae also. I wanted to keep this weekend focused on the investigation. I was hereby resolving to keep my distance from all things Riley Thomas. "What is it?"

"I called the hospital today and asked about Ginger. I ended up talking to Jim. Ginger died last night, Gabby."

I gasped. "No . . ."

He nodded grimly. "I'm sorry to be the one to tell you. But now we have two murders on our hands."

"Maybe three," I said.

"What do you mean?"

I explained my phone call with Rae Gray to him.

"That's crazy."

"There's more. I decided to look into the death of Dr. Turner's wife. She was killed because of a hit-and-run driver. The weird thing is that the police never discovered who killed her. The case is still open."

"What are you getting at?"

"I just wonder if she's connected with all of this somehow." It was just a vague theory, and I had nothing to prove it. I had to consider it as a possibility, though.

"It's a stretch, but maybe. I want to go back to something you said earlier. Blaine used to be Dr. Turner's patient?"

I nodded. "Apparently she does okay when she's on her medicine. But, otherwise, she's obsessive with an attachment disorder."

"It appears we have a new suspect then. But what about the boat? And finding her locked in the shed? If she's guilty, how do those things fit?"

"I'm not sure." I stared pensively at the window a moment, trying to process everything. "Our window of opportunity for solving this case is rapidly closing, though."

This was the last weekend of the retreat. Three women were dead. If I ruled out Dr. Turner's wife, what did Anna, Ginger, and Khloe have in common?

The answer hit me like a Mack truck. Why didn't I see it earlier? I knew the reason those women were murdered.

"What's going on in that brain of yours, Gabby?"

"I think I have a motive." I shook my head, trying to process it. "Riley, all three of the women who died were unfaithful to their spouses. That's what links these women together."

"You think someone is killing because of that?"

I shook my head again. "It's the only thing that makes sense."

"Why isn't someone killing the men who've been unfaithful?"

"I have no idea. But I think I know how we can test my theory." I rattled off a plan for Saturday evening. I had to collect some more information first. I had to know what I was getting into before I made myself an open target.

"It might work, but it sounds dangerous," Riley said.

"It may not be as dangerous as we think. If I can get this person to confess, then we can end this once and for all." My mind continued to turn everything over. My theory made sense. My plan could work, and if my hypothesis was accurate, putting myself out there wasn't entirely foolhardy. The problem came only if my assumptions proved incorrect.

How confident was I?

"There's only one way this will work," I finally said.

"How's that?"

"On a wing and a prayer."

Riley groaned. Yes, I'd used a bird reference. Maybe Dr. Turner was wearing off on me.

***

That evening at dinner, Riley and I were seated with Bo and Angelina. The men started talking about football, so I decided to take the opportunity to see what Angelina knew.

Anxiety churned in my stomach. There was a lot that could go wrong. But I was closer to finding answers than I'd been before. I just had to plan each of my moves carefully.

"Have you heard anything else about Leroy?" I asked, lowering my voice. Another man I'd never seen before had escorted us across the water today. Apparently, Dr. Turner had hired him out of one of the local marinas until he could find a permanent replacement.

Angelina's eyes lit with an excitement that only gossip could bring. "I heard the police let him go. I mean, he still has to have his day in court, but he's out on bail now."

"It's scary all this stuff happening, isn't it? Too many eerie things for my comfort." I took a bite of my prime rib with garlic mashed potatoes and lemon-drenched green beans.

"Tell me about it. Even the rich have their problems. Maybe even more than regular old folk like me."

"To be truthful, I grew up poor."

Angelina's eyes widened. "Shut up. I would have never guessed."

"There's probably a lot about me that would surprise you." I realized I was coming a little too close to the truth. "I feel like I can relate to you more than I can some of these other snooty people here. Growing up, my dad didn't even make twelve thousand dollars a year."

"Well, if I'd had to pay, I would never be here," she whispered.

"I thought everyone had to pay?"

She leaned back, a smug smile on her face as she shrugged. "When you have a big, brilliant brain, you can think of ways to get around these things."

I made sure to look impressed. "How'd you do it?"

She looked around briefly before leaning closer. "Between you and me, I found out something about Dr. Turner."

Excitement spiked in my blood. "What's that?"

"I ran into a man at the gas station where I work. It turned out he was dating Dr. Turner's wife."

"What?" My voice croaked out about five levels higher than normal.

She nodded. "It's true. They were having an affair."

She couldn't be telling the truth. It was like saying Mother Teresa harmed animals in her free time. The mental picture just wouldn't form. "Not Dr. Turner. He said he had a great relationship with his wife. All his books say so."

"Well, that's what he wants us to believe. Truth is, she was just as unfaithful as any of these other women here."

"How did that equate to you getting in here for free?"

"Well, I was going to go to the media with the story. They love stuff like that. Marriage guru fails at marriage. Doesn't that smack of irony?"

"But you went to Dr. Turner instead?"

"It was Bo's idea. We just prodded him in the right direction. He paid us a nice little check that will ensure a great vacation and let us come to the retreat."

"You got money. Why come here?"

"The chance to get away from our kids for a few weekends while being waited on hand and foot? Why would we pass that up?"

There were some people I'd never understand. "You mean you aren't having marriage troubles?"

She laughed loudly, before putting a hand over her mouth. "Not like these people! Honey, Bo and I leave here feeling better about our marriage. We know we've got it good after hearing all the problems some of these people have."

"Why was Dr. Turner so desperate to conceal his wife's affair?"

"Isn't it obvious? His credibility would be ruined, plus he said he wanted to preserve his wife's reputation. Isn't that sweet?"

I nodded. Well, I'd solved one mystery. The mystery of Bo and Angelina.

But another disturbing thought barreled into my mind. If Dr. Turner's wife was unfaithful, what if her death was somehow connected here also?

If that was the case, there was only one person I could think of who would be responsible. Someone who was obsessive, maybe even possessive.

Blaine Stewart.

CHAPTER 41

"Since you seemed interested in that skeleton we found a couple of weeks ago, I thought you might also be interested in an update," Dr. Turner said before the evening session started.

Riley and I were sitting on our couch in what was beginning to feel like a normal part of my routine. I straightened at Dr. Turner's proclamation, trying to forget what Angelina had said about the doctor earlier. That just couldn't be true. But it would explain his passion for strong marriages.

"I'd love an update," I said, remembering the skeleton. "I find anthropology very interesting. Probably because I've watched too many episodes of *Bones*." That sounded like a viable excuse, right?

"It turns out her name was Anita Nottingham. She was a housekeeper here on this island."

"Wow. That's pretty amazing," I said.

Dr. Turner nodded. "State authorities took some of the old records from the island with them during their investigation. They were able to do some DNA tests and match what happened with the records."

I was fascinated—not so much by the death, but by Anita's story. "Do they know how she died?"

"Apparently, she was dusting one of the bookshelves and was high on a ladder when she lost her balance. She hit her head and died instantly."

"Housework can be deadly," I mumbled. I was trying to be cute. Really, I was.

Dr. Turner did not look amused. "I believe marriages are happier when the woman takes on the duties of the house."

"That might be true in some cases, but not every woman was created to clean houses." My words sounded funny to my own ears, since I'd basically made a living by cleaning for the past several years. But Dr. Turner was essentially saying that women should cook and clean and look pretty for their husbands. While I couldn't say there wasn't merit in some of those things, I didn't like to pigeonhole people.

"I sense that your independence may tear your marriage apart," Dr. Turner said.

My jaw came unhinged. "Me again? Why is every problem in this . . ." I glanced at Riley, at a loss for words. ". . . in this *marriage* my fault?"

"I'm just giving you something to think about."

Riley put his hand on my arm, obviously trying to get me to settle down before I said or did something I regretted. As Dr. Turner moved on, I was still fuming.

Riley looked halfway amused. "What? You don't want to rub my feet after I work long and hard all day to pay the bills?"

"It's not even that," I muttered. "If that's what a person's marriage personality looks like, then fine. But I really get the feel from him that women are inferior."

"He grew up in a different age. A lot of marriages thrive under a more old-fashioned role model."

"Is that what you would want from me if we were married?" I'd lowered my voice.

"I'd respect whatever you want to do, Gabby. I know God created you to do big things. Maybe that will be through your career, through raising kids, or both. Only you will know that when that time approaches."

My racing heart slowed a moment. Until Riley leaned closer.

"And our problems were my doing, not yours," he whispered.

His words did something to me. They made my bones feel like jelly. They made months of worry and guilt and burdens disappear.

I knew it took two to tango. But I'd needed to hear what he'd said. I needed to know that he understood what his leaving had done to me.

He did, didn't he? Was that what he'd been trying to tell me this whole time?

***

After our session, Riley walked me back to my room, silence falling between us as well as tension.

He stopped outside my door. "You remember that homework Dr. Turner gave us?"

I nodded. "How could I forget?"

"I wanted to share a few things that I love about you." Riley pulled a piece of paper from his pocket and cleared his throat. "Things I love about Gabby. The way she quotes musicals. The goofy T-shirts she's so fond of. Her hair, especially when it's curly. Her steadfastness. Her work ethic. Her determination. The way she's real. When she enjoys her food and lets it show in its entirety. How she's not afraid to look crazy for the greater good. Should I go on?"

My resolve was crumbling and quickly. Did he really love all of those things about me, or was he just playing along? I couldn't be sure.

"That's . . . that's really sweet, Riley."

"Thanks for not totally writing me off. Not many people let their exes come back into their lives. You've stood by me, and I just wanted to say thank you."

"Then there's something I need to tell you." I reached into my pocket also and pulled out my list. I'd had it on hand in case Dr. Turner asked for it. I licked my lips before starting. "What I love about Riley Thomas. He has my back. He makes me feel safe. He pursues what's right over what's profitable. He'll fight tooth and nail for what he believes in. He loves Jesus. He took in a stray parrot. He's friends with people who aren't just like him. He looks after the least of these."

I glanced up, and the look in Riley's eyes took my breath away. He appeared transfixed. For a moment, it seemed like old times. It felt like he should lean closer and give me a goodnight kiss.

But Angelina and Bo clattered into the hallway at that moment and broke the spell. Riley took a step back and ran a hand through his hair. "I'll see you in the morning.

I nodded. "Right. I'll see you then."

I went into my room and changed into my yoga pants and a T-shirt and washed my face. I tried to get Riley out of my mind. So, of course, I thought about the investigation instead. It was my safe place.

This was my last shot to get this right. If I didn't find the killer this weekend, then Brad would never have answers. I'd feel obligated to give his money back. And I wouldn't get that new car I needed.

My suspect list was being narrowed each day. Only two of three people stood out in my mind now.

I was going to figure this out.

I pulled my covers back, ready to get in bed. What I saw

under the covers made me freeze.
It was a snake.
A water moccasin, if I wasn't mistaken.
It stared right at me, ready to strike.

CHAPTER 42

Steve successfully captured the snake and carried it out of my room an hour later. I'd run to get help, and a whole army of people ended up in my suite, trying to figure out the best way to remove the snake from my bed.

Finally, Steve had grabbed a box and a stick. He went into my room alone, made a lot of noise, and emerged successful.

Praise Jesus.

"This old building. That snake must have been living here before this was refurbished," Dr. Turner said before turning to leave with the rest of the men.

But I wasn't so sure about it. I would wager someone had put it there on purpose. Maybe someone who knew who I really was? Someone who wanted to get me off this island. The same person who'd been following me.

Steve seemed surprisingly at ease in handling the snake. Could he have anything to do with this? I wasn't ruling him out yet.

I stared at my door after everyone left, hesitant to go back inside. What else might someone have left there for me? Did I really want to find out?

At that moment, Farrah stepped out of her room with binoculars around her neck and a notebook in her hands. She must have heard me gasp because she jerked her head toward me.

"I thought there was another snake," she said with a feeble laugh.

"I'm just a little jumpy." I nodded toward the equipment around her neck. "Hot date?"

She laughed. "Secret hobby, actually."

"What's that?" Spying on people? Plotting out murders?

"I like to bird-watch."

"What?" Certainly I hadn't heard her correctly.

She nodded. "This island is incredible when it comes to waterfowl. I've seen egrets, herons, osprey, and a warbler. I just can't get enough of this."

"You're full of surprises. First, I find out you're a pediatrician, and now that you're a bird-watcher. What will I learn next? That you went to the Olympics when you were younger."

"No, that would be my younger sister."

I raised my eyebrows. "Fascinating. So is this really the only enjoyable part of this retreat, or was that an exaggeration?"

Farrah frowned and shrugged. "It's hard to say. Sometimes I want to believe that things can be like they used to. Other times, I feel like our marriage is hopeless and that I just need to accept that. If Atticus doesn't want to change, then none of this is going to work."

"Do you think he wants to make it work?" I pulled my legs under me, feeling a heart-to-heart talk coming on.

"He claims he does. I just don't know if I can truly believe him or truly trust him. He's powerful. He thinks he can get away with murder."

Her words made me shudder.

"Or affairs. Or living however he wants, really."

"Is he still seeing other women?"

"He claims he's not, but he's the only one who really knows that."

"How'd you hear about the retreat center anyway?"

"We've had several friends who've gone through this program. It's the 'in' thing in our circles back at home."

A realization began to beg for my attention. "You know other people who've gone through this? You mean, people from up in Baltimore?"

She nodded. "Yeah. We have our AA meetings, our spa days, and our therapy."

"I heard there was another incident up at his second retreat center. Something about a woman named Khloe?"

Farrah went pale. "You know about Khloe?"

I nodded. "I have a few friends up in Baltimore also."

"Blaine asked us not to tell anyone. We were actually good friends with Khloe and her husband. It was devastating when we heard what happened."

"Why in the world did Blaine ask you to keep quiet?" I was trying to connect all the dots, but the process wasn't happening fast enough for me.

"Because it would be unnerving to the other couples here, especially in light of everything else that has happened."

I pinched the skin between my eyes, thinking everything through. "So let me get this straight. Khloe had a heart attack. Anna committed suicide. And Ginger fell off a bluff?"

"It's strange, isn't it? But it's like Dr. Turner said, people who come here are at the end of their ropes. They've already been taxed emotionally. And the things that come up in therapy can be overwhelming. Ginger's was just a terrible accident. I've seen things like this play out before. As a doctor, I know the effect of human emotions on a person's physical well-being. It's not always pretty."

Apparently, the rest of the clients here hadn't gotten word that I'd seen someone push her. Maybe I could use that to my advantage.

But I also had another realization. Blaine and Dr. Turner weren't the only ones connected with all three deaths. So were Atticus and Farrah.

Atticus moved further up on my suspect list.

CHAPTER 43

The afternoon activity on Saturday had been pretty simple. There'd been obstacles set up and Riley and I had to help each other through them. Nothing dangerous had happened, and no one had been injured.

The anxiety in my stomach continued to grow, however, as I thought about what might go down tonight. Was I really prepared to handle myself? I supposed I would find out.

The good news was that Riley and I still hadn't had any time to talk other than the normal conversations that all the couples were having.

Right now we were all gathered in the Therapy Lounge for a surprise. I had no idea what that might mean.

Dr. Turner, Blaine, and Steve all marched in the door with a strange look of satisfaction in their eyes. Blaine held something in her arms. Books. Large books.

"We have a special gift for you," Dr. Turner announced. "Blaine, if you don't mind."

Blaine handed a book to Riley and me. With a touch of nervousness, I opened the first page and blinked at what I saw there.

It was a scrapbook of our time on the island. The photos inside showed Riley and I laughing, fishing, eating, and cuddling. Something about the images made my heart warm. We looked so happy in these photos, like a real couple.

I glanced up at Steve.

This was why he'd taken those photos? And I thought he was only the cook, or maybe involved in murder . . .

"Blaine and Steve have been working hard since you arrived to put this together for you," Dr. Turner said. "I instructed Steve, our photographer, to get as many candid shots as possible. I wanted to highlight your best moments. I think the books turned out wonderfully. Don't you?"

Everyone murmured in agreement.

"You're now dismissed for free time until this evening's activity," Dr. Turner said.

As the crowd thinned, Riley and I made our way toward Steve.

"Great job with the pictures," Riley told him.

He nodded. "Thanks."

"And to think, the whole time we had no idea," I added. "How did you manage it without us noticing?"

"I'm pretty good at being sneaky. I hung out inside a lot and took pictures out the windows. I hid around the corner a few times. Everyone is so distracted with their own issues that they didn't even notice me. The people here made my job easy."

My curiosity heightened. "Is that right?"

That must have been the glare I saw that day when Riley and I were fishing. It had been the reflection of the sun hitting his camera lens. Why hadn't I put that together earlier?

"Dr. Turner asked me to take the photos," Steve said. "He asked me to be subtle so we could surprise everyone. Photography isn't exactly in my job description, but Dr. Turner has done a lot for me."

"Has he?" Riley questioned.

Steve nodded. "Yeah, I used to be one of his patients.

He likes to help people out. He knew I was having trouble finding a job because of my record, but he also believed I was a changed man. I'm grateful for what he's done for me."

Would someone who was guilty admit he had a record? I wasn't sure. But I didn't think so.

**

That evening, we all met downstairs, dressed in our finest. Angelina wore a jean skirt with the word "Sexy" stitched across the butt and a white T-shirt. Bo had on baggy jeans and a White Sox shirt. Farrah wore a lovely pair of palazzo pants and an elegant top, while Atticus wore khakis and a Henley that probably cost more than I made in a month.

I glanced down at my dress. It was a white sundress that I'd topped with a black sweater. I'd slipped on some silver flip-flops. I thought it was, overall, a nice look.

But as I glanced around, I realized Riley wasn't here. Where was he? Was he okay?

Then he appeared coming down the stairs. He wore a white button-up shirt and some low-slung jeans. My throat went dry at the sight of him. He was . . . handsome. More than handsome.

He had my heart.

And when he looked at me and smiled, I felt like the luckiest girl alive. Was I setting myself up for failure? Maybe. But Riley and I did need to have a conversation. Soon. I had to stop avoiding it and face reality.

He stood beside me, his eyes still warm and captivating. I forced myself to look away, so I could figure out what was going on here tonight.

Dr. Turner grinned broadly, which made me even more

suspicious. *Mr. Rogers Goes to Happy Land.*

"Thank you all for coming," Dr. Turner started. "I think you've each come a long way throughout this experience. I wanted to end our time together with something very special and meaningful. At least, I hope it will be meaningful to you." He made eye contact with each of us. "Tonight, we'll have a vow renewal ceremony."

I sucked in a quick breath. Vow renewal? Really? I didn't know what to think about that. Before I could formulate my thoughts, we were ushered outside, down the steps, and to the sandy shore below. Steve had his camera out and was snapping pictures, and Blaine handed each of the women a bouquet of flowers.

Anxiety churned in my stomach. There were a lot of things I justified myself acting through. But this seemed so intimate and personal. I'd be face-to-face with Riley, saying words that I had hoped to say to him a different lifetime ago. What if he saw the truth in my eyes?

"I'd like you to face each other and take your spouse's hands into your own," Dr. Turner started.

With my throat constricting, I placed my flowers by my feet and turned toward Riley. My cheeks flushed when I looked up at him.

There was something about his eyes that captivated me. The look there was enough to sweep me away to a happy place I'd be content to never leave. But that wasn't realistic. I just needed my heart to get that message.

"You look beautiful," Riley whispered.

"Dearly beloved, we are gathered here today to celebrate the marriage of three fine couples who are determined to stick together for better or for worse," Dr. Turner started.

Tears started to push to my eyes. Really, this was too much for me. I'd imagined this moment so many times . . . only it had been real when I pictured it. I hadn't been undercover.

Dr. Turner continued talking in the background—something about birds again. I looked away from Riley before he could see my tears, but he let go of my hand long enough to nudge my chin up until my eyes met his.

He was just acting, I reminded myself. I didn't care how his eyes looked. That meant nothing.

"God has brought each of you together with your spouse for a special purpose. You'll grow together in the good times and the bad times. Now, repeat after me. I vow to remain faithful."

"I vow to remain faithful," I repeated. I wanted to break my gaze, but our eyes seemed locked together.

"I vow to love unselfishly, to hold on to hope, and to always forgive."

I stumbled over the words. Had I forgiven Riley? Had I been unselfish? I'd like to think that I had, but, deep down, I wasn't sure.

"I vow to make time for you, to let you know that you're an important part of my life."

Riley and I repeated the words together.

"I vow to put the past behind me, and focus instead on our future together."

Again, my stomach lurched. I was supposed to be concentrating on the mystery we had to solve, and, instead, all I could think about was Riley and our past relationship. Could I put the past behind me? Was it possible?

"Now, I'd like for you to each take a moment to quietly speak to your spouse and tell them what they mean to you," Dr. Turner instructed.

If Riley and I had actually been participants here, this would have been a beautiful moment. But right now I just wanted to run. Or dive into the bay. Or be carried away by giant seagulls.

"I'll start," Riley said softly.

He stepped closer, close enough that I could see the flecks in his eyes, see the stubble starting to form on his chin and cheeks, see a wisp of hair that straggled across his forehead.

My stomach clenched as I waited for him to begin. I wasn't sure I could handle this or that my resolve would be strong enough.

But I had no choice but to proceed.

CHAPTER 44

"Gabby, I have made a lot of mistakes since I met you," Riley said. "Until recently, I don't think I was ready to admit that. I wanted to think that I was better than those things, that I was too good of a person to hurt you. But things have changed in the past year."

For a moment, I felt like I was in some kind of strange version of *The Bachelorette*. All I needed were some video cameras recording all this and millions of viewers watching my every move. This was by far *my* most dramatic rose ceremony ever.

"I want to do right by you, Gabby," Riley continued. "I can't imagine my future without you."

"Go ahead and wrap up your talks," Dr. Turner instructed.

My head felt like it was spinning. No! Don't stop now, I silently pleaded. I needed to know what else he had to say.

Riley kept going, never pulling his eyes away. "You are who you are, and you don't let other people sway you. You're persistent. You don't back down from doing what's right, even when your life is on the line. You love with all your heart, and you've risen far above what most people in your shoes would have."

A tear drizzled down my cheek. I'd dreamed about this moment. In fact, maybe this was a dream.

"You're the only one I've ever wanted, Riley," I whispered. "I was trying to give you space, to do what was best for you. But it tore me apart inside. Just like being here at the retreat. It's only confirmed that I still have feelings for you."

"I'm glad to hear that." A wide grin crossed his lips.

"And by the power vested in me, I now remind you that you're husband and wife. Forever and into eternity. You may kiss your bride."

Oh no! Kiss the bride? What—?

Before I could worry too much, Riley pulled me into his arms. His lips found mine. The lips that I was at one time all too familiar with.

I fully expected him to pull away, to do an obligatory peck on the lips and then step back. End of acting scenario. Duty done.

But, instead, his hand traveled to my neck, and he tilted my head backward. Everything else around me disappeared at his touch. His kiss deepened, and even though some kind of protective instinct inside me told me to resist, I was powerless to do so.

In fact, somewhere in the process, I wrapped my arms around his neck and kissed him back. Not only did I kiss him back, I kissed him back like I meant it. Because I did.

Despite my reservations, despite my fears, despite the hurt of the past . . . this was what I wanted. *Riley* was what I wanted.

When Riley finally pulled back, I realized that everyone was staring at us. I felt myself blush, and I rubbed my lips, which were still tingling. I couldn't look at Riley. Not now.

Now there was no denying that I was in love. The stranger thing was Riley might be also.

***

"That was some pretty good acting you did back there." I had to admit it: I was fishing for a confirmation of the truth. I didn't want to assume anything here. I needed something concrete.

Dr. Turner had dismissed us for some time alone. Riley and I had headed to the library.

He closed the door and pulled me into his arms. His face lingered close to mine, so close that I wanted to reach up and kiss him again. And he had an impish smile playing at the corner of his lips. "I wasn't acting, Gabby."

My heart nearly stopped. "Really?" I sounded more breathless than I'd realized was possible.

"I've never been as happy as when I heard you and Garrett were definitely not together. As wrong as it might be, I was praying that might happen."

"You would never pray for something like that, would you?" I said in mock outrage. My fingers pulled more tightly around him, and I could hardly stand just talking. I wanted to feel his lips again, to step closer, to bask in his strength.

He nodded, his eyes still dancing. "Yeah, I have to admit that I did. Maybe I was selfish."

"You can be selfish like that."

A fire lit in his eyes. "Can I?"

His lips met mine again, this time with not as much trepidation.

"I love you, Gabby."

"I love you too, Riley."

His thumb traced the side of my face. "I'm so sorry for the ways I hurt you. I know I've done a lot of damage, but I want to change things. I'm changed."

"It was a difficult situation, Riley. Who knows how I

would have handled it if the roles had been reversed."

He leaned down and kissed me again. Seriously, I couldn't get enough of his kisses. But I had to think things through here. There'd be time for this later.

"I hate to break up this moment, but we have a plan to put in place." I stepped away, but his arms circled my waist again.

He pulled me back for another quick kiss. "I don't want this moment to end."

I giggled. Giggled? Me? But it was true. I felt giddy. Honestly, I could stay here forever. I never wanted to let go. But staying here alone too long with Riley was a bad idea.

I pushed him back. "We have to. This is why we're here."

He frowned, his eyes moving from playful to dead serious. "I have reservations about you going out. You're basically setting yourself up as bait, and a lot of things could go wrong."

"The Marine Police should be showing up to investigate more oyster poaching allegations in about an hour. If we play our cards right, we should be okay."

"There are too many ifs in there."

I squeezed his arm. "There are too many ifs in life in general. Let's do this."

CHAPTER 45

I stepped out of the library and into the hallway and readied myself for the performance of a lifetime.

"I'm sorry," I cried. "I never meant to hurt you, Riley!"

"You did. I can't believe you kept this from me. How could you?" Riley leaned out of the door, his voice loud and angry.

Even as he said the words, I saw the apology in his eyes. Ruining my reputation and good name was painful for him. That was a positive sign for our authentic relationship.

"I can explain," I started.

"There's nothing to explain. You cheated on me. I can't ever forgive that."

"Please, you've got to understand—"

"Understand this: We're through. As far as I'm concerned, our marriage is null and void. Over. I'm sorry we ever came on this retreat together." He stepped back into the doorway and mouthed the words, "I'm sorry."

Doors started opening. People began to pop their heads out, curious about the commotion.

Just what we'd hoped would happen.

"You heard what Dr. Turner said, Riley." I made sure my voice contained the proper amount of desperation. It even cracked once. "We're supposed to be able to work through issues like this."

"I thought we were on the right track. But I was wrong. You cheated on me, and I can't ever forgive that."

"Do you two need to talk?" Dr. Turner appeared. A wrinkle of worry had formed between his eyebrows.

"I'm done talking." Riley slammed the door.

I wrapped my arms over my chest and frowned. Trying to make this believable, I took a step back and hid my face. I couldn't force any tears to come—I wasn't that good. But I made sure my body language showed distress.

"I can't believe this," I whispered.

"Why don't the two of us go talk, Gabby?" His hand pressed on my shoulder.

I raised my head, but kept my fingers pinched between my eyes. "I don't know if there's anything to say. I messed up, Dr. Turner. I thought things were on the right track. I thought we were in a good place, so I ventured to tell him the truth. I was wrong. Our marriage can't survive what I did."

A couple of doors closed. Good. Hopefully, everyone had heard about what happened and this humiliation wasn't all for naught.

"Maybe you need a listening ear?"

"I think I just need some time alone. But thank you." Before he could say anything else, I hurried back up to my room and shut myself inside.

Now I needed to wait a little while before I started Phase 2.

***

Just past midnight, it was time to begin the next part of my plan. I reached between my mattresses to retrieve my gun. I reached. And reached.

All I felt was the silk material covering the box spring. My hand easily glided across the empty space.

I sucked in a quick breath.

My gun was gone.

But how? And who?

I wouldn't feel nearly as safe going downstairs without it.

But what else was I supposed to do?

With a touch of hesitation, I crept from my room. I had to admit that my entire body was tight with nerves as I realized what I was about to do. So many things could go wrong.

But so many things could go right as well. If my theory was correct, the killer was waiting for an opportunity to strike again. If this person was paying attention, he or she would know I was leaving right now and would follow.

I was 99 percent certain I knew who would be confronting me tonight. I thought I knew who the killer was and the nefarious reason behind the act.

A slight tremble raked through my body as I stepped outside. Goosebumps joined the party as I hurried across the grass. By the time I reached the stairs leading to the beach, nausea joined the crowd and I felt like a mess inside.

I glanced around the dark beach but saw no one. Hesitantly, I sat on the shore. The sand was slightly damp from high tide, and the smell of the sea was even stronger than usual. Or maybe it was the fact that adrenaline heightened my senses. If I'd timed all of this correctly, the marine police should be showing up in twenty minutes because of suspected oyster poaching.

There was so much that could go wrong. But I couldn't think like that. I had to stay positive.

If everything worked out, the killer should show up any

time now. Riley hid in the shadows, as well. It felt good to know I had someone covering my back.

The minutes ticked by. What if I'd been wrong? And if this didn't work, how would I find evidence to nail the perpetrator of these crimes? I couldn't let someone get away with this.

Just then I heard a footstep behind me.

CHAPTER 46

I looked up. Just as I suspected, Dr. Turner stood there. He wore a parka instead of his usual cardigan. He had a heavy flashlight in his hands and a different aura about him. Gone was the meek next-door neighbor, and in its place was someone malicious and conniving.

"Gabby, I thought I heard someone leave." He took a step closer. "With all the accidents happening around here lately, I wanted to make sure you were okay. It's dangerous out here, you know."

I nodded. "I realize that. Especially with all the tragedies here on this island."

He sat beside me. *Mr. Rogers Goes to the Beach.*

It didn't seem nearly as entertaining now as it had earlier.

A moment of silence fell as we both stared out at the water lapping the shoreline. I waited for him to make his next move. I had to remember to keep a cool head. It could mean the difference between life and death.

"Gabby, I realize you're going through a hard time," Dr. Turner finally said, his voice compassionate and concerned. "But it's no reason to want to end your life."

I swallowed hard, his words causing an eerie chill to wash over me. "I wasn't thinking of ending my life." My voice sounded gravely solemn. I didn't take things like ending my life lightly.

"Anyone in your state would consider it. Your marriage is falling apart. You've made mistakes that your husband will never forgive you for."

My muscles tightened even more as his words taunted me. Then I remembered I was playing a role here. I couldn't lash out and say the things I wanted. Not yet.

"I don't know that." My voice sounded melancholy. "I'm still hopeful that things will work out between Riley and me. Don't you think they will?"

"You don't deserve to be with Riley, Gabby. I'm sorry to tell you that, but I'd be doing an injustice if I didn't speak the truth."

My stomach lurched. Probably because what he said had echoed my own sentiments so many times in the past. But not anymore.

"What do you mean?" I stole a glance at Dr. Turner. His eyes looked intense and almost eager, which only made my instincts even more alert.

"Men want respect," Dr. Turner continued. "When a wife betrays her marriage vows, the husband will never again feel respected. God's design for marriage is that the two become one . . . but cheating puts a crack in the unity. A crack that can't be repaired."

I pulled my knees closer to my chest, wiping some stray sand granules from my hands. This whole conversation was disturbing on so many levels. "But I thought marriage was a matter of changing and forgiving and growing. Isn't that what you said?"

"It's different in this case. There's no undoing what you've done." A new gleam glistened in his eyes. "It was with Garrett, wasn't it? He's the man you cheated on Riley with."

"What?" His words truly shocked me. How had he remembered Garrett? How had he known exactly where to throw his sucker punch?

"Riley mentioned him once. Was he the man you cheated with?"

I wanted to say no, but then I remembered my ruse. My heart panged as I responded with, "Yes. He was."

"You know what the Bible says about adultery, right?" Dr. Turner said.

"That it's wrong." I swallowed hard again and continued to stare at the mesmerizing water. At the moment, I halfway wished it would swallow me up just so I could avoid this conversation.

And was Riley close enough to hear? If so, what was he thinking? Was Dr. Turner putting thoughts in his head and making him regret the rekindling of our relationship?

"The Bible says that adultery is punishable by death." His words were hard and unyielding. Dr. Turner believed what he was saying. He was convinced that his judgment was correct. "Hebrews 13:4 says God will judge the sexually immoral and adulterous. John 8:5 reminds us Moses commanded the stoning of such women. Proverbs 5:3 and 5, "For the lips of the adulterous woman drip honey . . . Her feet go down to death; her steps lead straight to the grave."

A chill rushed through me. "There are a lot of verses you left out. Jesus forgave. He commanded adulterers to leave their lives of sin. He commands that of all of us. Besides, there's always hope for redemption. That's the entire gospel message." I believed that. I had to believe that. Without that truth, then there'd be no hope for my life. Or anyone else's, for that matter. That was the reason that Christ had died for my sins.

Dr. Turner squeezed the flashlight in his hands, his jaw

clenched. "There are some sins that are abominations in the Lord's eyes. There are some things you can never undo. Gabby, no one would fault you for wanting to end your life because of this. They'd understand what drove you to do it."

I sucked in a deep breath. He really was implying what I'd thought: He wanted me to end my own life. The outrage in my voice was real. I couldn't hold it back any more. "To do what? I'm just sitting on the seashore reflecting on life. I'm not going to kill myself over some guy."

He turned toward me, his nostrils flaring. I stared at the flashlight in his hands, wondering what it would feel like if he banged it over my head. How could I protect myself? I had to be on guard here.

"He's not just some guy." Dr. Turner stared at me, bitterness in his eyes. The man was losing it, and I was going to be here to experience it. "He's your husband."

"No one's worth ending my life over." My words left no room for doubt.

"The guilt you're going to carry for the rest of your life is going to be overwhelming, too heavy of a burden."

"I can overcome anything through Christ. Right? That's what I read in the Bible." He was starting to mess with my head. I wasn't expecting this. I was expecting a direct assault.

"You don't want to live in disfavor with God. It's no way to live. No way to live at all, Gabby."

"You must know God differently than I do because I believe that God loves me despite my sin. That he loved me enough to die for me and take away the punishment I deserve."

"Don't fool yourself, Gabby. No one will be surprised if you sleepwalk right into these waters. There will be no shame in that. It will look like an accident." He pointed toward the dark water before making his fingers imitate me walking toward my death.

I'd had enough of this.

"Is this what you did to Anna? You convinced her to swallow those pills?" I hadn't planned on saying that, but I was starting to feel cross-eyed with his double-talk and innuendo.

Dr. Turner knew how to mess with people's heads, and that was a dangerous skill to possess. In fact, that must have been how he'd killed the other women. He'd been able to read their weaknesses and use those traits against them. That's why I knew I would survive tonight—as long as I could remain in control of my thoughts.

Something changed in his gaze. There was a spark of realization there. Either that, or the man was coming undone. "I don't know what you're talking about."

"Or how about Ginger? Did you try to convince her to end her life, but when it didn't work you pushed her off that bluff?"

"That would be crazy. No sane person would do that." His voice practically sounded like a growl now. "Besides, I wasn't here that night."

"But you were. You came back early. In fact, I'd bet there was no meeting. You just needed an alibi."

He smiled, but his eyes looked empty. "Nice theory. You can't prove it."

Mr. Rogers Stars in a Horror Movie.

"Then how about Khloe Wescott? I know she had a heart attack, but I'd even venture to say you gave her some pills. Maybe to relax her? You have our medical history so you must have known she'd have a reaction to whatever was in those pills. You probably encouraged her to take them, and now you think your hands are clean. You prey on women using the power of suggestion. It's a deadly trait to have, and you've mastered it."

"You've done some homework, haven't you?" He sneered. "But I would never purposefully hurt someone."

As his hands tightened on the flashlight again, I stood. "But you would. You're bitter about your wife's death. You're even more bitter about the fact that she had an affair. So now you're trying to punish any woman who's cheated on her husband?"

Something changed in his eyes at that moment. I'd struck a nerve. I knew I was getting closer and closer to the truth. With any luck, I was turning the tables on him.

"I loved her. I dedicated my life to her, and what did I get in return? Her unfaithfulness. She said I worked too much. That I cared more about other people's marriages than I cared about my own." He shook his head, his emotions bubbling to the surface. "She didn't understand me. If the news of what she'd done had gotten out, I would be ruined. Ruined."

"What she did was wrong. But you don't have to punish everyone else because of what your wife did."

"But I do! Women have to be punished for their indiscretions." His nostrils flared, and I knew I was getting to him.

"But not men?"

He slowly rose to his feet. Wearing that dark parka, he'd be hard to spot out here. Had he planned it that way? "The Bible speaks of a woman's unfaithfulness. It's punishable by death."

"Don't you remember what Jesus said to the adulterous woman?" I countered.

"Adultery is punishable by stoning," Dr. Turner continued.

"I'm not justifying unfaithfulness, but in the words of

Jesus, 'Let any one of you who is without sin be the first to throw a stone.'"

"You're going to walk into the water, Gabby." He pulled a gun from his jacket pocket. "I was hoping to do this the easy way, but I can see that won't be happening."

CHAPTER 47

I shook my head and took a step back. "I'm not walking into the water. You can shoot me. Then everyone will know what kind of person you really are. You won't be able to deny your involvement when they find out I've been shot."

"People will realize that you were the one who provoked this. This is your gun, Gabby."

I sucked in a deep breath, my eyes skittering down to the weapon in his hands. Sure enough, that was mine, a 9 mm Smith and Wesson I'd purchased after my ordeal with Scum. In all of my planning and calculating, I hadn't anticipated this. It was a game changer.

"How did you get my gun?"

He smirked, no longer seeming like the meek therapist I'd once thought he was. "I'm not as naïve as you might think. I know you came here to snoop around. I figured that out after your first weekend here."

He'd figured that out? I'd thought I was a better actor than that. But Dr. Turner was programmed to read people. That made him even more dangerous than your common criminal.

"But that doesn't explain how you got my gun."

"Blaine found it. She has a little problem with kleptomania, among other things. I've been working with her."

She must have been the one who took my necklace. And Steve's knives. And Anna's letter. "I thought she was obsessive . . ."

"That too. She's also very resourceful. There were multiple reasons I hired her. Besides, she owes me. Emotional leverage is always a powerful asset."

I had a feeling she was the one who'd been following me. Probably the one who'd stolen the list from my van. Obsessive, with sticky fingers, and unusually dedicated to Dr. Turner. It all made sense.

"Now let's get this over with," Dr. Turner said.

"Dr. Turner, put the gun down." Riley stepped from the shadows. "This is over. The police are on their way."

The doctor sighed. "I really didn't want to have to hurt two people. But murder-suicide it will be. The two of you set this all up for me this evening so very well with that argument in the hallway."

His words were true, weren't they? We had given him the perfect excuse if he went through with this. The man was smarter than I'd given him credit for.

"You'll never get away with it," I told him, casting a fleeting glance at Riley. He stood on the other side of Dr. Turner. We were too far away to truly protect each other. I prayed this whole situation turned out okay. I had a deep-seated fear that one day life wouldn't. That my carefully—or not so carefully—planned move would backfire. "You should just give up now."

Dr. Turner chuckled.

He was losing it, I realized. Maybe his head had never quite been screwed on straight. Just like mechanics had broken-down cars, landscapers had terrible lawns, and crime-scene cleaners had messy houses, maybe therapists also had messed-up mental states.

"But I have a plan. Don't you see?" Dr. Turner asked.

I looked at Riley again, desperately wishing we were closer. "Apparently, we don't."

"Well, you will soon enough."

What did that mean? I wasn't sure I wanted to find out. Where were the police? They were an extremely important part of this equation, especially now that Dr. Turner had a gun.

"So you were the one who went through my suitcase, who put a hole in that kayak—even though that was meant for Ginger. You probably even tampered with the throttle on Blaine's boat."

"She wasn't supposed to be aboard. That was intended for Leroy. I couldn't have him running illegal operations from the island."

"Why did Anna have two suicide notes?"

He let out a cackle. "One was part of a lesson we did here at the retreat. She was taking it with her, and she was going to leave the island. But I caught her before she could. I didn't know she'd stashed that letter in a kayak. I would have removed it, of course. Before that, I'd convinced her to write another letter."

"Convinced her?"

He nodded. "That's right. We talked through all her problems, and she finally saw things my way. She even put the pills in her mouth and swallowed. So you see, I'm not really guilty of anything."

"Except knowing how to manipulate people. It's almost like mind control. I may have even fallen for the power of suggestion a few times since I've come here. Nevermore, though." Yes, I'd found inspiration through Edgar Allan Poe.

"As people think, they do. Thoughts can be very powerful."

"Did you convince Ginger to jump off the cliff?"

"She was convinced I was going to push her. So she did it herself. Again, it wasn't my fault. It was all in her mind. But she needed to pay for what she'd done to Jim and Jill Wagnor."

"What about what Jim Wagnor did?"

"Ginger committed the ultimate disrespect to marriage." Dr. Turner shook his head. "You're clever, Gabby. I always knew you were. I could see it in your gaze that you were different than most people I've encountered. Too smart for your own good."

Just then I saw movement behind Riley. My eyes widened. It was Blaine!

And she was carrying a baseball bat.

"Riley, watch out!" As I started to lunge toward him, the gun fired. Fire ripped through my arm. But I kept moving.

I didn't need to, apparently,

Riley whirled around and grabbed the bat before Blaine could clobber him. He twisted it in her hands until she yelped and released it. Then he shoved Blaine to the ground and rushed toward Dr. Turner.

We reached him at the same time.

Riley grabbed his hands and pointed his gun upward just as it discharged again.

My heart lurched with fear.

Please say Riley wasn't shot. My heart can't handle that trauma again.

CHAPTER 48

I held my breath, waiting to understand and comprehend what had just happened. The next instant, Riley had Dr. Turner's hands pinched behind his back. Riley's other arm was tightly slung across the doctor's chest, holding him in place.

Where had Riley learned those moves?

It didn't matter. What mattered was that he was okay! He was okay!

"You're bleeding, Gabby." Riley nodded toward my arm.

I glanced down. Sure enough, that bullet had skimmed my arm. The wound stung, but I'd been through worse. A few inches difference would have brought me to my knees.

"It's just a flesh wound." I tried to keep my British *Monty Python* accent at bay.

"Gabby, behind you!" Riley yelled.

I turned in time to see Blaine charging toward me, a crazy look in her eyes. I grabbed the bat at my feet and swung it. The wood connected with her knees, and she yelped with pain before falling to the ground.

I halfway wanted to apologize because I knew that had to hurt. But she'd been ready to kill me. I'd been forced to take action.

She sneered at me from the ground. "I was on to you. I knew what you were doing. I tried to warn Dr. Turner."

"You were following me," I said.

"I found that list you made. I knew I had to take it as proof. You were going to ruin Dr. Turner's reputation."

"I think he did a good job doing that himself."

She sneered again. "He's a miracle worker."

"If by miracle worker you mean serial killer, then yes."

She narrowed her eyes. "You don't know what you're talking about."

"What I don't understand is how you ended up locked in that shed with cuts on your arms," I said, watching her carefully. "I'm guessing you were trying to steal something, although I can't imagine what."

At that moment, someone else appeared at the top of the stairs. Steve. He held a camera in his hands. "I've got documentation of all of this. There's no way Dr. Turner or Blaine will get away with this. And I was the one who locked Blaine in that shed."

"You're also the one who reported her missing," I said. "Why would you do both?"

"I knew she was behind the thefts here on the island. When I saw her in the shed about to steal some of the copper wire that had been left in there after upgrades, I wanted her to get caught red-handed. That's why I trapped her inside."

"So you were trying to put that wire in your pockets, and it ended up scratching you. But I didn't see any wire on you when I found you."

"I hid the wire, but when I went back to get it later, it was gone." Her fingers clawed the sand like a cat about to pounce.

Steve stood behind her now, the camera still strapped around her neck. "When I realized my plan didn't work, I went back and took the wire. It was the only satisfaction I could get out of any of this."

"Tell me one more thing," I said. "Did Dr. Turner kill his own wife?"

Surprise flashed in Blaine's gaze. "What?"

"That hit-and-run? They never did catch whoever was behind the wheel. But since Dr. Turner thinks adulterous women should be put to death, maybe she was his first kill."

In one last burst of strength, Blaine sprang at me. I jumped back before she could reach me, fearing another struggle might ensue. Before she could take it any further, Steve grabbed her and held her in place.

Behind us, lights filled the air. "Police. Everyone, put your hands up!"

***

As the police led Dr. Turner away in handcuffs, he looked back at us and smirked. "You two think you're so clever."

A medic attended to my wound under the bright police lights. "Not clever," I told him. "Just determined."

He stopped, despite his police escort. "Well, let this fact sink in. You two are married now."

I nearly snorted except the sting of getting stitches hurt too much. "No, we're not."

His eyes widened as he tried to drive home his point. "Remember, I'm licensed to perform marriages. At the vow renewal you stood before God and pledged forever to each other. Have fun."

I looked at Riley, and my lips parted with surprise. "That's not true, right?"

He looked equally as perplexed. "No, of course not."

But we both still froze, staring at each other uncertainly.

"I mean, legally, we're not married," I said as the medic put a bandage on my arm.

"But we did kind of take a vow before God, didn't we?"

I loved Riley. I knew I did. But was I really married to him after that ceremony? I didn't know what to think about that.

Apparently, Riley didn't either.

"Maybe we should take some time to think about that. Talk to Pastor Randy."

I nodded. "Good idea."

Because of all the ways I'd seen myself getting married, this was not one of them.

Before I could think about it too long, my phone rang. My phone! I'd found the magic reception spot—only it was too late.

Chad's number appeared on the screen.

"Gabby, we're going to the hospital." His voice contained an excitement unlike any I'd ever heard from him. "Sierra's in labor!"

"What? Already? Is she okay?" The questions rushed from my lips unchecked.

"She's fine. The doctor doesn't seem to be worried."

I heard Sierra yell something indiscernible in the background. The sound clearly indicated she was in pain.

Oh my. My friend was in labor. In labor!

"I've got to go," Chad rushed. "Pray for us!"

I turned toward Riley, hardly able to breath. Sierra was the closest thing I'd ever had to a sister. She felt like family to me, and I couldn't be more excited for her now. "Sierra's having her baby. We've got to get home!"

***

Riley and I had been questioned by the police for most of the night. As much as I wanted to be with Sierra, that didn't happen until the next morning. I barely had time to shower before we left the island.

I couldn't help but think about Dr. Turner's proclamation that Riley and I really were married as we headed toward home.

I didn't let myself think about that one too long. No, no, no. I couldn't let myself go there.

Instead, I thought about Riley. I thought about the way he'd tackled Dr. Turner last night—and he'd done it with confidence and skill.

"You were no joke last night. You've got some nice moves."

The muscle in his jaw flexed. "I never want to be defenseless again. I mean, I know it could happen—"

"There was nothing you could have done to stop that man from shooting you, Riley. He walked in and pulled the trigger. No one would have had time to react." I hadn't truly realized just how much that experience had affected Riley. I'd thought I understood. But seeing the long-term effects put everything into a new perspective.

He nodded. "I know that. But I want to do everything in my power to protect myself and the people I love in the future."

My face warmed. Was he talking about me? Could he still love me?

I reached across the car and took his hand. It felt so good to feel his fingers wrapped around mine.

"I've missed you, Gabby."

I smiled. "I've missed you too."

As soon as I said the words, my thoughts went back to

what Dr. Turner had said.

You two are married now.

I mentally shook my head. He was wrong. We were just playing parts. There was no way we were really married in God's sight. The idea was ludicrous.

"You're thinking about what Dr. Turner said, aren't you?" Riley asked.

"How'd you know?" We pulled into a parking space at the hospital.

"Because I've been thinking about it also."

I shifted in my seat so I could better face him. "What do you think, Riley? Was he just trying to mess with our heads some more?"

"Maybe. But maybe not. The more I think about it, the more I can see it both ways. We did take a vow. Even if we were officially using assumed identities."

"Maybe we can tell God it was a mistake." I climbed out and started toward the entrance, but the conversation kept going.

"But was it?"

Riley's question caused my heart to squeeze with emotion. Was he implying what I thought he was? That wasn't something I could let slip by. I had to know.

"You mean, you're toying with the idea that it was real? And that . . ."

He shook his head. "I don't know. I've wanted to marry you for a long time, Gabby. But I envisioned it happening at church with family and friends around. Not by accident."

My heart raced ahead of my logic. "Really?"

"Yes, really." He smiled and squeezed my hand. "Am I being too honest? I'm not trying to scare you."

"No. I like it. Please, be honest more."

He rubbed my hand with his thumb. "We shouldn't be rash here. Let's think about this, pray about this."

"Thinking and praying about it won't change the reality if we took vows before a minister—even if he turned out to be a psychopath. Either it happened or it didn't."

"But there's no marriage license." He shook his head. "We'll talk to Pastor Randy. We'll get this figured out, one way or another."

We found Sierra's room. When we walked in, my friend was holding a baby in her arms. My heart bounced at the sight. She was glowing. Absolutely glowing.

"Gabby. Riley. You made it."

I rushed to her bedside and stared at the gorgeous newborn cuddled to her chest. "How beautiful," I whispered.

Something inside me twisted, and an unknown emotion stirred. Could there actually be a part of me that desired to be a mom? To have a baby of my own?

The thought was so foreign. Despite that, my throat ached for a moment.

"Meet Thaddeus Reef Davis. We'll call him Reef," Chad said. "What do you think?"

"A little boy? Oh." My hand flew over my heart. I would have had the same reaction if the baby had been a girl. "He's just perfect. And I love the name. Thaddeus?"

"I had a little brother who was stillborn. His name was Thaddeus."

"That's precious, Chad."

"Do you want to hold him?" Sierra asked.

"Can I?" A flutter of nervousness claimed my stomach. I wasn't sure I'd ever held a baby this young, and I wasn't confident in my abilities.

"Of course, Aunt Gabby."

I grinned. "That has a nice ring to it."

While I washed my hands, Chad scooped up the baby like he'd done it a million times before. I sat in a rocker by the window, and Chad placed the little bundle in my arm. My insides melted when I saw the baby's sweet face. "Reef. You're going to be one loved baby."

Reef closed his eyes and cuddled up to me. I was toast. I knew it already. Aunt Gabby was going to spoil this baby.

Riley appeared behind me and put his hand on my shoulder. That action was enough to draw Sierra's eyes away from her baby for a moment.

"I knew it!" Her eyes were wide and her voice full of emotion.

I practiced mock cluelessness. "Knew what?"

"That the two of you would get back together. I was just waiting for it."

"He just put his hand on my shoulder. It doesn't mean necessarily that we're back together."

"But you are. Aren't you?"

I looked up at Riley and smiled. I couldn't deny it. My heart was bursting with joy. "Yeah, you could say that."

She narrowed her eyes. "What's that mean? There's something you're not telling me."

I shrugged nonchalantly. "We may have accidentally gotten married. We're still trying to work out those details."

"Oh, you've got some talking to do."

"We'll have plenty of time for that here in the next few weeks." I looked down at Reef and smiled again. "It seems like we all have a lot to celebrate."

CHAPTER 49

"So, let me get this straight," Pastor Randy said. "You fear you unintentionally got married?"

Riley and I exchanged a glance. We sat on the couch in his apartment, coffee in hand, and our pastor seated across from us. We'd had a week to think about everything that had happened on Bird's Nest Island, and neither of us had come to any firm conclusions.

Other things had happened during the week, though. For example, the investigation into Dr. Turner's wife had been reopened. And Farrah had texted me and let me know she and Atticus were actually going to give their marriage another chance. She said if Riley and I could risk our lives to do the right thing, the two of them could give their marriage all they had.

"'Fear we got married' would be putting it strongly," Riley said. "We just need some clarity. We know we're not legally married. But are we married in God's eyes?"

Pastor Randy—who looked just like Shaggy from Scooby Doo—leaned toward us with his elbows perched on his knees. He had a look of deep thought on his face. "Well, when you marry before God generally you need an ordained minister."

"We had that," I added.

Pastor Randy nodded slowly. "You recite vows, pledging to spend the rest of your lives together."

"We did that too, I suppose," Riley said.

The unease in my gut grew. It wasn't that the thought of marrying Riley was terrible. I just didn't want to do it accidentally.

"And you promise God that you'll do whatever it takes to make it work," Pastor Randy continued.

"That sounds like what we did. But we weren't sincere. We were in character . . . right?" I glanced at Riley, waiting for his confirmation.

"But were you really in character, Gabby?" Pastor Randy asked.

His question stunned me and actually left me speechless for a moment. "Of course. I mean, yes. We were undercover."

"There was no part of you that meant the words?"

I raised my hand, silently pleading for him to stop. "I don't know what to say."

"Marriage was ordained by God long before our government was ever in place with its laws. For many, many years, people were married, and there was no such thing as a license."

"That's true," I conceded.

"What's more important? A piece of paper that makes it legal under the law or promises you made before God?"

I guess I could see his point.

"Ultimately, this is between the two of you and God," the pastor continued. "God knows your hearts, and He's the one you have to answer to."

I shook my head, surprised by his answer. I didn't know what to say or think.

Riley reached over and squeezed my hand. "It sounds like we have some soul searching and praying to do."

His words brought me a certain comfort. I nodded.

"You're right. God and I need to talk about this one."

"May I add something . . . as a friend?" Pastor Randy asked, sitting up slightly.

"Of course," Riley said.

"It's obvious the two of you love each other. You have for a long time. You were once engaged. Maybe your marriage isn't official . . . but maybe you should make it official."

My mouth dropped open. "You mean . . ."

"You think we should . . ." Riley seemed unable to continue.

Pastor Randy smiled. "Just a thought. I think the two of you could be happy together. Really happy. I'd venture to say that there's a part of you both that liked the idea of accidentally getting married."

I thought about it and shrugged sheepishly. "Maybe."

Riley glanced at me, his eyes warm. "I'd be lying if I denied it."

"It would be really easy to make this no-doubt-about-it official. Pray about it. And, until then, just to be safe, I wouldn't date anyone else."

I shrugged. "I don't want to date anyone else."

"Me neither."

Pastor Randy smiled. "Then maybe the two of you have your answer."

My heart warmed. Maybe we did.

"I say we do it right, though," Riley said. "In fact, I might even have a song for this."

I raised my eyebrows. "A song? Do tell."

He began singing "Nothing's Gonna Stop Us Now," even holding an imaginary microphone in his hand.

I burst into laughter. I'd trained him well.

When the lyrics faded from his lips, he stepped toward

me. "I love you, Gabby St. Claire."

"I love you too, Riley."

With that final proclamation, his lips covered mine.

###

Now available:

If you enjoyed this book, you may also enjoy these other Squeaky Clean Mysteries:

Hazardous Duty (Book 1)

On her way to completing a degree in forensic science, Gabby St. Claire drops out of school and starts her own crime-scene cleaning business. When a routine cleaning job uncovers a murder weapon the police overlooked, she realizes that the wrong person is in jail. But the owner of the weapon is a powerful foe . . . and willing to do anything to keep Gabby quiet. With the help of her new neighbor, Riley Thomas, a man whose life and faith fascinate her, Gabby seeks to find the killer before another murder occurs.

Suspicious Minds (Book 2)

In this smart and suspenseful sequel to *Hazardous Duty*, crime-scene cleaner Gabby St. Claire finds herself stuck doing mold remediation to pay the bills. Her first day on the job, she uncovers a surprise in the crawlspace of a dilapidated home: Elvis, dead as a doornail and still wearing his blue-suede shoes. How could she possibly keep her nose out of a case like this?

It Came Upon a Midnight Crime (Book 2.5, a Novella)

Someone is intent on destroying the true meaning of Christmas—at least, destroying anything that hints of it. All around crime-scene cleaner Gabby St. Claire's hometown, anything pointing to Jesus as "the reason for the season" is being sabotaged. The crimes become more twisted as dismembered body parts are found at the vandalisms. Someone is determined to destroy Christmas . . . but Gabby is just as determined to find the Grinch and let peace on earth and goodwill prevail.

Organized Grime (Book 3)
Gabby St. Claire knows her best friend, Sierra, isn't guilty of killing three people in what appears to be an eco-terrorist attack. But Sierra has disappeared, her only contact a frantic phone call to Gabby proclaiming she's being hunted. Gabby is determined to prove her friend is innocent and to keep Sierra alive. While trying to track down the real perpetrator, Gabby notices a disturbing trend at the crime scenes she's cleaning, one that ties random crimes together—and points to Sierra as the guilty party. Just what has her friend gotten herself involved in?

Dirty Deeds (Book 4)
"Promise me one thing. No snooping. Just for one week."

Gabby St. Claire knows her fiancé's request is a simple one she should be able to honor. After all, Riley's law school reunion and attorneys' conference at a posh resort is a chance for them to get away from the mysteries Gabby often finds herself involved in as a crime-scene cleaner. Then an old friend of Riley's goes missing. Gabby suspects one of Riley's buddies might be behind the disappearance. When the missing woman's mom asks Gabby for help, how can she say no?

The Scum of All Fears (Book 5)
Gabby St. Claire is back to crime-scene cleaning and needs help after a weekend killing spree fills her work docket. A serial killer her fiancé put behind bars has escaped. His last words to Riley

were: *I'll get out, and I'll get even*. Pictures of Gabby are found in the man's prison cell; messages are left for Gabby at crime scenes; someone keeps slipping in and out of her apartment; and her temporary assistant disappears. The search for answers becomes darker when Gabby realizes she's dealing with a criminal who is truly the scum of the earth. He will do anything to make Gabby and Riley's lives a living nightmare.

To Love, Honor, and Perish (Book 6)
Just when Gabby St. Claire's life is on the right track, the unthinkable happens. Her fiancé, Riley Thomas, is shot and in life-threatening condition only a week before their wedding. Gabby is determined to figure out who pulled the trigger, even if investigating puts her own life at risk. As she digs deeper into the case, she discovers secrets better left alone. Doubts arise in her mind, and the one man with answers lies on death's doorstep. Then an old foe returns and tests everything Gabby is made of—physically, mentally, and spiritually. Will all she's worked for be destroyed?

Mucky Streak (Book 7)
Gabby St. Claire feels her life is smeared with the stain of tragedy. She takes a short-term gig as a private investigator—a cold case that's eluded detectives for ten years. The mass murder of a wealthy family seems impossible to solve, but Gabby brings more clues to light. Add to the mix a flirtatious client, travels to an exciting new city, and some quirky—albeit temporary—new sidekicks, and things get complicated. With every new development, Gabby prays that her "mucky streak" will end and the future will become clear. Yet every answer she uncovers leads her closer to danger—both for her life and for her heart.

CHRISTY BARRITT

Foul Play (Book 8)

Gabby St. Claire is crying "foul play" in every sense of the
phrase. When the crime-scene cleaner agrees to go undercover
at a local community theater, she discovers more than
backstage bickering, atrocious acting, and rotten writing. The
female lead is dead, and an old classmate who's staked
everything on the musical production's success is about to go
under. In her dual role of investigator and star of the show,
Gabby finds the stakes rising faster than the opening-night
curtain. She must face her past and make monumental
decisions, not just about the play but also concerning her future
relationships and career. Will Gabby find the killer before the
curtain goes down—not only on the play, but also on life as she
knows it?

Broom and Gloom (Book 9)

Gabby St. Claire is determined to get back in the saddle again.
While in Oklahoma for a forensic conference, she meets her
soon-to-be stepbrother, Trace Ryan, an up-and-coming country
singer. A woman he was dating has disappeared, and he
suspects a crazy fan may be behind it. Gabby agrees to
investigate, as she tries to juggle her conference, navigate being
alone in a new place, and locate a woman who may not want to
be found. She discovers that sometimes taking life by the horns
means staring danger in the face, no matter the consequences.

Thrill Squeaker (Book 11)

An abandoned theme park. An unsolved murder. A decision that
will change Gabby's life forever. Restoring an old amusement
park and turning it into a destination resort seems like a fun
idea for former crime-scene cleaner Gabby St. Claire. The side

job gives her the chance to spend time with her friends, something she's missed since beginning a new career. The job turns out to be more than Gabby bargained for when she finds a dead body on her first day. Add to the mix legends of Bigfoot, creepy clowns, and ghostlike remnants of happier times at the park, and her stay begins to feel like a rollercoaster ride. Someone doesn't want the decrepit Mythical Falls to open again, but just how far is this person willing to go to ensure this venture fails? As the stakes rise and danger creeps closer, will Gabby be able to restore things in her own life that time has destroyed—including broken relationships? Or is her future closer to the fate of the doomed Mythical Falls?

Swept Away, a Honeymoon Novella (Book 11.5)

Finding the perfect place for a honeymoon, away from any potential danger or mystery, is challenging. But Gabby's longtime love and newly minted husband, Riley Thomas, has done it. He has found a location with a nonexistent crime rate, a mostly retired population, and plenty of opportunities for relaxation in the warm sun. Within minutes of the newlyweds' arrival, a convoy of vehicles pulls up to a nearby house, and their honeymoon oasis is destroyed like a sandcastle in a storm. Despite Gabby's and Riley's determination to keep to themselves, trouble comes knocking at their door—literally— when a neighbor is abducted from the beach directly outside their rental. Will Gabby and Riley be swept away with each other during their honeymoon . . . or will a tide of danger and mayhem pull them under?

Cunning Attractions (Book 12)

Coming soon

While You Were Sweeping, a Riley Thomas Novella
Riley Thomas is trying to come to terms with life after a
traumatic brain injury turned his world upside down. Away from
everything familiar—including his crime-scene-cleaning former
fiancée and his career as a social-rights attorney—he's
determined to prove himself and regain his old life. But when he
claims he witnessed his neighbor shoot and kill someone,
everyone thinks he's crazy. When all evidence of the crime
disappears, even Riley has to wonder if he's losing his mind.

Note: *While You Were Sweeping* is a spin-off mystery written in
conjunction with the Squeaky Clean series featuring crime-
scene cleaner Gabby St. Claire.

The Gabby St. Claire Diaries

a tween mystery series

The Curtain Call Caper (Book 1)

Is a ghost haunting the Oceanside Middle School auditorium? What else could explain the disasters surrounding the play— everything from missing scripts to a falling spotlight and damaged props? Seventh-grader Gabby St. Claire has dreamed about being part of her school's musical, but a series of unfortunate events threatens to shut down the production. Will Gabby figure out who or what is sabotaging the show . . . or will it be curtains for her and the rest of the cast?

The Disappearing Dog Dilemma (Book 2)

Why are dogs disappearing around town? When two friends ask seventh-grader Gabby St. Claire for her help in finding their missing canines, Gabby decides to unleash her sleuthing skills to sniff out whoever is behind the act. But time management and relationships get tricky as worrisome weather, a part-time job, and a new crush interfere with Gabby's investigation. Will her determination crack the case? Or will shadowy villains, a penchant for overcommitting, and even her own heart put her in the doghouse?

The Bungled Bike Burglaries (Book 3)

Stolen bikes and a long-forgotten time capsule leave one amateur sleuth baffled and busy. Seventh-grader Gabby St. Claire is determined to bring a bike burglar to justice—and not just because mean girl Donabell Bullock is strong-arming her. But each new clue brings its own set of troubles. As if that's not enough, Gabby finds evidence of a decades-old murder within the contents of the time capsule, but no one seems to take her seriously. As her investigation heats up, will Gabby's knack for being in the wrong place at the wrong time with the wrong people crack the case? Or will it prove hazardous to her health?

The Sierra Files

Pounced (Book 1)
Animal-rights activist Sierra Nakamura never expected to stumble upon the dead body of a coworker while filming a project nor get involved in the investigation. But when someone threatens to kill her cats unless she hands over the "information," she becomes more bristly than an angry feline. With every answer she uncovers, old hurts rise to the surface and test her beliefs. Saving her cats might mean ruining everything else in her life. In the fight for survival, one thing is certain: Either pounce or be pounced.

Hunted (Book 2)
Who knew a stray dog could cause so much trouble? Newlywed animal-rights activist Sierra Nakamura Davis must face her worst nightmare: breaking the news she eloped to her ultra-opinionated tiger mom. Her perfectionist parents have planned a vow-renewal ceremony at Sierra's lush childhood home, but a neighborhood dog ruins the rehearsal dinner when he shows up toting what appears to be a fresh human bone. While dealing with the dog, a nosy neighbor, and an old flame turning up at the wrong times, Sierra hunts for answers. Her journey of discovery leads to more than just who committed the crime.

Pranced (Book 2.5, a Christmas novella)
Sierra Nakamura Davis thinks spending Christmas with her husband's relatives will be a real Yuletide treat. But when the animal-rights activist learns his family has a reindeer farm, she begins to feel more like the Grinch. Even worse, when Sierra arrives, she discovers the reindeer are missing. Sierra fears the animals might be suffering a worse fate than being used for

entertainment purposes. Can Sierra set aside her dogmatic opinions to help get the reindeer home in time for the holidays? Or will secrets tear the family apart and ruin Sierra's dream of the perfect Christmas?

Rattled (Book 3)

"What do you mean a thirteen-foot lavender albino ball python is missing?" Tough-as-nails Sierra Nakamura Davis isn't one to get flustered. But trying to balance being a wife and a new mom with her crusade to help animals is proving harder than she imagined. Add a missing python, a high maintenance intern, and a dead body to the mix, and Sierra becomes the definition of rattled. Can she balance it all—and solve a possible murder— without losing her mind?

Holly Anna Paladin Mysteries

Random Acts of Murder (Book 1)
When Holly Anna Paladin is given a year to live, she embraces her final days doing what she loves most—random acts of kindness. But one of her extreme good deeds goes horribly wrong, implicating her in a string of murders. Holly is suddenly thrust into a different kind of fight for her life. Could it also be random that the detective assigned to the case is her old high school crush and present-day nemesis? Will Holly find the killer before he ruins what is left of her life? Or will she spend her final days alone and behind bars?

Random Acts of Deceit (Book 2)
"Break up with Chase Dexter, or I'll kill him." Holly Anna Paladin never expected such a gut-wrenching ultimatum. With home invasions, hidden cameras, and bomb threats, Holly must make some serious choices. Whatever she decides, the consequences will either break her heart or break her soul. She tries to match wits with the Shadow Man, but the more she fights, the deeper she's drawn into the perilous situation. With her sister's wedding problems and the riots in the city, Holly has nearly reached the breaking point. She must stop this mystery man before someone she loves dies. But the deceit is threatening to pull her under . . . six feet under.

Random Acts of Malice (Book 3)
When Holly Anna Paladin's boyfriend, police detective Chase Dexter, says he's leaving for two weeks and can't give any details, she wants to trust him. But when she discovers Chase may be involved in some unwise and dangerous pursuits, she's compelled to intervene. Holly gets a run for her money as she's

swept into the world of horseracing. The stakes turn deadly when a dead body surfaces and suspicion is cast on Chase. At every turn, more trouble emerges, making Holly question what she holds true about her relationship and her future. Just when she thinks she's on the homestretch, a dark horse arises. Holly might lose everything in a nail-biting fight to the finish.

Random Acts of Scrooge (Book 3.5)
Christmas is supposed to be the most wonderful time of the year, but a real-life Scrooge is threatening to ruin the season's good will. Holly Anna Paladin can't wait to celebrate Christmas with family and friends. She loves everything about the season—celebrating the birth of Jesus, singing carols, and baking Christmas treats, just to name a few. But when a local family needs help, how can she say no? Holly's community has come together to help raise funds to save the home of Greg and Babette Sullivan, but a Bah-Humburgler has snatched the canisters of cash. Holly and her boyfriend, police detective Chase Dexter, team up to catch the Christmas crook. Will they succeed in collecting enough cash to cover the Sullivans' overdue bills? Or will someone succeed in ruining Christmas for all those involved?

Random Acts of Guilt (Book 4)
Help me. Don't trust anyone. Do-gooder Holly Anna Paladin can't believe her eyes when a healthy baby boy is left on her doorstep. What seems like good fortune quickly turns into concern when blood spatter is found on the bottom of the baby carrier. Something tragic—maybe deadly—happened in connection with the infant. The note left only adds to the confusion. What does it mean by "Don't trust anyone"? Holly is determined to figure out the identity of the baby. Is his mom

someone from the inner-city youth center where she volunteers? Or maybe the connection is through Holly's former job as a social worker? Even worse—what if the blood belongs to the baby's mom? Every answer Holly uncovers only leads to more questions. A sticky web of intrigue captures her imagination until she's sure of only one thing: she must protect the baby at all cost.

Carolina Moon Series:

Home Before Dark (Book 1)

Nothing good ever happens after dark. Country singer Daleigh McDermott's father often repeated those words. Now, her father is dead. As she's about to flee back to Nashville, she finds his hidden journal with hints that his death was no accident. Mechanic Ryan Shields is the only one who seems to believe Daleigh. Her father trusted the man, but her attraction to Ryan scares her. She knows her life and career are back in Nashville and her time in the sleepy North Carolina town is only temporary. As Daleigh and Ryan work to unravel the mystery, it becomes obvious that someone wants them dead. They must rely on each other—and on God—if they hope to make it home before the darkness swallows them.

Gone By Dark (Book 2)

Ten years ago, Charity White's best friend, Andrea, was abducted as they walked home from school. A decade later, when Charity receives a mysterious letter that promises answers, she returns to North Carolina in search of closure. With the help of her new neighbor, Police Officer Joshua Haven, Charity begins to track down mysterious clues concerning her friend's abduction. They soon discover that they must work together or both of them will be swallowed by the looming darkness.

Wait Until Dark (Book 3)

A woman grieving broken dreams. A man struggling to regain memories. A secret entrenched in folklore dating back two centuries. Antiquarian Felicity French has no clue the trouble she's inviting in when she rescues a man outside her grandma's old plantation house during a treacherous snowstorm. All she wants is to nurse her battered heart and wounded ego, as well as come to terms with her past. Now she's stuck inside with a stranger sporting an old bullet wound and forgotten hours. Coast Guardsman Brody Joyner can't remember why he was out in such perilous weather, how he injured his head, or how a strange key got into his pocket. He also has no idea why his pint-sized savior has such a huge chip on her shoulder. He has no choice but to make the best of things until the storm passes. Brody and Felicity's rocky start goes from tense to worse when danger closes in. Who else wants the mysterious key that somehow ended up in Brody's pocket? Why? The unlikely duo quickly becomes entrenched in an adventure of a lifetime, one that could have ties to local folklore and Felicity's ancestors. But sometimes the past leads to darkness . . . darkness that doesn't wait for anyone.

Cape Thomas Series:

Dubiosity (Book 1)
Savannah Harris vowed to leave behind her old life as an investigative reporter. But when two migrant workers go missing, her curiosity spikes. As more eerie incidents begin afflicting the area, each works to draw Savannah out of her seclusion and raise the stakes—for her and the surrounding community. Even as Savannah's new boarder, Clive Miller, makes her feel things she thought long forgotten, she suspects he's hiding something too, and he's not the only one. As secrets emerge and danger closes in, Savannah must choose between faith and uncertainty. One wrong decision might spell the end . . . not just for her but for everyone around her. Will she unravel the mystery in time, or will doubt get the best of her?

Disillusioned (Book 2)
Nikki Wright is desperate to help her brother, Bobby, who hasn't been the same since escaping from a detainment camp run by terrorists in Colombia. Rumor has it that he betrayed his navy brothers and conspired with those who held him hostage, and both the press and the military are hounding him for answers. All Nikki wants is to shield her brother so he has time to recover and heal. But soon they realize the paparazzi are the least of their worries. When a group of men try to abduct Nikki and her brother, Bobby insists that Kade Wheaton, another former SEAL, can keep them out of harm's way. But can Nikki trust Kade? After all, the man who broke her heart eight years ago is anything but safe...Hiding out in a farmhouse on the Chesapeake Bay, Nikki finds her loyalties—and the remnants of her long-held faith—tested as she and Kade put aside their differences to keep Bobby's increasingly erratic behavior under

wraps. But when Bobby disappears, Nikki will have to trust Kade completely if she wants to uncover the truth about a rumored conspiracy. Nikki's life—and the fate of the nation—depends on it.

Standalones:

The Good Girl
Tara Lancaster can sing "Amazing Grace" in three harmonies, two languages, and interpret it for the hearing impaired. She can list the Bible canon backward, forward, and alphabetized. The only time she ever missed church was when she had pneumonia and her mom made her stay home. Then her life shatters and her reputation is left in ruins. She flees halfway across the country to dog-sit, but the quiet anonymity she needs isn't waiting at her sister's house. Instead, she finds a knife with a threatening message, a fame-hungry friend, a too-hunky neighbor, and evidence of . . . a ghost? Following all the rules has gotten her nowhere. And nothing she learned in Sunday School can tell her where to go from there.

Death of the Couch Potato's Wife (Suburban Sleuth Mysteries)
You haven't seen desperate until you've met Laura Berry, a career-oriented city slicker turned suburbanite housewife. Well-trained in the big-city commandment, "mind your own business," Laura is persuaded by her spunky seventy-year-old neighbor, Babe, to check on another neighbor who hasn't been seen in days. She finds Candace Flynn, wife of the infamous "Couch King," dead, and at last has a reason to get up in the morning. Someone is determined to stop her from digging deeper into the death of her neighbor, but Laura is just as determined to figure out who is behind the death-by-poisoned-pork-rinds.

Imperfect
Since the death of her fiancé two years ago, novelist Morgan Blake's life has been in a holding pattern. She has a major case

of writer's block, and a book signing in the mountain town of Perfect sounds as perfect as its name. Her trip takes a wrong turn when she's involved in a hit-and-run: She hit a man, and he ran from the scene. Before fleeing, he mouthed the word "Help." First she must find him. In Perfect, she finds a small town that offers all she ever wanted. But is something sinister going on behind its cheery exterior? Was she invited as a guest of honor simply to do a book signing? Or was she lured to town for another purpose—a deadly purpose?

About the Author:

USA Today has called Christy Barritt's books "scary, funny, passionate, and quirky."

Christy writes both mystery and romantic suspense novels that are clean with underlying messages of faith. Her books have won the Daphne du Maurier Award for Excellence in Suspense and Mystery, have been twice nominated for the Romantic Times Reviewers' Choice Award, and have finaled for both a Carol Award and Foreword Magazine's Book of the Year.

She is married to her Prince Charming, a man who thinks she's hilarious—but only when she's not trying to be. Christy is a self-proclaimed klutz, an avid music lover who's known for spontaneously bursting into song, and a road trip aficionado. When she's not working or spending time with her family, she enjoys singing, playing the guitar, and exploring small, unsuspecting towns where people have no idea how accident-prone she is.

Find Christy online at:
www.christybarritt.com
www.facebook.com/christybarritt
www.twitter.com/cbarritt

Sign up for Christy's newsletter to get information on all of her latest releases here: **www.christybarritt.com/newsletter-sign-up/**

If you enjoyed this book, please consider leaving a review.

Made in United States
Troutdale, OR
02/22/2025